Bobbie Ayres

DISCARD

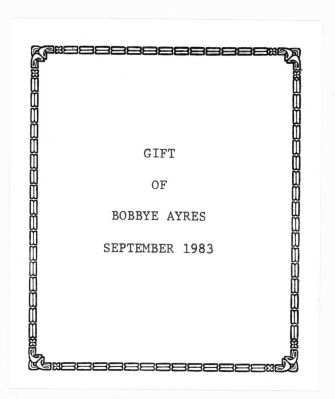

Books by John Yount

Wolf at the Door
The Trapper's Last Shot

The
Trapper's
Last Shot

The
Trapper's
Last Shot

by John
Yount

Random House

New York

Library of Congress Cataloging in Publication Data
Yount, John, 1935–
The trapper's last shot.

I. Title.
PZ4.Y85Tr [PS3575.089] 813'.5'4 72–11433
ISBN 0–394–46378–1

Manufactured in the United States of America

First Edition

*For John Luther Yount
and in memory of
Henry Richard Childs*

The author wishes to express his thanks to the Rockefeller Foundation for a grant enabling him to undertake the writing of this book.

Book
One

Chapter

One

The summer of 1960 was hot and
dry in Cocke County, Georgia. No rain fell from the second week
in June through the entire month of July. The loblolly pines
turned yellow in the drought. The grass scorched and withered
in the fields, and bare patches of red clay earth began to appear
and to crack and cake in the sun like the bottoms of dried up
lakes. The first day of August some clouds drifted in from the
mountains in Tennessee and the Carolinas, and the air grew still
and heavy, and for a while a thin rain fell as warm as sweat. But
before the rain had quite stopped, the sun came out again, and
steam began to rise from the fields and woods, from the dirt roads
and concrete slab highways, and the countryside cooked like so
many vegetables in a pot.

The next day five boys started out to go swimming in the south
fork of the Harpeth river. Except for a thin crust like a pastry
shell over the pink dust, there was no evidence of the rain. As
they walked toward the river, the heat droned and shimmered in
the fields, and locusts sprang up before them to chitter away and
drop down and then spring up again as they came on. When they
got among the trees on the river bank, the oldest of them, who
was fourteen, shucked quickly out of his britches and ran down

3

the bank and out on a low sycamore limb and, without breaking stride, tucked up his legs and did a cannonball into the water. The surface all around, even to the farthest edge, roiled when he hit as if the pool were alive, but they didn't see the snakes at first. The boy's face was white as bleached bone when he came up. "God," he said to them, "don't come in!" And though it was no more than a whisper, they all heard. He seemed to struggle and wallow and make pitifully small headway though he was a strong swimmer. When he got in waist deep water, they could see the snakes hanging on him, dozens of them, biting and holding on. He was already staggering and crying in a thin, wheezy voice, and he brushed and slapped at the snakes trying to knock them off. He got almost to the bank before he fell, and though they wanted to help him, they couldn't keep from backing away. But he didn't need them then. He tried only a little while to get up before the movement of his arms and legs lost purpose, and he began to shudder and then to stiffen and settle out. One moccasin, pinned under his chest, struck his cheek again and again, but they could see he didn't know it, for there was only the unresponsive bounce of flesh.

According to the coroner who saw the body, the boy had been bitten close to two hundred times.

Sheriff Tate Newcome and Deputy Earl Wagner dynamited the swimming hole that same afternoon and reported that just beneath the surface, there were hundreds, perhaps thousands of cottonmouth moccasins, the bodies of which practically formed a dam at the lower end of the hole and all but stopped the flow of water.

For days afterwards no one could think or talk of anything else. Some said they had heard of snakes congregating like that before, but nobody seemed to know what caused it. The drought, some offered. A biology professor at the college in Seneca was quoted in the paper as saying that it might have been a kind of breeding orgy that belonged, evolutionarily speaking, to a more primitive time. Some thought it was more than likely a consequence of the infernal testing of atomic bombs. And some felt very strongly that it was a judgement on them, connected somehow with the disrespect of the young for the old, the Communists taking over, the niggers getting too big for their britches—a sure sign given them to show the degeneration and sinful nature of the times.

But whatever their disagreement about its cause, everybody in Cocke County had heard what had happened, and they couldn't free their minds of the thought of it, nor their stomachs of a sick and shaky feeling that lasted for days and days. Even Deputy Earl Wagner—who, given any back talk, could come out of his hip pocket with a sap and beat a man almost to death and all the time be sucking his teeth as if he were bored—when he told about setting off the dynamite, would blink and swallow and rest the heel of his hand on the butt of his holstered pistol for comfort. "They was snakes all over the whole ███████████ river," he'd say, "blowed out on the bank and clean up in the trees, and that hole there, where that boy jumped in, after we taken and set off that dynamite, was solid snake bellies. Look like a bowl of spaghetti." The men standing about to listen in Sharaw, standing by the barbershop or in front of the courthouse, shook their heads when he told it and grunted as if they had been poked with a stick. And after, they seemed unable to walk away and looked at the ground or off at the horizon, their eyes glazed over with thought.

Book
Two

Chapter

Two

It was a morning in the middle of
August that same year when Beau Jim Early signed his separation papers at Fort Jackson, South Carolina, and stepped out of
that last yellow frame army building and stood with the hot sun
cooking the top of his head. He looked around at the quadrangle,
the squat, ugly buildings in stiff rows, the grounds without tree
or shrub, and the scattered army personnel he could see here and
there upon the narrow gravel walks; and he tried to believe he
was free to go. He had been in the army six years, and it didn't
seem possible that he could just walk away and go home to Cocke
County, Georgia. Just like that. The process of clearing post, the
equipment and clothing check, the signing of papers, the counting out of his mustering out pay had seemed plain, ordinary,
army routine, and there was no feeling of having reached a precise end. He wondered if he could have forgotten to perform
some last official act. He rubbed the back of his neck thoughtfully. He had signed his separation papers. He even had a card
in his pocket that said he was separated. There should have been
nothing to do beyond that, but he puzzled a moment more. Finally, abruptly, he took hold of the duffel bag he'd left leaning
against the side of the building and swung it to his shoulder. *I'm*

gone, he thought, *and if you get me back again, you'll have to burn the woods and sift the ashes.* He started walking, though he felt less sure of himself than he wanted to feel.

He hadn't the least idea which way to go to get off the post, and he didn't even think about direction until he'd walked a hundred yards or so; still, he was in no mood to worry about such a small detail, and he never slacked his pace. Sooner or later he knew he'd run across a bus to catch or a taxi to hail that would take him into Columbia. He felt confused and numb and not quite all there, as if he had left a little of himself all along his back trail from Germany where he'd been two weeks before—some of him still riding the ship across, some still gawking at New York City, some still strung out and lingering along the train track from Pennsylvania Station down the country to Fort Jackson where he'd been sent to be released. He had been in the army ever since his brother signed for him to enlist when he was seventeen (at twenty, in a moment of terrific irresponsibility, he had signed up for three more years; they had given him six hundred dollars in cash and put him in for sergeant stripes, but he lost the six hundred in a poker game and the promotion didn't come through until eighteen months later); and now that he was finally out, he felt strange, as though he didn't know exactly who he was taking home.

Up ahead there was a wider thoroughfare, and he picked up his pace, hunching his shoulder under the duffel bag to settle it more comfortably, and at the same time reaching around with his left hand to adjust the wallet in his hip pocket. It was thick with money, and his pants didn't fit right. He had won over four hundred dollars in a crap game the night before, and that morning the army had given him five hundred and thirty-six dollars and some cents in mustering out pay, and there was a pressure at his hip, a discomforting sensation. When he got to the corner and saw the Post Exchange just down the street, he knew immediately what he would do.

He bought the grandest things that caught his eye and took great pleasure in counting out the frayed crap game money which accounted for much more bulk than the crisp new bills the army had given him. He got a new double barrel shotgun for his brother, Dan; a set of china for his sister-in-law, Charlene; and for his seven year old niece, Sheila, a stuffed pink tiger that must

have weighed twenty pounds and was as big as a heifer calf. He
was lucky, for when he got all that carried outside, he saw himself
a taxi to wave down and didn't have to call one. The driver, a
small, sour looking man, helped him get his presents in the back
seat and trunk. But Beau Jim took no notice of him. He got in
the front seat, pushed his cap to the back of his head and stuck
his elbow out the window.

"Head her toward the greyhound bus station," he said, "and
if you get caught for speedin, I'll pay the fine."

The driver gave him the fisheye and pulled off slowly.

Downtown, the driver helped him carry his things just inside
the door of the bus station sandwich shop and pile them by the
nickelodeon. It took them two trips apiece, and the packages
attracted some attention, particularly the tiger, which was bigger
than the driver who carried it and which he set on top of the
boxes of china as if he were planting a marker, a flag. And though
Beau Jim gave him a two dollar tip, when the little rooster of a
man walked away, he looked toward the waitress and the two or
three customers sitting at the counter and gave a toss of his head
back over his shoulder toward Beau Jim as if to say, "Get a load
of the big man here," and they gave Beau Jim a quick look before
they flicked their eyes to one another and smiled. Immediately,
as though they were so many mirrors, he saw himself from another angle and was shamed. He abandoned his presents in the
coffee shop and went into the bus station lobby.

At the ticket counter he found that there was an express from
Columbia to Atlanta in an hour; from Atlanta to Sharaw he
would have to take a milk run bus, but that was all right with
him, and he bought his tickets. He found that the baggage clerk,
however, had stepped out somewhere for a break, and after waiting two or three minutes for him to return, the urge to get his
presents out of sight became so strong, he decided to put them
in a baggage locker and check them through later. Once they
were safe and he was released from them, he could go out and
walk around the streets, get a taste of freedom, see what being a
civilian felt like. He gave himself a moment to get ready.

He lit a cigarette, tucked it into the corner of his mouth and
went back into the sandwich shop. He looked at no one, picked
up his huge pink tiger and started out again. It's girth was twice
his and he could get his arm no more than halfway around it; still,

he carried it as nonchalantly as possible against his hip. It's tail,
long and loose and as big around as his forearm, wagged and
jounced when he walked and threatened to trip him, and the
irises inside its goggle-eyes were loose, and they shifted, so that
the tiger was with one step, cross-eyed, and with the next, wall-
eyed; and they made a noise too, like a baby's rattle, though he
could only barely hear it over the self conscious buzz in his ears.
By the time he got to the baggage lockers, his ears warmed the
side of his head. He put his money in the slot, turned and withdrew the key, and opened the door, but one look at the clean,
rectangular space, and he knew the tiger wouldn't fit. He left the
door standing open and tried one of a row of larger lockers on
the end. Even there he had difficulty, for the elbows of the tiger
were bent and stiffly braced for lying down, and he had to put
the thing in catty-cornered, one elbow in the lower right hand
corner, and one elbow in the upper left hand corner, and had to
bring some of his weight to bear in order to force it in. Still, he
was careful. They could not cause him to despise Sheila's toy, or
harm it. Finally he got it in, its tail coiled behind it. It filled the
locker completely. He went back for his duffel bag and his brother's shotgun, and back again for Charlene's china. It took three
lockers in all, although one was less than half filled.

Once he was out upon the sidewalk again, his anonymity returned and he breathed easier and thought to himself that a man
who cared about his privacy ought to travel light. The more you
carried with you, the more you gave away about yourself. But it
was a thought with only a little bitterness, for he was out of the
army and free. Still it was a very hard thing to understand or
believe. He rubbed his chin and mused, trying to get his mind
around it. The ring finger on his left hand was missing at the first
joint, and somehow, more with that insensitive fleshy nub than
with the other fingers, he felt stubble, as though the whiskers
didn't slide so easily across the deadish skin there and translated
better to the sensitive layers beneath. He had allowed himself the
luxury of not shaving that morning, his first, funny expression
of freedom, since, after spending most of the night hunkered
down by the metal legs of an army cot watching dice bounce off
the wall, it would have made him feel better to shave. Tall, tired,
a little rumpled, he walked the sidewalks as though he expected,
without knowing it, to meet himself, the old civilian self, six

years abandoned, and get reacquainted. The odd scraps of memory that came to him of Sharaw seemed strong, if unimportant. High school football games on a Saturday night, the lights around the field making a kind of false gauzy ceiling up in the night sky. On the cinder playing field behind the gymnasium, a fist fight he had lost to Foots Taylor—picking cinders out of the heel of his hand afterwards, such bright pain, it caused his mouth to water. Honky-Tonks. Riding around in a buddy's forty-nine Ford which had a chrome Tennessee Walking Horse as a hood ornament, tooling down the streets looking for some vague and imperfectly imagined adventure which stayed always just a little out of reach.

Oddly then, a little at a time, he did begin to get the sweet, sad taste of being out of the army and going home. It was something like the first clear cold days of Fall when he could catch in his nostrils the spice of dying leaves and grass, and feel, somehow, more permanent than those things, feel full of possibility and promise. He was, by God, going home. And he was going to make something of himself. He was going to amount to something, for he had grown tired of being nobody.

Strangely, it seemed exactly right that he should look up in that moment and see her coming toward him, for she was exactly the way he remembered them from High School, and something about her made him shy. She was wearing a kerchief over the rollers in her hair, short shorts and sandals. She couldn't have been more than seventeen or eighteen, but she was confident in her near prettiness already. Her legs were smooth and tanned, and she had a short, pert, sexy body, even though her face looked a little muggy as if the stations of her brain hadn't quite opened for business. Her jaws were worrying a piece of chewing gum, her sandals skuffing and slapping the pavement, her eyes roaming the store windows. It struck him that there were no girls anywhere like American girls, and when she passed and gave him no more than a bored glance, it broke his heart in such a familiar way, he felt suddenly almost at home again. He would make something of himself, no doubt about it; and when he did, he would forgive all the girls who had the power to break his heart, although he felt satisfied that they would not forgive themselves. He was as certain of his future as if he had it in writing, and it made him very happy. "Hot Damn!" he said to himself, barely able to keep from doing a little dance in the middle of the sidewalk.

Around a corner a Negro boy sitting on a wooden box with a loop of rope attached to the side, saw him coming, sprang up, and slipped the loop of rope over his shoulder.

"Hey soldier, lemme shine them shoes!" he demanded.

The boy was so threatening he was funny, and Beau Jim laughed. "Not today, I reckon," he said.

"Come awn, fifty cent," the boy said.

Beau Jim winked at him and shook his head, *no*, but the boy didn't go away. He was in front of him, facing him, and walking rapidly backwards. "Twenty-five cent!" the boy said, his face and the tone of his voice, fierce.

"Not today, ole buddy," Beau Jim told him, although he couldn't help smiling.

"Look!" the boy said as if he were giving Beau Jim one last chance to be reasonable, "If I kin tell you where you got them shoes, will you let me shine em?"

The shoes were not army issue. The boy would likely know that since they were long in the toe and there was a buckle across each instep instead of laces. But Beau Jim had gotten them in San Antonio, Texas, and the boy could not possibly know that.

"All right," he said.

"You got em on yo feets," the boy said, unslinging his box and putting it down in front of Beau Jim to block his path. He picked up one of Beau Jim's feet and put it down on top of the box, and in a motion too quick to follow he produced a can of open polish and slapped his fingers in it, slapping the toe of Beau Jim's shoe almost in the same moment. A dozen times the can of polish and then his shoe got lightly slapped, and finally a toothbrush dipped in something to stain the sole got drawn in one continuous motion—though the boy had to change it from one hand to the other—around his shoe; and then the boy was lifting up on the toe in such a fashion as to make Beau Jim step back quickly or fall. The other shoe took no longer, and again the sudden leverage on his toe, up and back toward his shin, light as it was, made Beau Jim take his foot away quickly in order to recover his balance. The shining took only a little longer, but the shoes did shine.

"Fifty cent," the boy said, fierce and threatening.

Beau Jim squinted at him, making a tough face of his own. "Yore last price was a quarter, Hoss," he told him.

"Man, what make you want to cheat a nigger boy? Fifty ████████
cent!" the boy insisted.

Beau Jim didn't have a quarter in his pocket anyway. He had
a fifty cent piece, a dime, a nickel and some pennies. He dropped
the half dollar in the outstretched palm, expecting then, some of
the grace a winner can afford to show a loser, but again, almost
too quickly for the eye to follow, the coin disappeared in the boy's
pocket, and almost as quickly the boy himself was gone, stepping
to one side and behind Beau Jim and seeming to leave only his
small but intimidating voice in the space he had just vacated:
"Hey Mista!" he called to someone out of Beau Jim's vision. And
Beau Jim was abandoned, feeling a little funny in the feet.

He turned and saw the small blue-black shoeshine boy already
walking backwards and haranguing a business man in a summer
suit. The man walked steadily on while the boy made quick,
violent gesticulations as if he were accusing the man of having
stolen something from him, stepped on his foot, insulted him.
Without slacking his pace or even inclining his head to the boy,
the man said finally, "Get the Hell out of here," and the boy
stepped obediently aside as if the remark meant less than nothing
to him, except as a sign he was wasting his pitch. He scratched
his crotch absently and looked up and down the sidewalk for
other business possibilities. He must not have seen any, for he
unslung his box and sat down on it. The position caused his
britches to ride up and show his scaley, thin, sockless shanks
between his ragged cuffs and the tops of his black tennis shoes.

For some reason Beau Jim found himself going over the
amount of money he had left when he walked away, as though
the shoeshine boy had taken him for much more than fifty cents.
Somehow, it felt like more than that. He was going to have to
look out for himself, he decided. It was a tough world. Even the
little kids had to be tough in order to get along. But that too was
the way he remembered it, and that was all right. People were
only people, and that he was freshly out of the army and again
among them, just wasn't going to move them much. He blew a
little snort of laughter through his nose, suspecting he'd thought
otherwise. A sign over the entrance of a bank gave the time, and
he saw that he had about forty-five minutes until his bus left. He
decided to cut over a block and get back to the station. He didn't
want to go back exactly the way he had come.

He speculated that in six hours he would be in Cocke County,

Georgia. It was a good thought. He pushed his hat back on his head and stuck his hands in his pockets, and almost nothing within sight or sound escaped his notice or appreciation. He looked at the people, window shopped, and even strolled into a used car lot just off the sidewalk. There wasn't a jeep or a three quarter ton among them; they were good-time machines of chrome and color. They appealed to him instantly, and he patted their fenders and kicked their tires as fondly as if they too were children of the larger civilian world, like the girl, the shoeshine boy, and now——~~Jesus~~, it was hard to believe—himself. It was fun to taste the possibility of owning one.

Chapter
Three

About five miles outside of Co-
lumbia, Beau Jim learned that the front end was shot. He was
going the speed limit when the green fifty-three Studebaker
Commander hit a bump and went into convulsions. It trembled,
then shook, then shuddered so hard that steering it was next to
impossible. When the crisis passed and the car settled down and
the steering wheel quit jerking and shaking, his hair was standing
on end. He learned to watch for every bump and swale in the
road and dodge them if he could, or slow way down if he
couldn't.

The second thing he learned was that if he really kicked the gas
pedal—in order to pass quickly, say—the motor seemed to flood
out for a moment, before, with an explosion like a cannon shot,
it caught again. The first time that happened, his feet jumped up
from the floorboard, and his heart missed half a dozen beats. The
third time the Studebaker backfired, the motor began to rumble
and chortle through a hole in the muffler.

About a hundred and fifty miles from Columbia, he was going
around a little town on the truck route, listening to the guttural
sounds of his engine and watching carefully for bumps, when he
saw a stop sign ahead where the truck route dead ended into a

four lane highway. He stepped on the brakes. The brake pedal
went all the way to the floor and stuck. The green, fifty-three
Studebaker not only didn't hesitate, it seemed to gain weight and
momentum, and when he saw the city bus coming down the
highway on a collision course, his balls climbed out of his scro-
tum, shinnied right up into his stomach like yo-yos up strings.
"Whoa, shit, whoa!" he told the car, but smooth as a sigh, slick
as a kid on a slide, it went right by the stop sign, taking him
where he didn't want to go. The bus was going to roll through
his window. If you can't slow down, speed up, he thought, and
kicked the gas pedal. The motor flooded out and then cut in again
with a backfire, and he swung so hard into the left hand turn, he
slid out from under the steering wheel, across the cheap new seat
covers and landed with a bump on the floorboard, but he still held
onto the steering wheel and still steered, looking out of the top
of the windshield at the tops of trees and telephone poles on
either side of the highway and keeping the Studebaker in the blue
alley of sky between them. He heard car horns and air brakes and
screeching tires while he steered and floundered, and he tried to
dodge the sound of them. He tried to push himself off the floor
with his right hand and steer with four fingers and the nub of his
left. The nub was hurting just the way it had three years before
when he'd picked up the tongue of the trailer and the three
quarter ton truck had rolled back when it should have pulled
forward. It was a record twenty-seven degrees below zero, and
a little while before the accident, he had taken off his gloves to
light a cigarette and hadn't put them back on again before trying
to disconnect the trailer hitch. He had unscrewed the clamp and
picked up the tongue, and the ~~fucking~~ three quarter ton truck
was supposed to pull away, but it had rolled back and pinched
one of his cold fingers. It hurt. But not enough. Not nearly
enough for that crooked little piece of finger lying half on the toe
of his boot and half in the snow to belong to him. The finger was
all wrong, completely out of place, like a new born creature, all
hairless and defenseless and out of its nest. "Hah, whoa now,"
he'd said as though someone had made a mistake they were going
to have to correct. The nub was hurting just the same way when
finally, miraculously, he got himself back on the seat just in time
to keep from hitting a new Chrysler head-on. In his proper lane
at last, he got his toe under the brake pedal, pried it up, and

pumped it until it offered a little spongy resistance. He pulled
into a handy service station and stopped. He was shaking. The
bus driver pulled in behind him, and leaning from his high window, cursed him without mercy. The man in the new Chrysler
had made a U-turn and stopped to yell at him from the street, and
the service station attendant, who must have seen it all, came
toward him waving his arms and wanting to know if he was
drunk or what? Crazy or what?

He was going to say his brakes went out, and that's what he
said, just as soon as his finger quit hurting—not the part he still
had, but the part buried in a C ration can in the woods in Germany, which had begun to hurt too, in a dull, far off way, like
an echo. It was a funny feeling, and he shook his head and smiled
and told the attendant that his brakes had gone out. The brake
pedal had sunk again to the floorboard, and he managed to open
his door and point at it.

"Theeeeaay?" the service station man said in surprise and wonderment. "Hey, Orville!" he called to the bus driver, "It won't
this feller's fault. His brakes went out!"

Beau Jim sat where he was and took a couple of deep breaths
while the bus driver, still cursing over the whining engine of his
bus, pulled off in a cloud of acrid fumes. The new Chrysler
squealed tires and left an angry vacuum where it had been, and
the service station attendant said, "You lucky you ain't hamburger."

Beau Jim did not feel like adding up the quality of his luck to
see if it was good or bad.

"I didn't see nobody in the car till just before you pulled in.
Where wuz you anyhow?" the attendant wanted to know.

"I slid off on the floor," Beau Jim said.

"They Lord God," the service station attendant said, "you
shoulda been hamburger meat."

While the air was being bled out of his brake lines and fluid
added, Beau Jim sat in a diner across the street. He had ordered
coffee, and though it was bitter, cankerous stuff with a blue film
floating on top like a thin oil, he drank it while his stomach
settled down and the sweat at his temples grew hard and sticky
in the air conditioning. That he had almost five hundred dollars
less than he'd had only a few hours ago seemed entirely too
painful to be true, even though the evidence of it was parked just

across the street. He thought about the presents piled on the floorboard and in the back seat. What was Sheila going to do with a toy she couldn't even pick up, and which, if the frapping thing fell off the bed on her, would probably smother her to death under twenty pounds of kapok and pink fur? And Charlene and eight place settings of fancy china didn't want to go together in his mind. She wasn't much for entertaining. And Dan, his good brother, already had himself a shotgun, an old pump he'd had for years. Dan was a careful and easily contented man who likely wouldn't even know what to do with a second shotgun. What was he supposed to do, carry one in each hand? It would seem a waste to Dan. Beau Jim took a sip of his bitter coffee, admitting to himself that his presents probably weren't very good ones. Sadly, only the impulse seemed right. But in one way, they were better than the Studebaker, if only because, once he had bought them, he was through paying for them. That damned car could absorb his last penny in doomed, useless repairs, until—on some un-handy stretch of road—the son of a bitch would let one last explosive fart and fall over.

"But you won't cost me much more money," he told it softly, speaking aloud to himself, "I will dismount and walk-the-fuck-away first."

Strange how money won in a poker game or shooting craps lost its value. He doubted if he would have spent so much if it hadn't been for that. Money that he'd won never seemed real. Only if he had lost did money translate back into the stuff without which, a man was broke. He sucked his teeth and looked at himself in the mirror across the counter, seeing the man he knew: Beau Jim Early, a fellow he'd taught to roll with the punches. Nothing was going to get him down for long. Ninety percent of what was across the road he'd paid for with crap game money, so no real harm was done. He was still out of the army, still going home, still, by God, going to try his hand in college at Senneca where he'd already made application. He was going to go there and get smarter, learn a few things. He was going to make something of himself because he wanted to.

He got to thinking about buying the Studebaker and managed some wry humor. He supposed that when that son of a bitch of a salesman jumped out of his little white frame shanty and said, "Yessir, soldier, what can I do for you?" he'd felt like a trespasser or something. And having been taken by surprise, he'd said, "Oh just lookin," and as if to prove it, bent to look in the window of a black fifty-five Ford convertible.

"I couldn't sell you that one, soldier," the salesman said. "I suspicion the transmission. We could probably drive all over town and it wouldn't do it, but every now and again, she jumps out of gear."

Funny how things worked. He'd felt a little guilty and wanted to establish his right to kick tires and pat fenders—at least after he'd been caught at it—he wanted to let the man know that he had money and was to be taken seriously. And lo that's how the man had taken him, which obliged him to look a little further.

The next car down the line was a fifty-six Chevrolet Bel Aire. "That's a honey," the salesman told him. "The only thing to my knowledge that's wrong with it is that the clutch slips a little, and we could either get it fixed for you or take the price of the job off the car." The salesman was a nice looking fellow, his white hair in a crew cut, a gold tooth in the bottom center of his smile, and tough friendly wrinkles bunched at the corners of his eyes.

"What's it worth?" Beau Jim asked him.

"Twelve ninety-five. But I'll tell you what." He gave Beau Jim a long, serious look, smiling at last, as though Beau Jim weren't just anybody, but someone for whom he had a sudden special affection. "If you want to worry with the clutch, I'll let her go for twelve."

Though he'd had no intention of buying the car, it embarrassed and hurt him that he didn't have near that much money. He hadn't even wanted it until he found he couldn't afford it. He looked at the red and white Chevrolet not knowing exactly what to say to escape his silly embarrassment. The salesman didn't say a word, offered nothing to lift the weight of his proposition. Beau Jim fingered the sweaty hair over his ear and studied the chrome nuts on the hubcapless wheels for a long fruitless moment before he admitted—blushing as if he were admitting something unnatural about his mother—"That's more money than I've got to spend."

"Why sure. All right. Sure," the salesman said generously. The salesman stood with his forefinger crooked and pressed against his lips, and his eyes thoughtfully going over the cars down the lot. Beau Jim watched him with increasing fear and discomfort while a voice inside his head gave its advice: *Get the shit outta here!*

The salesman straightened the forefinger he had curled against his lower lip and held it up as the symbol of an idea. "You know," he said, "I've got a runnin little car down yonder that I'm certain would be just what you're after. It's not as snappy as these up here, but it's just a hell of a lot of transportation for the money."

Yes, it had gone a lot of miles, the salesman told him as he was looking in the window of the Studebaker at the speedometer, but that only went to show what a good car it was. And to be honest, it did use a little oil, he told Beau Jim who was looking then at the black smudge on the rear bumper just above the tailpipe; but Hell for two hundred and fifty dollars, he couldn't expect a new car could he?

No, Beau Jim agreed reasonably, he could not. Would it run, Beau Jim wanted to know.

Sheeeeit! the man had said, would it run? The actual fact of the matter was, it would probably outrun any car on the lot. He'd make him a bet about that green rascal. If it wouldn't do ninety-two miles an hour in second gear, over-drive of course, why, by God, he'd give it to him. Beau Jim looked at the green Studebaker, squatting on the oily gravel. It would be nice to go home in his own car rather than in a bus. He'd never owned a car, not in his life. The voice inside his head, full of the warning edge of involvement, saw it differently. *Thank the man*, it told him, *tell him you'll have to think it over, and make tracks out of here.* But Beau Jim wasn't talking, the salesman was. He was telling him that the Studebaker was fast enough to where his brother-in-law, who was a deputy sheriff, even used it now and again when his patrol car was in the shop. His wife used it too, the salesman said, and he'd put new seatcovers on it so his wife could use it to take herself and a lady or two who rode with her to choir practice at the church. She was going to be cross with him when she found out he'd sold it, he told Beau Jim, cross as a cat. His gold tooth flashed in a grin, and he shook his head as if it was his nature to let good things get away from him. He put his arm around Beau Jim and walked him back toward the shanty and suddenly he wasn't talking about the Studebaker any more. He was on his way to becoming a friend, even almost a relative. He was telling Beau Jim about his wife and children, his sister and her children, even to his nine year old nephew, who at such an early age, had one of the biggest paper routes in the city, though he gave most of what he earned to the church, and so made them all very proud that he was going to be honest and hard working and good, as it was implied the rest of the family was, particularly the nephew's uncle. They were back in the little frame office, and Beau Jim still hadn't made up his mind about the car, although the salesman seemed to think he had. It didn't seem like a bad idea, but the salesman never shut up a moment or gave him a chance to think. He was getting papers out of his desk and writing on them, and impossible as it seemed, he was confiding to Beau Jim that his wife had some sort of fungus in her crotch. He admitted that he had caught it himself, not a venereal disease, of course, but uncomfortable and hard to get rid of, and the medicine was terrifically expensive.

He was writing on forms, checking boxes, and as if the process reminded him of the car, he wagged his head and said that the little Studebaker was certainly a steal. If any ordinary used car salesman had it, why they'd take a blow torch and burn out the exhaust pipe until it was chalky and clean, get the smudge off the bumper, give the car a wax job, black the tires and floor mats, and jack the price up two, three hundred dollars; and the car wouldn't be one bit better. The man handed him a pen, got up, and giving Beau Jim's arm a gentle squeeze just above the elbow, all but signed his name for him, telling him all the time about how his five year old daughter was upset because she was too young to give a pint of blood to the Red Cross. His wife said, of course, that his bad habits were already rubbing off on the little girl. Now that had to be nonsense, absolute nonsense, but there didn't seem to be any way to turn it off; and still not having made up his mind, and against his better judgement, he yielded up his money.

Temporary tags in place, title in his shirt pocket where the man had stuck it, he had driven out of the used car lot, tappets tapping, valves clattering, rods knocking, and the exhaust pipe laying down gauzy barrel rolls of smoke. Even the voice inside his head was struck dumb, and unlike that morning, there was an awful amputated feeling in his billfold.

He looked at himself in the mirror, his short, dark hair, whorled in stubborn, tangential cowlicks, lantern jawed as any hick. He'd never had a chance. There seemed never to have been a time when he could reject the car without rejecting the man, his friendliness, his family, the kid with the paper route, his wife's poor fungusey crotch. The salesman had obligated, confused, and maybe even embarrassed him into buying the car. Beau Jim took a sip of his coffee, thinking it was almost magical for one man to surround him like that. "Shitass," he said aloud.

The waitress, leaning on the far end of the counter cut her eyes slowly and disdainfully around to Beau Jim and said, "If ya don't like it, don't drink it." And with a haughty little toss of her head, turned her bored eyes again to the window that looked out upon the street.

"The coffee?" Beau Jim asked, getting up and leaving change for the coffee and tip on the counter. "Hell, it's delicious."

"It is, ain't it?" the waitress said without even looking around.

It cost six dollars and fifty cents for bleeding the lines and adding brake fluid. The man told him the master cylinder probably had a very slow leak and needed to be replaced, and Beau Jim said he'd certainly get it seen to when he got home. He filled up with gas and oil and pulled out of the service station with the motor sounding as guttural through the torn muffler as a hotrod or some fantastic racing machine. When he hit second, he kicked the gas pedal to the floor and took some strange sort of pleasure in the backfire that resulted. "Hot Damn!" he said, "speak again sweet lips," and he shifted into high and kicked the gas pedal once more. He got two backfires. The first one was only a pop, but the second was a cannon shot he could feel through the floorboard and the soles of his shoes.

It was about five hours later when he crossed the South Carolina-Georgia line, and in about a quarter of a mile, the north fork of the Harpeth River. His stomach was edgy from too much coffee and too little sleep. His butt was full of the pin pricks of disrupted circulation. There was a sore little horn of a pimple pushing toward the surface of his chin. His eyes were grainy from having been open close to forty hours. But when the Studebaker dropped down the south pitch of the bridge in its shuddering lope, all those things ceased to bother him, as if they were left behind. Behind too was his long time away spent in dayrooms and gasthäuses, whorehouses, tents and foxholes, among all manners and mixtures of men as foreign to Cocke County and his youth as a New York skyscraper would have been or a Roman ruin, or the escargot he had eaten once on a bet. But though behind him and having no application whatsoever to the red clay earth, nor the yellowed loblolly pines, nor the gone-by cotton patch he was passing with its tatters of cotton strewn like white rags upon the pithy, scraggly stalks, and no application to the unpainted grey shack beyond the cotton field in its space of scorched grass and ant hills, the thin shade of a mimosa tree spreading over one sagging corner of the porch where the white freezer sat—though all those foreign people and places were somehow not negotiable experience here—they still carried a weight like some sin he had been guilty of and would somehow be held accountable for, so that he felt such a mixture of joy and sadness and something very close to shame that he could not have analyzed or named the feeling. It was a little as if he had loved no other place but this, and that having been away constituted some sort of effrontery, a broken faith, for which he could never quite be forgiven.

"Hot Damn," he said, when around a curve Barnett's store appeared on the left; its ancient Sky Chief gas pumps dented and battered, the red one turning a milky wine. It looked exactly as it had when he was in high school. There was a cold drink cooler on one end of the sagging gallery of the store, and there were watermelons on the other, just as always. The old metal signs nailed to the side of the building advertising Dr. Pepper, Red Apple chewing tobacco, Camel cigarettes, Purina Hog Chow, were just as they should have been. Then Barnett's store was behind, and all sorts of familiar things began to happen and come into view, even the concrete highway felt right, the measured thump of his tires across the tarred strips between the sections of slab was a thing so well remembered it made his eyes moist. He knew that Cane Creek was coming up, and he dropped down over a little hill and there it was. He knew that over the brim of the next hill he would be able to see the Dan Dee Drive-in Theater, and sure enough, it was there, looking as shoddy as ever. But past it, where he had hunted quail and rabbits, there was a housing development whose light colored brick and aluminum siding and pastel roofs looked hot even in the late afternoon sun. The development covered maybe a hundred acres that he could see and seemed to go across the ridge and down toward the old Eaton Chemical Company Plant in patterns of streets and planes of roofs, and little squares of lawn, and nowhere was there a tree over six feet tall. Just past that, there was a belt of a new four lane highway he'd never seen before, and past that, a new shopping center where a lumber yard should have been.

He began to feel Sharaw had been swallowed up or mislaid; and not until he got downtown, did things start looking right again. The old narrow, mellowed brick buildings, the black marble front of the Rexall Drug Store, then the jewelry store, the cleaners, the dimestore, the theater with its ancient marquee. And right there he saw someone he knew! Fat and placid as ever, sitting inside the ticket booth as if it were some darkly magic throne, was Edith, the ticket-lady. The sight of her made him feel important and shy, as though, if she saw him, she would wave and shout and call to others, and the people he had known would begin to rush into the street to greet him. When the traffic light at the corner by the theater caught him and he had to sit almost in front of her, he got nervous. He felt somehow famous, although he couldn't think why, but Edith, who seemed to be looking right at him, shouted no hurrahs. She had always spoken to him and seemed very friendly when he'd bought his tickets, from the time he was a child all the way into high school, but she seemed not to know him. The light changed without incident, and feeling the contradiction of being obscurely famous, he pulled away.

Judge Taylor's Hardware Store was in the next block, and above it, the shotgun apartment where he had lived and grown up. It was hard to get through his head that he could not stop the car, open the sidewalk door between Judge Taylor's and the shoe shop, climb those dark stairs, pungent with the odor of rotting wood and ancient dirt, and be home. It was hard to get through his head that Dan had bought a farm and didn't live there anymore. His bedroom window was just out of view, too high to see out of the right hand window of the car, and that was all right, he didn't want to see it, for someone else was probably living there now. Like the theater and Edith, he passed it by, suddenly very anxious to see his brother who would not be faithless like ticket-ladies and old dwellings, but would know him, slap him on the back, welcome him home. He speeded up through the next block and a half to Willard's service station where his brother worked, and pulled in and stopped by the pumps. It had not changed, although the Negro attendant who came out was new to him. "Is ole Dan Early around here somewhere," he asked, for some reason unable to keep from laughing.

"No suh, he home," the Negro said with gentle rising inflection as if he were asking a question, himself. He stuck the rag he had withdrawn to wipe the windshield with, back in his hip pocket. "He don't work on a Saturday no moe."

"Well," Beau Jim said, "well, fill it up, I guess." He sat in the Studebaker thinking he was going to have to go in and see Cass Willard and ask directions to his brother's farm, and he didn't want to do that. He never had liked Willard, and he didn't want him to be the first man to greet him home. But he couldn't think of any way around it.

Just as he opened the door to get out, the Negro said, "You ain't Mista Dan's brother, is ya?"

"I am," Beau Jim said, and feeling somehow that the two of them ought to shake on that, he offered his hand. The Negro looked at it for a long, awkward moment before he fumbled with the gas pump filling Beau Jim's tank, and stuck out his own, as tough and lifeless as a piece of leather, and allowed Beau Jim to take it and shake it. Beau Jim felt suddenly stupid, but the black man took him in stride.

"Yawl don't favor much," he said.

"I'm a lot better looking for sure," Beau Jim said.

The Negro stamped his foot and wagged his head in a silent pantomime of laughter.

"You wouldn't know how to get out to his place, would you?" Beau Jim asked, thinking immediately that, like the handshake, the question was a mistake. There was no reason for the man to have that information.

"Yes suh," the Negro said. "He live right across the road from me. My boy do his milkin of an evenin. You just take out like you wuz goin to Foscoe, nen turn off toward de Spermint Station, and it's about a mile down the highway, settin way back off de road."

Beau Jim couldn't remember how to get on the road to Foscoe, or how to get to the Experiment Station, but the black man went through it all again.

About twenty minutes later, he turned off the hardtop onto a dirt road, and with the pink dust boiling out behind him, he drew toward a small single story frame farmhouse. The sun was setting and seemed caught in the branches of an old dead chestnut snag

at the bottom of a cornfield on his left. Its light, awry, glowed
orange in the windows of the farm house and glinted from the
tin roof. There was an old black pickup truck parked under the
two huge pecan trees in front of the house where the road he was
on played out. He could see a tire swing hung from one of the
thick lower branches of a mimosa tree just out from the left rear
corner of the house, and there were chickens already gone to
roost in the tree and a few others scattered here and there in the
scrappy grass of the yard. As he came closer he could see that
maybe ten or fifteen years before, the house had been painted
white, but most of the paint was gone now, and the foundations
were stained rust where the rain dripping from the eaves had
splashed up the red clay mud. And he could see a man coming
from the direction of the barn, past the corner of the house and
the tire swing, and out toward the front of the house to meet him.
He was wearing patched bib overalls and a long-sleeved khaki
shirt, and what with his heavy slumped shoulders and the unhur-
ried long slow stride, and the way he looked at the ground but
still let you know, somehow, that you had been seen and ac-
knowledged, it could be no one but Dan.

The next moments were blurred by excitement and embarrassment and emotions he couldn't even name. He had pulled up and
stopped behind the pickup and gotten out, and Charlene had
stepped through the screen door to the porch, and behind her and
holding to her skirt, though her hand in the next instant got
brushed away, was Sheila. Then Beau Jim was standing by the
Studebaker, smiling but without one word to speak to his
brother, and they were reaching out their hands to shake. If the
Negro attendant's hand had been tough as leather, his brother's
hand was nothing as human as that. It was like shaking hands
with an old rusty hayrake or a cedar fence post. His brother did
not grip his hand, as if some shy respect kept him from it, and
somehow that was very important and disappointing. It made
Beau Jim shy, himself, and touched him suddenly with an unwelcome sense of their differences: he, himself, in uniform, four
inches taller and ten pounds lighter than Dan; he, having been
half way around the world and back, and Dan more than likely
having never been fifty miles distant from Sharaw in all those six
years; the aroma hanging over him of tobacco and sweat, of the
barn, of cow, of ancient pungent hay. There was no judgement

or condescension in his awareness of their differences; the awareness was just suddenly there between them, and he could think
of no words to speak.

"Well," his brother said finally, wonderment and disbelief
drawing out the word, "Jimbo, you're a growed up man."

Then neither of them had anything to say until, after a moment, Dan colored and said that it sure was a right nice looking
automobile that he had come home in, and Beau Jim laughed and
said that though he'd only paid two hundred and fifty dollars for
it, he'd been took to the cleaners because the car was about ready
to fall down. Then Beau Jim asked him how he liked living on
the farm, and Dan said, all right; and Charlene broke in and said,
all right her foot, it wasn't nothing but a wore out patch of
misery. And Beau Jim asked him how much land did he own, and
Dan told him how much he and the bank owned, and Beau Jim
said he didn't know his brother had got to be the owner of half
of Cocke County, Georgia; and Charlene said that a man could
own it all and still not have nothing. Then nobody said anything
for a while until Beau Jim jumped, remembering the presents
he'd brought, and opened the rear door of the car and brought
out the mammoth pink tiger and tried to give it to Sheila, who
had slipped out a little in front of her mother to sit on the steps.

But though Dan said, "Well, little Shirley Early, would you
look at that!" she wouldn't take it, so Beau Jim sat it down by her,
and she shrank back timidly and sucked her thumb and looked
at it.

Then he reached in the back seat again and began to slide out
boxes of china for Charlene, and he carried them over and set
them on the edge of the porch and said they were for her.

Dan grew a little redder and said, "Wellllll," the word rising
like fluff from a dandelion floating upward on a current of air.

Charlene said, "Would you ever?" and came forward to open
them.

Finally, Beau Jim brought out the box for Dan that had the
new double barrel shotgun in it and handed it to him, and Dan
looked altogether embarrassed and said, "Boy, you ought not to
have spent yore money that-away."

By then Charlene had opened one of her boxes. "Theeeyy," she
said, "it's full of dishes." But Beau Jim could not miss the way
her voice trailed off.

Dan gave his head a little shake. "Lord," he said softly, and he probed at the snuff tucked inside his lower lip with his tongue. He shook his head again. "You shouldn'ta spent yore good money like that." He caught his nose thoughtfully between his thumb and forefinger and blew soft little jets of air through his nostrils, and looking toward Beau Jim but not quite at him, he said, "We're obliged."

Beau Jim smiled and waved his hand, and after another moment of awkward quiet, Dan said, "Well, less us go on in the house. Charlene's got you a room fixed up."

As though they didn't quite know how to lay claim to them, not one of the three of them picked up their presents. Charlene went inside, and Beau Jim took the tiger from the steps and held it while Dan went up. As her father passed, Sheila took hold of the back of his overalls, and never taking her eyes off the tiger, allowed herself to be pulled, shuffling after him, across the porch and through the screen door.

When they got inside, Dan picked her up and sat down in his ragged over-stuffed chair with her in his lap, and Beau Jim carried the tiger up to her and wagged it from side to side and smiled at her, thinking she would smile back and take it, or at least touch it, but she simply quit looking at him and studied the space of floor between them instead.

"That's yore uncle Jimbo," Dan said to her, "and he brung you that big play toy." But Sheila would neither look at Beau Jim or the tiger. "She'll git use to you after a bit," Dan told him.

But it seemed to Beau Jim that Sheila's behavior was only symptomatic of what they all felt. It was as if they were all strangers who were only pretending to be themselves. He wanted to do or say something that would rid them of the need to be uncomfortably polite, but he couldn't manage it. Charlene offered him something to eat, but he told her that he'd already had his supper since he could see they had had theirs long ago.

Until she was put to bed, he tried to overcome Sheila's shyness, but he could never quite catch her eyes upon him. Somehow he felt if he could make a friend of her, things would be easier all around. He could feel her watching him, but when he turned to smile at her, he would find that she was no longer looking at him but at empty space just to the right or left of him, her cheek pressed against her father's chest, and the one round hazel eye he could see as wide and startled as a rabbit's, or a young doe's.

After Sheila was put to bed, they talked into the night, though often there were lags in the conversation when no one seemed to know what to say. Still they stayed up with him and talked until he realized that, as he had had to save the conversation from its awkward silences, he would have to release them from it. So he rose and forced a yawn and told them that he was so tired he couldn't think straight and he was going to have to get some sleep. He stretched out his hand to his brother, who gave him again his hard, shy hand to grip, and he told them how glad he was to be home. Charlene didn't say anything, but Dan told him they were just proud to have him. He went out and brought their gifts in from the porch and pulled his heavy duffel bag from the car.

When he had stretched himself out on the cot they had made up for him, he heard across the dark the single complaint of the bed springs in their room and then the *kalomph*, one after the other of what would be Dan's heavy work shoes against the floor, and he felt oddly homesick, suddenly and deeply homesick. He listened to them settle down in the next room until they were quiet, and then he listened to the sounds outside his window, the crickets grating and grating, a soft crystal sound like small creatures somewhere in the dark, made of glass, having a chill. And way up on the highway, he heard a car go by. In its wake of quiet he was conscious of the countryside stretching away, of vast distances, of oceans and continents, and it was hard for him to rest, as though the substance of his body, his flesh and bone, still retained momentum. The motion of the boat, the train, the car from Columbia still flowed in him. Through his open window he could smell kudzu and honeysuckle, and he could smell the house itself, an odor old, pungent and earthy as a root cellar, and it reminded him of home. Not of this house, nor even the apartment over Judge Taylor's Hardware Store, but of his first home which he had not seen since he was six and could not even recall except in the most disparate and disorderly way. He could remember the kitchen table, the look and feel of it, better than he could remember his mother. He could remember his father's gum rubber boots standing by the kitchen door, the rotting, warped wood beneath them, his big faded denim jumper over the back of a chair, better than he could remember his father. His parents were only sets of feelings with him, vague nostalgic presences of shifty outline. His father had a very crooked nose; he could remember that.

He couldn't even remember much of the fire that burned the house to the ground when he was six and Dan was twenty-one. He remembered Dan pushing him through their bedroom window to the roof over the kitchen, and he remembered Dan calling to him to jump from the eaves, and he remembered doing it, and Dan, already on the ground, catching him. The fire must have started in their parent's bedroom wing since it was only a moment after he and Dan were clear that the roof beam of that part collapsed. There was no chance for Dan to help them. Probably they were dead long before the sounds of fire woke him.

The month-long stay at their uncle Gaither's house, or the trip from Watauga County, North Carolina, to Cocke County, Georgia, he did not recall at all. But there was one memory he had from before the fire that was stronger than all the rest, and later when he use to tell his brother about it, Dan would never fail to give his head a shake, and thoughtfully, almost in disbelief, probe the roll of snuff tucked inside his lower lip against his teeth. What Beau Jim remembered was a picture. It had been hung in the musty smelling, seldom used parlor, and he could describe it to its smallest detail. He thought of it now, lying on his cot in the quiet dark of the house. It was an old print, done in brown and black, and it showed a mountain man in buckskins astride a horse that was wading across a deep slow stream. The sun was gone, and the wilderness around was lit obliquely, and there was on the still surface of the water a faint sheen, like silver. Over the rump of the horse behind the saddle, two huge bundles of furs had been tied, along with traps and a bedroll and other gear. It was a big horse and strong, but it was loaded down and belly deep in the water, and though the trapper had given it his heel and its eyes were bulged and its nostrils flared and it had gathered itself to hunch for speed, the mind could see what would happen in the next moment, for the load was too heavy and the water too deep, and the horse could only stumble and flounder. Having dug his heel in the horse's ribs, the mountain man was turned half around in the saddle to look behind him, his right hand swinging his long rifle around, and his left moving up to cradle the forehand piece. There was strength in his bearded face, or there would have been if it weren't for a telltale shine in the trapper's eye like the shine on the surface of the water. And Beau Jim had understood, even then, what that was about. It was fear that had dashed that moisture across the man's eye. There had been no moment of wonder or simple surprise; the fear was ready-made, as though the mountain man had long dreaded what was falling to him, so that even at the instant he was swinging his long rifle around, his thumb cocking the hammer, his eyes had already bleared with the sure and certain knowledge that he was dead. Behind him on the bank the half dozen Indians, lean and light and all but naked on their bareback ponies, had already raised their bows and lances over their heads in anticipation of the kill.

Beau Jim turned on his side, conscious of the sound of his own respiration and the beat of his heart and conscious of the odor of ancient wood and dirt as fragrant as tobacco, the image upon him of the trapper, perhaps the one strong impression he had brought from childhood forward into his majority, as though it stood him instead of parents, or even religion, a kind of talisman, if not to keep him from evil, at least to serve as a yardstick by which to measure his own fortune, and to find, inevitably, that he was not so badly off as he thought himself to be.

He still felt homesick. He felt homesick twice over, once for Sharaw and for his brother, and once for a time and place he couldn't even half remember. But after a while he got to thinking that maybe when a man reached a certain age, he was simply going to suffer from a certain amount of homesickness, as he would suffer the accumulation of his years. He was thinking of that, when, just before sleep, he heard a big tractor and trailer rig up on the highway, balling-the-jack, the diesel engine throbbing across the dark, the mosquito whine of the dual tires, and for a moment the headlights reached way across the honeysuckle and kudzu and scrub pine and brushed his window and circled the walls of his room and gave him again the feeling of motion. In the thickening quiet of the truck's wake, he went to sleep.

Chapter Four

The next Monday morning Dan came in from milking and began getting ready to go to Foscoe Grammar School. He was nervous, but he was stubbornly righteous and determined, and he seldom answered Charlene who followed him about and chided him. He got his suit out of the chifforobe and laid it across the unmade bed and unhitched the galluses of his overalls.

"Shoot," Charlene said, "now that suit's gonna help a lot when you walk in there to tell those people their business. You think you goan fool em any?"

From the top right-hand drawer of the chifforobe he took the only three items it held: a white shirt, a pair of dark-blue socks with powder-blue arrows on the ankles, and a powder blue tie with dark blue diamonds down the middle. He had bought the suit and the rest of it from Penney's Department Store to get married in and except for his wedding and the time he went to the bank to get a mortgage so he could buy the farm, it had been laid carefully away.

"The child missed half the school days. She don't even know all her letters. You act like they held her back for meanness." Charlene folded her arms across her stomach and leaned into the

34

doorjamb. "You just goan show your ignorance for nuthin and act a fool," she said, and she smacked her lips disgustedly.

Dan was buttoning up the white shirt. He had grown thicker since he had bought it, and when he buttoned the collar button, his face grew a deeper shade of red. Even the cuffs were tight and hard to button over his wrists.

"You got nobody to thank but yourself neither," she said. "You taken her out of the town school when you bought this good-for-nuthin place and then let her stay home every time she acted sick."

"She had the ear ache," Dan said.

"Shoot," Charlene said, "she was play actin the biggest part of the time cause she was afraid of the new place, and if she's got to go to school with little niggers, you've got yourself to blame. Buy a piece of wore out red clay mud that won't even grow a decent crop of briars and then act surprised when you make everybody suffer for it." She narrowed her eyes and made little pecking motions with her index finger in his direction. "That's what you done, Mister. That's just exactly what you done!"

He took the coat and trousers off the hanger, sat down on the bed and pulled the trousers on over his work shoes. Even as wide as the cuffs were, he had some difficulty. When he stood up and buttoned the pants at the top, Charlene saw the fierce horizontal creases just above the knees where they had been so long across the hanger.

"Get out of em," she said, "and I'll press em for you."

"They're all right," he said. He took a rag from the hip pocket of his overalls and went down the hall to the bathroom where he wet the rag and cleaned his shoes. Charlene was still leaning against the doorjamb when he came back and picked up his tie. He looped it around the bedpost, laid the wide end across the narrow end and then stood still and studied it, his tongue compacting the snuff inside his lower lip. He wrapped the wide end around the narrow end twice and then studied it again, rubbing the material between his huge callused thumbs as if he were testing its quality, before he remembered and brought the wide end around from the back and pulled it down through the knot. He took it off the bedpost and put it over his head, but when he drew the knot up tight, the narrow end was four inches longer than the other, and he had to take it off and untie the knot and start again. He probed his snuff and thought a long time, pulling the narrow end and then the wide end of the tie around the bedpost toward him before he began to knot it again. The second time, the narrow end was five inches shorter than the wide one, but he decided it would do, and he put on his coat and went into the bathroom to comb his hair.

"They ain't gonna pass no chile into the second grade who don't know one letter from another and couldn't add two and two," Charlene said as he passed her. "Seems to me you'd have sense enough to see that."

He ran his comb under the spigot and combed his hair. He used too much water and it wet his ears and crept out of the hair on the back of his neck to disperse in the deep crosshatched wrinkles and wet his collar.

"Hit's four," Sheila said. Neither of them had noticed her standing in the doorway to the living room.

"What's four and three if you're so smart, Missy?" Charlene said.

Sheila's eyes grew opaque and she put her thumb in her mouth.

"She kin make hit up," Dan said. "That's what I'm gonna tell em. She's bright as a button and she kin make it up."

"Shoot," Charlene said.

"She's just shy," Dan said, "Just cause she don't talk all the time, don't mean she's not as smart as any of them. We kin hep her, and she kin make it up."

"Shoot," Charlene said and she turned away to look down the hall into the kitchen, and it seemed, through the kitchen walls and far away.

"I'll be on back," Dan said. He buttoned up the two buttons on his coat and went through the living room and out the front door.

After a moment they heard the pickup start up and back around, and the license tag rattling as he drove off.

Sheila withdrew her thumb from her mouth. "Hit's six," she said.

"What?" Charlene said.

"Four and three," Sheila said. "Hit's six."

"It's seven," Charlene said.

The door to Beau Jim's room bumped and opened, and Beau Jim stepped out into the hall stuffing his shirt tail in and hitching up his pants in back. He yawned and rubbed his face vigorously. "Where did Dan go?" he asked Charlene. He saw Sheila standing in the door to the living room and winked at her.

"Off to act a fool," Charlene said. "Come on in the kitchen, and I'll get your breakfast."

She sent Sheila out to play, and while she fixed his eggs, Beau Jim sat at the kitchen table sipping coffee and watching Sheila through the window. She was sitting in the tire swing, sucking her thumb and moving in lazy circles, looking at the ground. With what seemed an abstracted and irritated efficiency, Charlene set food before him: a plate of biscuits, a jar of honey, an old cracked tureen of gravy, and a plate of eggs and bacon, the bacon being thick and salty and as tough in its lean part as leather.

Charlene half leaned and half sat on the kitchen counter across from him. She took a cigarette out of a pack on the sideboard and lit it, arching her lips grotesquely to keep from smearing her lipstick. "Work like a nigger and live out here in the middle of nuthin," she muttered to herself. "Shoot," she said, and she fluffed at the hair over her ear and flicked on the radio which sat back from the sink. For a moment she stared into space and made spitting noises trying to rid her mouth of a piece of tobacco. Finally she picked it off her tongue with the thumb and little finger of the hand that held the cigarette. "Do you know how long it's been since I've even been to a movie show?" she asked him suddenly, as if the fault were clearly his.

"No," he said. But she didn't tell him how long.

"From February till April it didn't do nuthin but rain, every single day. Damn tin roof. Like being shut up in a tin can with somebody peckin on it all the time. Then when it finally quit, it quit altogether. When I get through cookin of an evenin, you cain't breathe in this kitchen. Work like a nigger and live out here in the middle of nuthin." She poured herself some coffee. "You got any idea how long it's been since I've even seen a movie show?" she asked him again.

"No," Beau Jim said.

"Shoot," Charlene said in a dreamy bitter voice. Then suddenly she said, "Get up from there!"

Beau Jim put down his fork and sat still with an anxious and embarrassed smile on his face. Did she want to fight him, or what? He didn't know what to do.

"Get up," she said, "I want to show you something." She caught him by the arm and led him to the back screen door. "I just want you to see for yourself," she said, and she pointed out a line of trees, a thousand yards distant, where the south fork of the Harpeth River ran, and told him about the boy that had jumped into the cottonmouth moccasins and gotten bitten to death right there on the edge of their property, and she asked him what he thought of that. He'd never heard anything like it, he told her, wondering what she wanted him to say. Finally, he said he thought it was a bad thing, a terrible thing.

Charlene seemed gratified for a few moments as though she had won an argument, and Beau Jim sat back down to finish his breakfast, but before long she was telling him how, ever since they had bought the farm, they hadn't had two half dollars to rub together at the same time, and how it wasn't ever going to get any better either, and Dan was too dumb to see it. She told him how talking to his brother about some things was like talking to a cedar fence post.

"You just cain't tell Mr. Big-Britches Early that wore out red clay mud will soak up money and work like a sponge, and not give you nuthin back!" she said. "Maybe you can explain it to him, cause I can't." She stubbed out the cigarette she was smoking and lit another one. "Huh!" she said, and she began to pick up the kitchen, taking things from the table, putting pots and pans in the sink. And she said nothing more, as though it had occurred to her that talking to him, like talking to his brother, was a waste of breath. She took the plate from between his elbows at the very moment he took his last bite, and when he thanked her for the breakfast and told her he thought he'd go into Sharaw and look around a little, she didn't even answer.

Chapter

Five

Though the prospect of having to talk to Sheila's teacher and maybe even to Mr. Haggerman, the principal, made him so nervous his ears rang, he had steeled himself to do it. It was necessary, he thought, and if a thing was necessary, no matter what it cost, a man had better take hold of it. But he dreaded it. He was no good at talking. He was not a clever man, and he knew he wasn't. He didn't fool himself about that. He had discovered early that there were all sorts of things that he just couldn't get his mind around, and though it grieved him and he wished it weren't so, he accepted it. He even extended to himself a certain tolerance in this matter of intelligence. *I ain't got but two thinkin gears,* he'd say, *one's low and the tuther's double low, and they both growl when I use em.* But being truthful as well as humble, he might show his enormous, knobknuckley hands and add, *but they's not a whole lot of work these dogs cain't catch.* Charlene didn't think that kind of talk was very funny. *It's not as if you got to advertise that you're not blessed with sense,* she'd say. *Who do you think it is in Cocke County that don't already know it?* But he didn't mean to be advertising anything; it was just that, every now and again, he wanted to set the record straight and let it be known what he would be held accountable for and what not. He didn't

39

even envy smart people so much anymore. Though it was slow and painful for him, he could read a little and write some. Since there was no help for it, he had to be satisfied with that. "I'll let the folks that can handle it do the head work, and I'll do the kind where you take your hand and grab on to it," he said, addressing himself to the pickup—the dusty streaked dashboard, the worn seats, the look of the hood, the familiar steering wheel and pedals and mechanical quirks which possessed a personality that was benign, even sympathetic, and very easy to talk to. "But this here won't kill me," he said, trying to console himself, but he could make himself feel no easier about speaking to Sheila's teacher, and by the time he pulled in to park at Foscoe Grammar School, his shirt and even his suit coat was sweated through.

When he got out of his pickup, his hand was shaky on the door handle, and he thought he'd better hold up a little while and try to get straight in his head what he wanted to say. He reached back in the pickup and got the tin of Copenhagen off the seat. He tucked a pinch inside his lower lip and tried to organize his speech, but all of his arguments were gone, and he felt foolish and embarrassed. *Maybe*, he thought, *this ain't a good time; maybe Wednesday when school commences would be better.* He tucked at the snuff inside his lower lip with his tongue and spat, *Sheila's teacher probably ain't even here since it's two days till it starts.* But he had glimpsed Haggerman's blue Plymouth below the line of yellow school buses when he pulled in, and he'd noticed Mr. Stoval's, the science teacher's, Ford too, and there were lots of other cars around. He wouldn't let himself leave. *They all here*, he thought, *gettin ready to commence a'Wednesday.* He looked at the school and then way off down the road where the heat shimmered and made the pavement look wet. *Twon't be no easier then*, he admitted. He flipped the snuff out, rolled his lower lip this way and that, ran his tongue over his teeth, spat, and started out toward the school.

It consisted of two very dissimilar buildings, though they were joined. The older part was two stories and made of dark red, lusterless brick with steps, window ledges and corner stones of granite. The windows were inset, solemn, dark, stern. Attached to the old building's left side was a one story annex. It was made of aluminum, had colored panels below the flush windows of smoked glass; and if the old structure seemed certain that no child wanted what it was determined to give, the new part seemed smugly certain that the opposite was true. Dan Early went nervously up the steps and through the double doors of the old structure.

With his first step inside the door he inhaled the odor of oiled floors, pencil shavings, chalk, galoshes, the close smell of bodies from seasons past, and if it had an odor, the odor of confinement, discipline, and humiliation. By the time he reached the point where the broad entrance hall met a narrower one that ran the length of the building, his resolve was gutted. It was as if he had lost all the intervening years between the time he was in grammar school and the present; it was as if they had simply evaporated. The unlifting despair of sitting before a problem in mathematics he could not begin to solve was immediately upon him, and when he was called upon to read aloud, the struggle to decipher the sound and sense of each syllable of each word, until the teacher, out of mercy or impatience, would call upon another and leave him all but sick with relief and shame. Through two years in the fourth grade and three years in the fifth, he had worked hard and waited patiently to find the trick to reading and mathematics, thinking surely there was some trick, some simple rule, which, once discovered, would make these subjects as plain to him as straining milk, or grading tobacco or butchering a hog. But while he searched and waited for the key, his schoolmates, who seemed already to have found it, or not to need one, left him far, far behind. He sat day after day afflicted with such frustration and woe that finally he began to think of himself as something less than human, a different creature than his fellows. After his third year in the fifth grade when fractions were no clearer to him and reading came very little easier, he told his teacher and his parents that he had had enough schooling. Though the three of them protested his decision, they did so out of tact more than conviction; he had always been serious and responsible, and they let him have his way.

Standing at the juncture of the two hallways, it took him a few moments to get himself in hand, and remember why he had come. The atmosphere of the place had affected him like a momentary sickness, a fever, which he had to let pass. Just inside the front door he had noticed two offices. The one on his left had a sign about waist high beneath the glass, and he turned and began to sound out the word. Half way through he realized it said:

PRINCIPAL. He had not seen Haggerman inside. He had seen a gray-haired lady sitting at a desk who had seen him too and watched him pass the door with her forehead wrinkled as if she wondered what he wanted. He did not want to talk to Haggerman if he didn't have to. He had hopes that he could settle it with Miss Wheeler, Sheila's first grade teacher, but he didn't know how to go about finding her. Before he could make up his mind what to do, the office door opened and the gray-haired lady leaned the upper part of her body out into the hall and looked at him. He looked at her, not knowing exactly what to say. Finally she came out into the hall and said, "Can I help you?" as if she very much doubted that she could.

"I come to see Miss Wheeler," he said, leaving the end of the sentence up in the air as if it were a question. She looked as though she doubted that too, and feeling very uncomfortable he asked, "Kin you tell me where she's at?"

"She's in a meeting," the lady said.

He didn't know what to do about that. He pulled at his ear and looked at his feet and thought.

"Can *I* help you with something?" the lady asked, not unkindly, but as though she wanted him to state his business.

He wondered if she could, but he decided after a moment that what concerned his daughter was not to be discussed with anyone but her teacher, and if he got no satisfaction, then with the principal himself. "When will she be done?" he asked her.

"The meeting's just started," she said. "It will be an hour, maybe two."

"If you kin tell me where her school room is at," he said, looking just to one side of her, "I'll wait there till she's aloose."

As though she were giving up information against her will, she told him where Miss Wheeler's class room was, though she said she thought it would be better if he went away and came back later.

"Nome," he said, "If it's all the same to you, I'll just wait."

She stood before him a moment more, and he felt called upon to say something, but he couldn't think of anything to say. The atmosphere of the building seemed to crowd in upon him. He felt constricted by his clothes; the cuffs of his shirt were so tight around his wrists, he could feel his hands swelling, and the collar was so tight about his neck, he felt he badly needed to hock and spit, though he did not.

As though she were assenting against her better judgment, or as though out of kindness, she had decided not to point out his foolishness, she said, "All right." She turned back toward her office, and the old wooden floors popped and groaned. He felt he should thank her, but she was gone before he could get the words out.

He waited miserably beside the door to Miss Wheeler's room for almost an hour before the pressure in his bladder reached the threshold of pain, and he had to go look for a toilet. He found one at the end of the new annex and relieved himself, feeling guilty and ashamed as though for a grown, rough and ignorant man like himself to use the school's toilet, constituted some sort of desecration; still, when he was done, he didn't want to go back out into the public hall and had to make himself do it. He waited another hour before a few people, teachers he could tell, began appearing in the halls, and a young woman with dark hair and eyes that looked large and blurred behind her glasses, approached him.

"Did you want to see me?" she asked, and she smiled and opened the door of her classroom and stepped inside and with a motion of her hand, beckoned him in.

His stomach felt empty and jumpy, and he couldn't concentrate on walking and talking at the same time, so he stayed where he was. "I come to see you about Sheila Early," he said; and, as with the other woman, he left the end of the sentence up in the air, deferentially, as though it were a question.

"Oh," she said, "Sheila's a very sweet little girl."

"Yes'um, she is, and she's smart as a whip too," he said. He hadn't meant to say that so soon, and having said it, his face grew hot immediately, but he forced himself to look her in the eye in order to show her how serious the subject was. But she was not looking at him.

"Oh," she said, and as if embarrassment were infectious, her cheeks began to gain a little color themselves. Along her jaw, back toward her ears, her cheeks were downy as the skin of a peach, and color began to rise there from her neck. "She's a very quiet, sweet little girl." She adjusted her glasses. Her neck turned rosy. "Come in," she said, and she smiled nervously at him.

He followed her into the class room and sat stiffly in the chair she offered beside her desk. His ears were ringing, and his vision had strangely altered so that it was fuzzy around the edges and bright in the middle, and when he heard himself speak, his voice sounded strange. "I want to see about gettin her passed on into the second grade," he said. "She's bright as she kin be, and she kin make up anything she don't know." The eyes in his head felt hot as coals, and the things he said, he seemed not to have said at all, but to have overheard, and he was surprised with himself for speaking so well. "She was sick and missed a lot, but she kin make it up. There's no need for her to go to school with no niggers," he said.

"Oh my, Mr. Early," Miss Wheeler said, "Sheila's a darling child, but she had a hard time last year. She did miss a lot as you said . . ."

"She don't need no punishment," he heard himself say. "If you'll just let her pass on into the second grade, I'll hep her with her studies myself."

"It isn't a matter of punishment at all," Miss Wheeler said, "it's a matter of what's best for Sheila. It would be much easier for her to begin fresh, than start out way behind. She'd be much happier. It's very hard on a child to expect them to make up things they've missed and keep up with new things as well." Her big blurred eyes were upon him, but he wasn't looking at her now.

It was as if what he had said had been a speech which he had memorized without knowing it. It had cost him so much effort to come and see her, so much embarrassment to speak, that he had nothing else to say. He had spent all his logic and all his words, and he had no more to spend. He sat not looking at her, not looking at anything, as though his eyes had lost the ability to focus and saw everything and nothing at once. What was she telling him? That he was trying to hurt Sheila? It boggled his mind. He felt wrapped in a hot vapor through which he could hear her still talking. "It makes a child very unhappy not to be able to do what the others are doing. You would be punishing her by putting her in the second grade when she's not prepared," she was saying. But he had heard Cass Willard explaining things to Haggerman, the principal, in the service station just last week *"Now a white man's skull has got five bones in it, and a nigger's ain't got but four, like a monkey's. Now you cain't put niggers in a white school and expect em to learn like a white chile," Cass had said. "They just ain't got it," he'd said, tapping his head with his forefinger.*

"It will be hard for a while. It's a shame it has to come," Haggerman said.

"*Hell, it ain't no shame!*" *Cass had said.* "*It'ud be a fuckin shame if ever nigger in the world died of whoopin cough next Saturday night, but this here ain't no shame! Shame, Shitass!*" *Cass said, and he snorted and turned his head away, looking over his right shoulder at the place above the candy machine where the corner of the walls met the ceiling, and bobbing his head as if he had told that corner of the room what sort of remark a principal was likely to make and now he was reminding that section of wall and ceiling that he had predicted it.*

Haggerman had had an oil change and a grease job, and after a moment of looking at the back of Cass Willard's bobbing head, he said, "*Would you put that on my bill, please?*" *He acted as if he weren't angry, only a little amused.*

He had started to leave when Willard turned around and said, "*I reckon you'd say it was a shame that Jesus Christ was nailed on the cross!*"

"*No sir,*" *Haggerman said, with just the barest hint of a smile on his lips,* "*I'd say as sinful as you and I are, it was a merciful thing that he was.*"

"*Well, you gonna have to lick yore calf over again,*" *Cass said to him as Haggerman was going out the door. Cass rounded the counter himself and followed him outside and called after him,* "*The onliest ones that are smart enough to learn anything are going to be the white children, and the onliest thing they're gonna have a chance to learn is how to act like niggers!*" *he shouted.*

Haggerman drove away smiling, but red-faced and shaking his head. Cass was in a bad temper for hours, and Sammy, who was blue black— a purple-gummed nigger, Cass called him—had been in the second stall washing a car during the whole thing, and he kept his distance and didn't say two words for the rest of the day.

"Some children mature earlier than others, Mr. Early," Sheila's teacher was saying. "Sheila was awfully shy. I think you'll find she'll do much better and be much happier this year," she said.

"Not with niggers," Dan Early heard himself say with neither heat nor enthusiasm.

"Oh, that will work itself out," she said.

But he was no longer listening to her. He was thinking how the only help for it was to go back and do last year over again in such a way as to keep Sheila from failing, and then she would know what she had to know and wouldn't have to go to school with the niggers. He began to wonder how he could have changed it. He began to wonder how it might have been if he had not bought the farm, or had bought it the year before so that Sheila would not have had to change schools in the middle of the year. And he began to see how difficult things were, how each action depended on another, and on another, and another until the complexity of it overwhelmed him, *and he was not even thinking about Sheila anymore at all, as if his mind had just lost its grip on all of that, and he was thinking, instead, of how he used to hose down the pavement of the service station in the mornings, back when they still lived in town; a May morning, Sharaw just beginning to wake up, and the steamy smell of the wet concrete in the early sun. Then he was thinking of the way the cow would blow softly in her feeding trough in the mornings when he milked her, and when it was cold, how her breath would steam. He was thinking about the wooden gravelly sound she made in eating, and "Saaawwhh" he'd say to comfort and quiet her, and he'd lean his head into her side, and she would smell of hay, feed, mud, dung, warmth; and milk would spew into the pail, not like the stream of water on the pavement before the service station, but a small sound like:* spew, spew, spew; *and she would be chewing with that sideways motion of her jaws.*

Sheila's teacher was saying something, but he didn't hear what. He rose and extended his huge callused hand, and she put her's, as small and frail as a bird, in it. He nodded his head at her, forgetting even to be embarrassed. "I'm obliged," he said, and he left her room and the school building, feeling strange, jarring himself a little when he walked as though his legs had gone to sleep, and blinking in the harsh outside light as though he had come out of a cave.

Chapter

Six

Beau Jim had spent the morning wandering around town, and he'd seen at least a half dozen people he knew, people like Judge Taylor and Hack Dennis who ran the shoe shop. The encounters were very friendly, but embarrassing, unsatisfying, and always gave him the urge to move on. Jerry Bartlett was the only one of his high school classmates he'd seen. Beau Jim had recognized him squatting in the window of a clothing store arranging a display of shoes. But they had never been very good friends, and they didn't talk long before Jerry began trying to sell him a suit.

After that he walked idly about the streets, content merely to see faces he recognized, and to roam around Sharaw again. He went all the way up Clairmont St. to the high school and circled its grounds, gazing for long moments at the stark buildings and the empty cinder practice field. A little before noon, though he wasn't quite hungry, he stopped in a diner on Main Street and ordered a cup of coffee and a hamburger; and from a booth by the window, he watched the people pass to and fro, thinking that probably he didn't need the two or three weeks of Hell raising and lying around that he'd promised himself back in Germany. It would only be a waste. He had almost a month before Senneca

College started its fall session, and he decided that probably it wouldn't hurt him to take a job. Dan had told him the day before that Bond Chemical Co. was putting up three new buildings, and the general contractor was hiring unskilled laborers almost every morning. He didn't see why he couldn't get on. He wouldn't have to tell them he only wanted a few week's work, and he could use the extra money. The notion made him restless, and he began to tap his coffee cup with his fingers and shift his feet under the table. There wasn't any reason why he couldn't go out there, right then, and see about it. It would be something to do. He pushed the half-eaten hamburger away, paid up and left.

It had been hot before, but after the air-conditioned diner, the heat bore down from the sky and pounded up from the sidewalk, and he seemed to swim through it back to his car. The door handle was almost too hot to touch, and the inside was a blast furnace that brought sweat from every pore. He seemed to be breathing, not air, but the musty stuffings of the upholstery. There was one moment, before he got the window rolled down, when he thought he might pass out. So long a time in Germany had made his blood too thick for Georgia weather, he decided.

He drove out the highway to the Bond Chemical Co. plant, but somehow he couldn't make himself turn in their private road. He went on down the highway a ways and turned around, but he couldn't make himself turn in on the way back either. *Hell, they're not likely to hire a man that comes strollin up in the middle of the afternoon,* he told himself, *they like to see em already hunkered down and waitin when they get there early in the mornin, whites and niggers, all anxious and ready to go, not comin in like a banker in the middle of the day.* But he knew he wouldn't want to turn down that road tomorrow morning either. Digging ditches was the sort of thing he wanted to keep from doing; it was the point of going to college in the first place. What he really needed to do, he decided, was go over to Senneca and take a look at the campus. He leaned back in the seat and pressed the accelerator, feeling almost justified.

Oddly, he'd driven only a few miles when he began thinking of Brewer, of Johnny Reisen, and Hoots. Brewer, when last seen, was a sergeant first class, but he'd be busted to a private more than once before he retired. At that very moment Brewer was likely sitting on his bunk, talking to himself and searching his hairy body for crabs. Jesus, the poor bastard had hair everywhere, on his chest, belly, back, shoulders; there were even a few thin, stiff hairs growing out of the top of his nose, and high on his cheeks under the eyes, there was fuzz where he left off shaving. And even though he kept his bunk dusted with so much DDT powder that, if a man should give it a pat, a white cloud would puff up, Brewer always thought he felt an itch, something crawling on him, and he would tear off his clothes and search his pelt, one hand holding the thick hair on his belly or chest out taut, and the other shining a flashlight through it. "If I was to get the crabs, they'd kill me," he'd explain, a note of real hysteria in his voice, and then he'd go back to looking and talking to himself: "What's that? Dandruff? Can you have dandruff on your belly? It ain't movin. Gotcha! Squeeze the mother to death! Thank Jesus, ain't nuthin but a cruddy piece of lint. What's that?" His trouble was that as much as he feared crabs, he loved prostitutes, and he was always looking for one or the other. Wars could come and go and be no more to Brewer than a kind of climate in which he looked for whores and crabs. Brewer would still be in the army all right, suspended somehow in time, and just as he had left him.

Brewer had been one of them, the small group of friends. And Johnny Reisen, who had suffered the army as if it were a long bad summer camp his parents had sent him to, was another. He would be out now and part way through medical school. Dale Hoots was out too, probably riding a tractor on his father's farm in North Dakota, his baby blue eyes as innocent and cheerful as ever. He would have married a farm girl by now and be spawning slightly fat, healthy, contented, blue-eyed Hootses on whom the sun would never shine too hot, nor the wind blow too cold, nor nothing, no time, ever get the best of, because it was the nature of a Hoots to accept whatever came along and not to know any better than to be happy with it and do well. They were an unlikely bunch, the four of them, nothing alike, but they got along, and it gave him comfort to think of them, and to think that though each of them might be diminished by separation, they would all survive and do well by themselves too.

He remembered a time they were in the Dolley Bar in Munich, and Johnny about got bested by a German whore. He wasn't more than five-five and couldn't have weighed more than a hundred and ten pounds, but his small, bright ferret eyes never missed anything, and his strange Jewish wit often made them laugh till they ached. But just that once, for a moment or two anyway, he ran up against a naturally superior creature. She had walked past their table with her sweater stretched over breasts nearly the size of basketballs, and Johnny had said to Hoots, "The Virgin birth, maybe; but *that* I don't believe." All four of them flinched when she stopped on a dime, and whirled, the tips of her enormous breasts almost brushing the end of Johnny's thin arched nose.

"Vot you said?" she demanded, and Johnny, instantly pale, could only blink.

"Hah," she said, "discover it then for yourself," and she lifted the bottom of her sweater up and over his head in one quick motion as if she had caught a bird, and for maybe half a minute, she banged and wallowed his face between her tremendous tits, before she lifted her sweater again and stepped back and asked: "Now vot?"

His high narrow forehead was no longer white, but flushed, his thin hair was mussed, but after a moment he found a squeaky voice. "Brünnhilde," he said, "I think I'm in love. Can you make chicken soup?"

"Vot you said?" she asked, her eyebrow arched, her jaw rigid.

Beau Jim was afraid she was going to hit him.

"Spätzchen," Johnny said, "I want you should shave your armpits and come home with me to Boston to meet my mother." He was smiling and holding out his arms to her.

Beau Jim was certain she was going to hit him, but suddenly she laughed and sat on his lap, and when he grimaced as if he were being crushed, she laughed harder and pinched his cheek.

She called to her friends, and pretty soon they had a girl apiece, and Hoots's, naturally, was almost pretty. Beau Jim's had a birthmark just under the point of her chin about the size of a quarter with half a dozen stiff black hairs growing out of it, and she had feet bigger than his, but she wasn't altogether ugly. Still he couldn't get in the swing of things. And though he drank as much as usual, he didn't get high. When the rest of them decided to give their girls sixty marks each for all night stands, he went along, though his heart wasn't in it. And when Johnny talked his Brünnhilde into carrying him out of the bar and down the street like a babe in arms, it was funny, but not as funny as it should have been.

His girl mistrusted him because of his gloomy mood, thinking probably that he was not satisfied with her and would be mean or cheat her; and in her room, when he was only good for one time, she grew bitchy until he gave her the sixty marks; after that she seemed only sullen, and before long she was on her stomach, snoring. He, himself, did not sleep; but in the little space she had left him, lay on his back with his hands behind his head and wondered what was the matter. It was a simple thing, and maybe for that reason it took hours to sort it out, but when it came to him, he knew it was right. What came to him was that he had become a man, that without his noticing it, a threshold had been passed. Johnny and Hoots were short timers, would be getting out of the army soon and going home—Johnny to medical school and Hoots to his good rich farm—and only he and Brewer would be left. Give Brewer a whore, a flashlight and some DDT powder, and he was happy; and Hell, he wouldn't knock it: a man should do what he wanted. But what about him? He had more than a belly full of the army. He had a long time to go, but he'd had a belly full and wanted no more. But he had a basic mistrust of making plans too; he'd always had it, as long as he could remember. And fellows like Hoots and Johnny Reisen, although he admired them, seemed to have a kind of ignorant faith in the permanence of things. It was a faith so ignorant they didn't even know they had it. He lay with his hands behind his head and thought about it, how even in grammar school he'd felt indulgent toward his teachers for what they were trying to teach, and indulgent toward his classmates for what they were trying to learn, since all of it seemed unimportant when it was placed over against what he already knew. And what was that, he asked himself. Funny that he couldn't name it, never had been able to. But he knew it was there and had been with him always. It seemed almost to be the sure and certain knowledge that everything there was, was going to fail. But who could do anything with a thought like that?

For a long time then he lay quietly and listened to the girl's soft snoring, a noise like, far far away the noisy hinge of a door opening and closing. He listened to that and was conscious of the quality of light changing outside the window. And he found himself thinking there was no reason, after all, he couldn't play his hand out as far as it went. It seemed so easy and so simple that he didn't know why he hadn't thought of it before. He could play his hand any way he wished. He could take the G.E.D. test, get the equivalent of a high school diploma and go to college. Of course he could. He had the G.I. bill. There was no reason not to. There was no reason not to see what he could make of himself.

He felt so good, all at once, that he began quickly to collect his clothes and put them on. He left without waking her—her light snoring grinding softly on its hinges—and walked out upon the early morning streets. When he found a place open, he had himself a good breakfast; and at ten o'clock, he met the other three of them at the train station as they had arranged. Johnny was still with his big whore, whom he had not yet paid. He told her he would have to go to the bank in the train station and cash some traveler's checks. But he'd had no intention of paying her, and while she waited self-consciously outside the bank, he escaped by another door.

When he caught up with them again outside, he was very proud of himself. No one but Beau Jim had had any breakfast so they started out to get some before catching their train back to Ülm. Only about a half a block up the street, Brewer happened to look behind them and saw Johnny's whore coming fast. "Hey, Johnny," he said, "you better run! Here she comes, Hoss!" But Johnny thought Brewer was only kidding and made mincing little steps up the sidewalk, wiggling his tiny ass. When he looked back to show Brewer he hadn't been taken in, she was almost on top of him. She chased him up the street, screaming curses, slapping and hitting at him. Johnny and his whore went out of sight around a corner that way, and they saw no more of him in Munich, didn't see him again, in fact, until they got back to the base. He'd gotten away, but he had long red streaks down his back where she'd gotten close enough to mark him with her tube of lipstick.

Beau Jim drove the grumbling Studebaker through the heat and thought of that, and for a little while the four of them still seemed pertinent to each other, as though what affected one of them might still somehow affect the others, though a moment more, and he knew such a thought was only foolishness. Above the jack pines on the horizon, he could see a water tank with SENNECA COLLEGE written on it, and he felt perfectly alone.

A mile or so further on he began to pass Negro shacks on either side of the road. They were small and mostly unpainted and very close together with a scrawny hedge, or a chicken wire fence, or nothing at all separating the yards of hard-packed mud. Seldom was there a yard with any grass in it, but often there were white-washed tires lying flat with flowers growing from their centers, and every now and again two upright whitewashed tires, half sunk in the ground, formed a gate into someone's space of bare ground. Here and there, an old person sat slumped and vacant on a porch like charred wood on a cold hearth. Through its torn muffler the Studebaker grumbled and chortled between the houses and toward half a dozen children who seemed to be making suckers out of the melted tar on the road. He could see them twisting sticks into the soft tar in order to form balls on the ends, and he slowed almost to a stop. A little girl in a blue print dress was nibbling daintily at such a lollipop, and sitting behind her on the curb in a pair of filthy cotton drawers, a child of no more than two was smiling up at her with tarry teeth. It caused his stomach to knot.

"Hey youngins, don't eat that stuff! It might kill ya," he said to them out the window.

"Nawh t'wont," the little girl answered.

"Ain't none a his beeswax," a small skinny-chested boy said to her. "Hit's the same as lickerish."

Another bigger boy in a pair of brown short pants with the fly gaped open where buttons were missing said, "Hell, lickrish is what it am, man," and went on spinning himself a sucker.

"I'm comin back in just a minute," Beau Jim said, stopping completely and leaning out his window, "and if I catch you youngins still eating the road, I'm goan stop and tell your mommas." They all gave him a look. "I mean it," he told them.

Just beyond them and over a railroad bridge, the streets had been widened and were dazzling in the sun. For some reason, he couldn't think why, there were four lanes for two blocks. There was a John Deere tractor place and a block long vacant lot on one side; and a used car lot, a service station, and a drive-in bank on the other. There were two lanes through the down-town business district; then, after a few blocks of that, the lawns and shade trees, buildings and walks of the college spread with dignity and elegance on either side of the street. Again he felt absolutely alone. He drove around and through the quiet shady streets of the campus wondering if he had any business, after all, trying to go to college. But he had sent them fifty dollars pre-registration fee from Germany.

"Awwh, they can't eatcha," he told himself.

He took another slow drive around the campus and then turned back toward town. Halfway through the business district a smoked plate glass window with TUCKER'S TAVERN painted across the top and a small, red, glowing neon beer sign beneath it, caught his eye. "Ole Trapper, ole lonesome traveler," he told himself, "less us have a beer."

It was a relief just to step through the door from the brutal sidewalk into the dim, cool, beer-stale inside of Tucker's Tavern. The place was empty but for a man sitting on a stool behind the counter. He was watching a small television set with the sound cut off, which was tucked up on a dusty shelf in the corner. Beau Jim went to the bar, sat down, and ordered a Budweiser. The man winked and bobbed his head, whipped the beer out of the cooler, popped the cap off with an opener hung from his waist, and set it before Beau Jim without a word, without even looking at him. Instead, he held his hand suspended over the counter as if he were about to smack a fly. Beau Jim put his thirty cents there and the man's hand flopped down on it and scooped it off the edge. He punched the cash register open, slapped the change in, and flipped the cash drawer closed again. Before Beau Jim had taken one swallow of his beer, the man was back on his stool watching television. Still, there was nothing unfriendly about him. In fact, his actions seemed, somehow, a kind of pantomime of friendliness, and even humor, as if the two of them were old friends who had no need of talk. Beau Jim liked him immediately, an old man who got your beer and took your money with style, as if he were performing a sleight of hand trick. He was a small man with tattooed forearms, a butcher's apron on, and a paper hat advertising potato chips cocked forward on his head like a sailor's cap. An old man who watched television with the sound cut off. Probably he'd got in the habit to keep the television from competing with the jukebox, or maybe he just liked it quiet. Whatever, Beau Jim liked it somehow himself, and watched along with him. The beer was so cold, it ached in his throat, and by the time he had his second, he could feel roots growing out of his feet and into the friendly floor.

It was hours later, and the little alcohol burning motor in his

head was warm and purring when he heard another customer
come in and draw up beside his shoulder, but he was watching
a western on television and didn't even glance around until whoever it was said in a quiet, amazed voice, "Well, get a stick and
kill it fore it multiplies!"

Even through the warm beery fumes in his head, the voice
sounded familiar, but when he turned and saw the big-pored face,
looking both young and old, like an apple picked green but shriveled by the frost, and the blond hair still cut so short the scalp
showed through—the face of an honest to God friend—it hit him
so hard, he had to swallow and could not speak for a moment.

"Jimbo, where you been so long?"

"Claire," Beau Jim said, "Christ's sake, Claire Buckner."

"Shit, where?" Claire said, frowning and pulling his head
quickly into his shoulders as if Claire Buckner were someone best
forgotten, someone they both knew was no damned good, and
Beau Jim recognized again, with joy, the peculiar quality of
Claire's eyes, the recognition in them of some fundamental joke,
no matter what expression the rest of his face might be wearing.
"What are you up to, back in these parts?" Claire asked him.

"I was wondering that myself." Beau Jim said, "I'm drinking
a beer or two, I guess."

"Well, I can help you do that. Less us get us some fresh ones,
and come on over to a table. You can catch me up on what you've
been doin. I been settin in here for six years, myself."

The two of them ordered beers, and the bar keeper served them
up with little flourishes, as if he were performing a magician's
trick, or awarding them a prize. And within the next two hours,
the day turned itself around, all wrongs were righted, and Beau
Jim was as drunk and as happy as he had ever been.

He had discovered that Claire had been going to Senneca College for four years. And it didn't scare him at all that in four years
Claire had only accumulated enough credits to be a sophomore.
Claire didn't take such things seriously, never had. He couldn't
remember Claire, even once, giving the right answer in high
school. No one expected him to, students or teachers. What they
expected was what they got: some slow, wry answer that was
almost always good for a laugh so that even the teachers did not
get angry, somehow. Claire was not dumb, but if he was in
college, all things seemed possible, and Beau Jim was able to put

worry aside and listen in deep contentment while Claire told him what had become of all the people they had known.

Except for two, who had died in a car wreck; and one, who was in the penitentiary, they had all gotten married. Had mortgages, jobs and children. They mowed the grass, taught Sunday School, and gave Tupper Ware parties, Claire told him.

Beau Jim's ears had begun to itch where they were anchored to his head—they always did when he was drunk—and they felt as mobile in their sockets as the ears of a mule. He was certain he could turn them this way and that, and he often smiled with satisfaction at how clever it must look to turn an ear around, mule-like, as if he were listening to something behind him.

Claire, sitting across from him, had his crotch cupped comfortably in his left hand and a bottle of beer in his right, and after he had accounted for everyone he could think of, he was silent for a moment. Then, he shook his head, and with slow deliberation, lifted his leg and farted.

Beau Jim wouldn't have made such a comment himself, but he wiggled his itchy ears and nodded solemnly. It seemed to him, in that moment, that the two of them were survivors of some great natural disaster, the last defenders of old values, and that he and Claire alone, among all the people in Sharaw, had the virtue of loyalty.

Claire stuck his middle finger in his bottle of beer and lifted it that way to his mouth where he withdrew the finger with a little pop, and holding the bottle by the neck, his thumb on the bottom and two fingers on top, as a man might hold a cigar, he tipped it and drank. With one little explosion inside the bottle, the beer drained away. When it was empty, he stuck his finger in it again and began to rap his head with it. His lips formed various size O's, and slowly, and with feeling, he was playing "Sweet LeiLani, Heavenly Flower," in hollow gourd-like sounds on his head.

"Jesus, that was beautiful," Beau Jim said when Claire had finished.

"It was, wasn't it?" Claire said. His blood-shot blue eyes were just a fraction out of focus in his muggy face. "Would you like to hear 'If I Had The Wings Of An Angel'?"

"If it wouldn't hurt you too much," Beau Jim said.

"A musician pays no attention to pain," Claire said, "but them high notes does hurt. To make them boys come out, you got to beat the piss out of the ole head bone. But a musician pays no attention to pain."

It was as if they had dealt with the past long enough, had caught up now with the present moment, and put all other questions aside in order to consider art and pain.

"You just can't let it bother you," Claire said. "Did I ever tell you about my uncle Theodore?"

Beau Jim wagged his head *no.*

"Man," Claire said, "now he could play head. He didn't use his knuckles or a spoon or a beer bottle or anything chickenshit like that to hit hisself with." Claire wagged his head from side to side. "He was a truck driver, and he used a tire iron. He sounded like a fuckin xylophone; I mean it would bring tears to your eyes to see him play." Claire lifted his leg again, but nothing happened and he let the foot flop back to the floor. "Got drunk one time and beat hisself to death playing 'Cherri Beeri Bee.' " Claire shook his head reverently, gave his crotch a squeeze, closed his doleful, blood-shot blue eyes and played, "If I Had The Wings Of An Angel."

Beau Jim was moved and seemed on the verge of some wise and true thought about old songs, coming home, friends, drinking beer in good places, the real dead center of a man where he kept, like hunger, his need to make something of himself, something finer than anything he could conceive—all of those things together, amounted to one profound statement he could feel stir in his head and wanted to say. All homesickness, ambitions, friends and enemies were wound up in it. "Claire," he said, and leaned across the table and took Claire by the arm.

"What?" Claire said.

"Claire, life is a son of a bitch!"

Claire looked at the floor thoughtfully and bobbed his head.

"No, I mean it," Beau Jim insisted, "I mean it."

He tried to expand what he wanted to say, and missed again, but they agreed anyway and nodded their heads solemnly.

They drank and talked and agreed, until, with no transition whatsoever, he was blinking at the ceiling of his room, his tongue dry and foul in his mouth, the creases of his neck slick with sweat, and his head hurting so badly, that even to move his eyes, was pain. He had no memory of coming home, and for a few moments had no idea where everything had gone. The inside of his head seemed stuffed with a beery horse blanket in whose folds were little fragments of the evening: driving the rumbling Studebaker through the countryside and winging empty beer bottles out of the window to skitter and tinkle in the dark ditches—it was as if the sound of them still lingered—Claire telling him how he'd gotten out of the army by pissing his bed at night; how sometimes, when he couldn't make water, he'd roam the latrines at three in the morning, searching for someone else's unflushed urine to carry back to his bunk in a butt can. That didn't sound right. But in the folds of the horse blanket in his head, he found the word "incontinent," and he owned no such word as that. It had to be Claire's word. While he was searching for its meaning, he went back to sleep.

When he woke again, it was to the familiar, grumbling sound of the Studebaker, and a moment later Claire came in, looking pink and healthy and carrying a cold bottle of buttermilk.

Chapter
Seven

It was hot and glaring, and if Dan Early chanced to look up from his work toward his house and barn, the sun, glancing from their metal roofs, struck him through the eyes with light as sharp and penetrating as a knife blade. Nothing moved in the heat besides himself. And except for the two sows that lolled, and dreamed, and grunted from the shadow and stench of the low hog house—they had got out that morning and ruined the late pole beans in the kitchen garden— there were no sounds besides the sounds he made: his posthole digger going *thunk* down into the ground and the wooden handles clacking together at the top. He worked steadily, sunk so deep in thought he didn't feel the sweat frying on the back of his neck. His cotton flannel shirt stuck to him like a wet second skin, and even his overalls, which were loose enough to fit a much larger man, were soaked and heavy with sweat.

Twenty-five feet away Sheila sat under a locust tree on some feed sacks he had spread out for her. Her right leg was badly swollen where, Tuesday afternoon, a ground hornet had stung her on the ankle, and though she was better, she still could not walk very well. She was sitting absolutely still, her right leg, rosy with swelling and the same size from foot to knee, stretched out before her and her left pulled up and hugged against her chest. She rested her cheek on her knee, sucked her thumb and watched her father, almost never blinking her round hazel eyes. And as if her constant soft attention roused him, he sent his posthole digger down into the ground, wiped his face on his sleeve and asked, "How you doin, Darlin?"

She nodded her head.

"Don'cha want me to carry you on back up to the house?" he asked.

She wagged her head from side to side.

"You sure, Honey?" he asked her.

Momentarily confused about which way to shake her head to show that she was sure, she sat absolutely still. Her lips parted and she almost withdrew her thumb, but the confusion passed, and she nodded her head that she was sure.

He regarded her thoughtfully, rearranged the snuff inside his lower lip and spat, and for an instant his teeth cropped, as yellow and worn down looking as the teeth of an old horse. "Well," he said deferentially, though he worried that she was too hot. He went back to work, distracted and fretful about her comfort. Again and again he sent the posthole digger into the ground, but he was paying no attention to what he was doing. He was thinking instead about the ground hornet clinging to her slender ankle and inflicting its outrageous pain, and such a volatile anger seized him that it rattled in his throat and all but blinded him.

He had roamed around the yard until after midnight Tuesday night, searching out the ground hornet holes with a flashlight, pouring kerosene down them and waiting for the ground hornets to crawl out so he could grind them under his heel. He said to each one through his clenched teeth, "I teach you to God Damn sting!"

They were striped like yellow jackets but big, two inches long, and when they came out, they were covered with the oily blue film of kerosene, which would, itself, have killed them, though he couldn't wait for that. He brought his heel down on each one like a sledge hammer, and when he cursed them through his teeth, the spit flew. He had gotten most all of them the first night, and the next morning when Sheila was much too sick to go to school, he had gotten the few that remained—his anger cold and patient by then, but no less fierce, he would stand motionless, probing his snuff, his bleak, almost colorless hazel eyes watching the hornets fly ceaseless patterns over the few remaining stubborn clumps of Johnson grass until they dropped down at last to the thresholds of their nests and crawled in; and he, having marked the spot without fail, would pour down the kerosene, and when they emerged, grind them slowly and deliberately into the earth, able to hear and even feel through his shoe sole, their hard insect bodies crunch and crackle.

Around ten o'clock Charlene came out on the porch and stood with her hands on her hips and watched him for a while before she said, "If that ain't somethin! A grown man standin around all mornin just to kill a few bugs! You gonna make a profession out of it?" But he had made her no answer nor even taken his eyes off the hornet he was watching. And in a little she snorted in disgust and went back in the house, the screen door slapping shut behind her.

Sheila had been unable to go to school the following Thursday or Friday, and so had missed the first three days of school. At night she groaned and whimpered in her sleep, but when she was awake, she didn't complain. She was nothing like other children in that respect. She never seemed surprised when something bad or hurtful happened to her, as though she expected it. She seemed only to grow more quiet, to withdraw deep inside her small body and wait for whatever it was to pass away. That she had learned to tolerate so much, made him feel guilty and ashamed. Children didn't have any business being so companionable with pain that they didn't cry. He didn't know how, or through what, she had come to be so tolerant of it. He didn't know, and yet he had the disturbing feeling that he should know, and that somehow beyond the range of admissible knowledge, he did know. Yet she had always been that way. Like the time when she was four, and he had taken her with him to visit a farm that was up for sale. He had gotten out of the truck and shut the door, but it didn't sound right, and when he turned to see what was wrong, he discovered that she had slipped across the seat to get out behind him, and the door had closed on her small hand. He, himself, had cried out and clawed at the handle until he'd gotten hold of it and snatched the door open again. Her round brimming eyes were upon him, and she held her hand out before her, her arm drawn up as though it were her shoulder or her elbow that had been injured. At the sight of her fingers, mashed and dented hideously across and already turning blue, his stomach shrunk away to nothing, but still she did not make a sound. She let him take her hand in his, and he moved the fingers gently, dreading to feel the ends of bones gravitating, but the bones were so small and supple that the fingers appeared not to be broken, though blood blisters were already beginning to form. "Go on and cry, Punkin," he'd told her, but she had not, as though already pain were nothing new. She didn't even look at her hand, as though she had learned to renounce ownership of things that hurt. She looked at him instead, as if only his part in it surprised her. He had rushed her to the doctor, and the doctor had X-rayed the hand, opened the blisters, and bandaged it; and through it all, she had made no sound.

He sent his posthole digger into the ground again and again, his arms swelling with fatigue, and the hair on his forearms bristling with dirt and sweat. But the work gave him no pleasure or release. He was distracted by Sheila and felt he must get her in the house and out of the awful heat. He looked at her out of the corner of his eye, and flinging down his posthole digger, he tried a shuffling little dance step. He wagged his head clownishly from side to side and spat tobacco juice at the hole he'd dug, cutting his eyes around to her to see what effect he'd had on her quiet seriousness. She didn't laugh or remove her thumb, but at the corners of her mouth there were little curls of a smile. He wasn't any good at clowning.

"Ain't you thirsty?" he asked.

She shook her head immediately *yes*.

"Me too," he said, though it wasn't true. The snuff kept moisture in his mouth. "I'm near'bout dry enough to spit dust," he said. "Let's us go on up to the house and get Momma to make us some good, cool lemonade."

He wiped his hands on his thighs and wiped his forearms awkwardly on his chest to clean away the scorifications of sweat and grime so that he could carry her without getting her soiled, but when he went forward to pick her up, she withdrew her white wrinkled thumb from her mouth and said, "No, I want to stay and work with you."

"I'm wore out," he said. "Gotta rest!"

"No you ain't," she said.

"And I'm haungry!" he said, drawing out the word and exaggerating it. She allowed him to pick her up, though he knew she was on to him. He carried her held a little way out from his soaking chest, up past the hoghouse and through the barnyard where the hens clucked and cocked their heads and studied them with round insolent chicken eyes. At the top of the back steps, he kicked the screen door by way of knocking.

"You know you *could* set her down," Charlene said, coming out of the kitchen to face them through the screen. "You don't have to kick the door in."

"Well," he said.

She pushed the door aside to let them in, smacking her lips disgustedly.

After they had their lemonade and an early lunch, he left Sheila in her dim bedroom with a wet towel sprinkled with baking soda wrapped about her leg. Also he'd taken the small oscillating fan from the sideboard in the kitchen and set it on a chair by her bed, though it only stirred the heat around a little and did not cool the room. He'd hoped she would sleep, but he'd left her sucking her thumb and staring off the edge of the bed at nothing as though she were prepared to wait out the rest of the day, but not to sleep.

Outside, it was even hotter than before. The sky was no longer blue, but a pale whitish-yellow, as if all the blue had been cooked out of it. He worked steadily in the smothering heat, finishing the postholes, setting the cedar posts and tamping the red clay around them to hold them as solidly as if they'd been set in concrete, and last of all, stretching the woven wire and stapling it to the posts so that it was tight as a fiddle string.

Usually when he worked, he didn't think. More often than not he would hum some single phrase of a song over and over again, all through the morning or afternoon and gear his labor to the rhythm of it. He had learned, early, how to take his conscious mind away, let his muscle and sinew perform, and let the sweat roll. But lately things had changed. For whole days he didn't feel right. There was a certain tightness in his head and a frailty in his stomach that working could not relieve. The feelings did not constitute pain. It would have been better if they were pain, because pain was only an affliction of meat and could be borne. But this was an affliction of another sort. It seemed urgent that

he draw some circle of protection around his home and the people he loved, and he didn't know how to do it. The feeling was
so strong that sometimes he would wake up in the night with it.
He'd find himself suddenly awake with every muscle tense and
a feeling in his throat as though he had been about to cry out; and
though he knew he had caught himself in time and had made no
sound, he seemed to hear what it might have been: a keening ache
existing almost audibly in the quiet and darkness of his house.
And he would lie awake, often until time to rise, feeling seriously
bereaved, and sometimes it would almost come to him what he
was losing, but it never quite came. Now and again just before
dawn, one of Sammy's scrofulous, bony hounds would bay from
across the road and remind him of the sound he had waked up
in time to keep from making, as though it still existed in the
texture of the dark and needed only the howling of some nigger's
half-starved hound to set it keening again like a tuning fork. After
a little then, he would get up in the graying light of their bedroom and pull on his sweat-rank work clothes, but he would feel
full of despair, as though all the lessons he had learned in his
lifetime would no longer do to keep him and his, as though the
whole order of nature was askew, and hard labor would no longer
be rewarded. And he would keep that feeling all through the day.

He had it when he dug the postholes and set the posts and
stretched the wire. And though regret and mooning over things
that were past were useless in his eyes, the sort of occupation left
to a man when he had given up, or could do nothing to help
himself, all through the afternoon he was visited by unwelcome
recollections.

He brought up a heavy pinch of hard caked red clay and
banged it loose beside the hole, and before he could guard himself
against it, he was thinking of Deep Gap, North Carolina, and the
good rich loam his father's plow would turn in the twenty acres
or so of creek bottom they once owned. The thought of the black
earth rolling easily back from the moldboard of the plow, made
his throat thicken. His father had put in his tobacco allotment
there, which was only six tenths of an acre, and the rest of the
creek bottom was left to grow ragweed almost as tall and thick
as a canebrake. And there had been another thirty acres up behind the house that was good crop land too, but except for a
kitchen garden that Dan's mother mostly took care of and canned
from, that plot was never planted either, and grew up in scrub

and briars. It made him seem to lose strength just to think of such waste. He shook his head, and sweat spilled into his eyes and stung, but he kept working and didn't bother to wipe them. Then he was thinking about Beau Jim coming into the house stumbling drunk just before dawn Tuesday morning, and though it made him feel disloyal and unworthy, he resented it. Having Beau Jim back unsettled him too; it was another distraction, something else to mar the predictability of his days.

"You raised him wonst!" Charlene whispered to him as the two of them lay courting sleep after Beau Jim had awakened them. "He eats like a fattenen hog, and if you're too shy to tell him this ain't no hotel, I will," Charlene said.

"No you won't," he said.

"Well, the devil I won't!" she said.

"No you won't," he said, and he laid his hand gently on her belly, but she turned over on her side, her rump bouncing high and the bed shaking for moments afterwards.

He picked up his long-handled spoon shovel, and carrying it and the posthole digger, he paced off ten feet and began another hole, thinking against his will of evenings in North Carolina and his mother at the gate behind the barn calling, *"Sook Jerz! Sook-sook-sook-sook-sooky,"* and the cow, with slow clumsy grace and full udders swinging, coming down to the barn to be given grain and milked. And his mother milking her, saying maybe once or twice: "Now I wonder where that Vernon could be," though both of them knew. Sometimes he'd come in before Dan went to bed, his eyes glassy and his face flushed with whiskey and unruly good humor. He was a tall, lanky, black-haired man; and after squinting at Dan, who was blond and heavy set like his mother, he'd likely fix his wife with his dark eyes out from under his bushy brows and say:*

"Bernice, are you just altogether and absolutely certain that somethin didn't jump over the fence and git to you when you wuz in heat?"

But Dan's mother would simply raise her head from where she would be maybe snapping beans, and sniff through one nostril after her fashion and say: "Vernon, I won't even trouble to answer that."

But Vernon would not be put off so easily, and though he would have come home full to the eyes of corn whisky, she would be the one answering questions. "Bernice," he'd go on, "you drive a good man to drink never giving him the straight of a thing like that. I won't hold you to blame. Just tell me who it was that got to you and let me kill him."

"Hush," Dan's mother would say. "Hush yore nasty mouth." But color

would be climbing out of the square neck of her dress, and her movements would get flustered and jerky.

"God forgive you, Bernice. Yore a Jezebel," Vernon would say, and Dan's good mother, plain as biscuit dough, would all but die of the flattery and shame of it, never in her life having had a beau but Vernon, and knowing that Vernon knew it as well as she did.

Another man might have been full of excuses and promises, or been mean and hard to handle and left his wife scared and unhappy; but when Vernon rose, sighing as if his heart labored under a great weight, and made for the bedroom to sleep it off, he left Bernice only a little flustered, snapping beans and rocking herself ever so slightly back and forth, as if now, with Vernon in the house and gone to bed, she had all the contentment she could ask for.

No matter that he neglected the farm, ran it into debt, mortgaged it, and sold pieces of it outright to bail him out of one failed business scheme or another. No matter that it wasn't even his to throw away, but Bernice's, left to her by her father who had been well off enough to have two farms to leave: one for his daughter, and one for his son, Gaither, which was the biggest and best and on down the road from them toward Boone. Bernice never complained. Not when the coal hauling business went sour and Vernon sold the ten acres up by the curve of the road where the big limestone spring was, and where they built a cannery when the property sold a second time for three times what Vernon got. Not when the root and herb business failed and caused them to mortgage the whole place.

Even the summer Vernon got wild drunk and took it in his head to cut the porch off the Daniel Boone Hotel with his Model A Ford and circle saw, and the State of North Carolina brought suit against him for damage to two bridges and eleven and six tenths miles of public highway, and she had to sell the creek bottom to pay his fines; even then, she forgave him, for Vernon Early was no man to follow a mule down a furrow, he was something special.

He'd seen his father go by from high up in the pasture behind the barn. He had slipped the rope halter over the cow's big-boned, dusty crown and over her muscular ears to take her to the pasture below the road, for the upper pasture had got so full of wild onions that her milk was getting barely fit to drink, and even in that moment the soft green porcupine quills of them, warm in the sun and bruised under foot made the air rife with their odor. High in the pasture, nearly drunk with warmth, and odor of onion, and cow-shitty hocks, and made dizzy by yellow and brown butterflies swirling up from old cow flops, he had been hearing the thin, high, quavering wail a long time somehow thinking it was inside his own

*head. But when the Model A broke around the curve by the cannery, he
knew that sound didn't belong to him, but to his father's mobile sawmill
coming fast. The big circle saw was not strapped on top where it belonged
—except when the Model A was blocked up and sawing lumber—it was
on the right rear wheel and screaming like a woman; and the Model A
was wide open and floating the valves. Even as far above it as he was,
it put his teeth on edge when it went by, but he didn't get to carry the
news to his mother, for by the time he had the cow in the lower pasture
by the creek and had got back to the house, his father was back himself.*

*"Hawh, Momma, now wouldn't it a give them suckers a little change
a pace though if I'da cut that porch off." His nose was on sideways and
still blowing little bubbles of blood, like rubies, from the not quite clotted
gash between his eyes. The men who had gotten him out of the wreck, had
helped him to sit down at the kitchen table. "Them rich suckers settin up
there all day with darkies in red coats waitin on em hand and foot! Can't
you see em scatter, Momma, when I drove up that ramp with that circle
saw a'eaten wood?" His head rotated on his neck, and his eyes rolled up
in his head for a moment. "Hellkatoot!" he said.*

*But the men who had brought him in were talking, and Bernice was
standing stock still with her red chapped hands, one upon the other, over
her mouth. They had been down at Daltey's store and had heard him
coming and seen him go through the railing of the bridge over Winkler's
creek. "Boy, he wuz burnin the breeze," Irey Morritz said. "It'uz probly
the throttle lever on the steerin wheel, done his nose that way," Dallas
Ayres said. "Goin off that bridge woulda kilt a sober man," Irey said.*

*"Hellkatoot!" Vernon said, his eyes rolling open again, "I'da laid that
circle saw up against the wall, gone around that porch twicet or three
times, and cut that sucker off like peelin a apple!"*

*"Hell, he mighta done it!" Irey said, "Hit's built just like a wagon
wheel around a hub; ain't nuthin a holdin it up but them braces under-
neath just like spokes."*

*"Not after drivin all the way to Boone on the Goddanged sawblade,
he wouldn't," Dallas said calmly. "It would've been ruint."*

*"I'da dropped that sucker right on the ground," Vernon said, blinking
his eyes and trying to focus on Dallas. "With the right man running it,
that Model A and circle saw a mine'll cut animal, vegitable, or mineral."*

"Humph," Dallas said, "not no more, it won't."

*"Hellkatoot, Momma," Vernon said, waving his hand awkwardly at
a bubble of blood expanding from the bridge of his nose. He brushed at
it and began to slide, bonelessly, out of his chair.*

On a bench at the back of the courtroom, his mother wiped her brow

*with a handkerchief or twisted it between her red, mannish fingers, and
he waited for his father to touch the proceedings with humor.*

*Vernon had been made to pay the damages presented by the State for
repairs to two bridges: the first one he'd crossed, had badly sliced planking,
and the one above Daltey's store, had damaged planking and the last third
of the rail carried away. He was given a six-month jail sentence, suspended. There was also a gash in the highway, four inches deep and eleven
and six tenth miles long, but since it constituted no real hazard, it was
not repaired, and Vernon was not held liable for that damage.*

*After sentence was passed, there was a pause during which the judge
looked over the top of his glasses at Vernon, and Vernon looked at the floor.
His nose had healed—it had been six weeks since the accident—but it was
twisted and knobby at the bridge and lay almost completely on its side.
It caused him difficulty in breathing, and from time to time, he had to
take a handkerchief from his pocket and wipe his eyes, for they were red
and rheumy as though the wound still caused them to smart. He was
dressed in his best clothes, his hair combed, and his face shaved smooth and
pink by a town barber; but he only looked at the floor and wiped his eyes
until finally the judge said that, all things considered, he thought the State
of North Carolina had been lenient; but he felt it necessary to add that
if the defendant ever appeared on the highways of that sovereign state
riding on anything more destructive than the conventional rubber tire,
he would see to it that the defendant spent some time repairing and
maintaining the roadways under strict supervision. Irey, who was sitting
on Dan's right, leaned forward at that, stretching his neck toward Dallas
who was sitting on the bench in front of them. "What?" he whispered.
"Chain gang," Dallas said out of the corner of his mouth without turning
around.*

*But Dan was tense and ready to snicker—a feeling like feathers in his
nose—at what his father would say to turn the tables:* ARE YOU AL-
TOGETHER AND ABSOLUTELY CERTAIN, YORE HONOR, THAT SOMETHIN
DIDN'T JUMP OVER THE FENCE AND GIT TO YOUR MOMMA WHEN SHE
WUZ IN HEAT? *He waited and waited. His palms misty, the strain getting
to his back, his kidneys burning. But the judge went on laying down rules
for his father's behavior, and his father went on standing with his head
hung, his big chapped hands folded before him, and his breath whistling
softly and wearily through his twisted nose. The suspense had reached the
threshold of pain before the chemistry of it began to change and burn him
with fear. He tried with all his strength to will a funny comment out of
his father. He scrounged in his head for something his father might say,*

but he could think of nothing but the unworthy expressions he had heard
at Deep Gap Grammar School. Still he tried to urge even them through
the humiliation and punishment of the court room to his father. He didn't
even feel the release of his kidneys when it came, though he smelled it. He
didn't hear his mother say, "Why Dan, child?" He was giving what
concentration, what gifts, he had to his father in one long soundless cry:
YOU CAN'T SHIT ME, JUDGE, I'VE GOT A TURD IN EACH POCKET. RUN,
JUDGE, HERE COME A SHIT EATIN HOUND. UP THE OAK AND DOWN THE
PINE, I'LL KISS YORES, IF YOU'LL KISS MINE. *But Vernon stood still and*
silent, and when the judge had had his say, Vernon fished in his pocket
and drew out his handkerchief and wiped pus out of his eye.

Well, what to do with that? A man couldn't do anything with it. Just
as, after he'd quit school and was working on the farm full time, he
couldn't do anything with the sight of his uncle Gaither plowing the rich
creek bottom across the road that Bernice had had to sell him to pay
Vernon's fine. Plowing it with his matched pair of Percherons. He couldn't
do anything but turn back to his own work behind his father's one, old,
sulky mule. Even then, if his father had done nothing, he could have
brought the farm back. He was doing it, rescuing it every month from
scrub and second growth, from collapsed fences, and leaky roofs and rotten
sills, but his father always had one more scheme to try.

And what to do with that? Nothing. And even when he tamped
the red clay around the cedar fence posts and couldn't help thinking that the poorest land on his mother's farm was better than
what he stamped under foot, there was no proper thought to
think. He was only tired. Weary. It was a feeling far beyond what
could be contained in muscle and bone, or explained by the fact
that it had taken him almost until he was forty to get back any
kind of land at all to work, it was a weariness that woke him in
the night, that came from dreading something he couldn't even
name. He worked every weekday from noon until ten at night at
Willard's service station. Every morning and all day Saturday
and Sunday, he worked on his farm, but he could stand all of that
if it only bore even the smallest amount of fruit.

Chapter
Eight

It's cause they can live on nuthin, Charlene told herself, thinking about how drab Sheila looked beside them. *Give um some turnip greens and a groundhog, and they won't need nuthin more for a week if they got some cornbread and buttermilk to stretch it out. It's some lady she works for probably give her them clothes anyway,* she thought. She wondered again, with a snort of bitter humor, how they could have three children, all the right age for first grade, and all brothers and sisters, and none of them twins. *They importin em from some'ers.* She snorted again. *Unless little niggers just happen like horsehair snakes.* Every morning since she had been well enough to go, there were three out there on Sheila's side of the road, all shined up in new looking clothes and ready to get on her bus with her. Only the oldest boy was standing on the other side of the road to catch the nigger bus going the other way.

If they had what we got, they'd be riding around in a Cadillac car, and they'd still be gettin stuff give to em, cause they niggers, she thought, and wanted to laugh, but she couldn't. She didn't know if Dan had noticed that Sammy's pickininnies were better dressed than his own child or not, but she knew he was aware that his precious daughter was outnumbered four to one, if you counted the oldest one standing on the other side of the road; and she couldn't deny the deep little buzz of joy and revenge it gave her.

She looked at the breakfast dishes on the chipped kitchen table, sighed, and began to clear them, but after making one trip to the sideboard with dirty dishes, she poured herself a cup of coffee and lit a cigarette and went back to the cluttered table and sat down. Dan was in her thoughts, but abruptly she had a vision of herself pressing her thumbs into Sheila's soft small stomach and spongy ribs until the infant cry became a nonhuman sound, the sort of wheeze a certain kind of stuffed toy might make if it were squeezed. Her teeth gritted at the thought of it, and she had again the little buzz of joy, though it scared her too. She puffed on her cigarette and tried to forget about it, but she could see herself looking down on Sheila where she lay in the frilly bassinet Dan had insisted on buying. She was an ugly creature, a small, red, noisy thing that cried for no reason; and she could see herself slamming her palm down viciously, squarely over the puckered, monkey features and leaning her weight on the rubbery face until the bawling was stifled. Only then would she lift her hand away with a final wicked twist of the palm and wipe it frantically on her dress front—as though the smeared tears and slobber on her hand were the venom of a snake—and watch the small shocked creature lying rigid for a moment before it gulped the huge breath for which its lungs were starved, and its face dissolved in puckers and red lines, and the bawling reached an hysterical pitch. She might take the child up then and rock it gently until it quieted.

Again, she shut such visions out of her head and took a deep drag on her cigarette. Up on the highway she could hear the bus doors close and the peculiar whinny of the school bus engine as it pulled away. She looked out the window, past the tire swing hung from the mimosa tree to where the land began to fall gently away toward the stunted and scraggly field of corn. She could hear Dan clanking around in the barn, working on the rusty hulk of a tractor the last owner had abandoned as worthless. She could see the litters of the two sows, now half grown, roaming through the corn field. They were long-eared, but otherwise, as lean and wary as razorbacks. Because of the drought, the corn hadn't made, and Dan had decided to hog it down and save himself the expense and labor of both picking the corn and feeding the hogs, but she wasn't really thinking about that, but about the apartment in Sharaw where, while she cooked or ironed, she could look out upon the main street and watch the people pass to and fro and watch the cars go by. It was so pleasant to be right up over the center of things. The dimestore was two doors away, the Rexall drugstore was three, the Capitol theater, four. She could see its marquee from her kitchen window, and if she pressed her face against the glass, she could see an edge of the ticket booth, the bottom squares of black plastic made to look like marble, and the top, a half octagon of glass and soft light built a little way out into the sidewalk, where Edith, round and dimpled, overflowed her stool, sold tickets and popped her chewing gum. For six years Charlene had gone to the movies never less than twice a week, since Dan was content and even pleased to stay home and keep Sheila. And never a day went by that she didn't have a leisurely CoCola in the drugstore and joke back and forth with Madeline who waited on the counter and Don, the thin and pimply-faced sodajerk. And at night the neon lights from the beer joint across the street touched the venetian blinds in their bedroom and made patterns on the wall. Every season was nice in the apartment. Even when it was cold or rainy, there was bustle on the sidewalks below, and it was never like the farm where, in bad weather, there was nothing outside the windows but the wet stretching away of fields and trees, and at night, the infinite dark. The first month on the farm had been the worst. February was one continual cold rain, an idiot rain that beat on the tin roof on purpose to annoy her, and not another soul around to talk to, save when Sheila pretended to be sick so she could stay home from school, and Sheila was precious little company.

When she was alone, she had gotten so nervous and restless sometimes, she would go out and walk around the house and barn, her breath fogging, and the icy mud curling around her shoes. She had thought often of leaving Dan, of running off to some big town: Atlanta maybe, or Chattanooga, or maybe even Nashville; but she didn't know what she could do in such a place. She felt too old, too ignorant, and she admitted bitterly, not pretty enough, to be able to better herself. The last of the winter had been an awful time. And the summer was little, if any, better. It was blistering hot outside, and inside, close and stifling, so that even when she woke in the morning the sheets were damp and she was already greasy with sweat.

Even when she went to Sharaw anymore, it was no good. She felt country, just like the people who came in on Saturday to do their trading and looked half scared about being there, as if there were no place in the whole town to sit down and rest without having to pay money to do it. She couldn't quite forgive Sharaw for showing its business face to her as if she had never belonged, or for getting along so well without her. Yet she held to the idea that she could teach Dan his error, one day, and they would move back. Perhaps they would take the apartment again over Judge Taylor's Hardware Store. Perhaps they would find someone fool enough to buy the farm and give them even a little more than they had in it, since Dan had made so many improvements. And maybe he would have enough stake to lease a Service Station of his own, and they would have some money for a change, like Cass Willard. It was possible. Maybe they would even have a nice car and not a pickup, and she could learn to drive and go over to Senneca and maybe even down to Atlanta, now and again. They might go to Florida for a vacation where Cass and his wife went for a week every winter and came back with bright new clothes, and baskets of grapefruit, and oranges they had picked from the very trees, and funny faces made of coconut husks.

She sat at the table and sighed into her raised coffee cup, holding it and the cigarette in the same hand. She fluffed at her hair in back with the fingers of the other hand, being careful not to hurt the protuberant little mole growing on her neck at the hair line. But she could hear Dan working on the rusty hulk of a tractor, and a little shiver went through her, and she put down her coffee cup and stubbed out her cigarette violently in the saucer.

When she took another load of dishes to the sideboard and turned on the faucet to fill up the sink, the water spurted and spit and made her jump. It ran for a moment, and then it began to spit and gurgle, and then it quit running and the plumbing began to vibrate. She knew immediately it was the well. Lots of them around the county had been going dry. Her face flushed with anger and she started across the room to yell at Dan to come and cut the pump off before it burned up, but halfway to the back door a different thought struck her and made the roots of her hair tingle and her face feel stiff as if she had been sitting before an open fire. She could hear the pump laboring in the crawlway under the house, and she could hear Dan clanking around in the barn, fussing with the tractor, and she went back to the sideboard and turned on the radio and lit another cigarette. Inside her stomach the buzzing feeling began again, and it was almost as exquisite as pain.

Chapter Nine

He was learning to live with the heat again, which, like living with constant pain, was a matter of not thinking of it, nor dwelling on it; otherwise it would break the spirit. If it reached a hundred and ten in the shade, a man might grin and say, "God, ain't it hot though," but only in order to show that he could take it, that it did him no harm. Still, as the two of them drove toward Greenville, South Carolina, the loblolly and rough scaly-barked jack pines, the kudzu and stubborn red clay, too rude and poor to yield any man a decent living, made him shake his head in wonder to think that people would actually choose to live in northern Georgia and that he, himself, had been homesick for it. He looked out the window at a weathered barn, stained rust around the bottom, leaning toward the rear as if it were about to sit down. There was a sign painted on its roof that said: SEE ROCK CITY. *Must be all in what a man gets used to,* he thought, and he knew it was so. But there was more to it than that, although it was hard to pin down. Maybe it was just that, though a fellow might ignore a more hospitable place, there was something about red clay country that got inside a man and stirred him, marked him, and wouldn't let him go. He could see it even in Claire. Beneath all his easy going good humor, there was another quality, a quality somehow in stubborn complicity with the terrible heat and red clay; as though, if he could choose, Claire would choose no better climate nor richer earth; and if that were true, there was something ruthless about it too, as there might be about a cottonmouth, given a choice, choosing to be a cottonmouth, or a stone choosing to be a stone. There was something self-satisfied and dangerous in it. And though Beau Jim could not think it into words, he could feel it, even in Claire, and could feel the lack of it in himself. Coming home after so long away had given him a disagreeable tendency to think too much.

But Claire was a puzzle. Apparently it was true that he had gotten out of the army as a bed wetter. Beau Jim hadn't dreamed it. Claire had been drafted, saw after a day or two that he didn't like the army, and so, without any particular fuss or bother, he figured a way to get out again. It was simple. He spent everyday telling everyone how much he liked the army and spent every night pissing his bed. The poor bastard on the bunk beneath him had to find another place to sleep, while Claire kept promising his platoon sergeant, the first sergeant, and the company commander, he could control himself, if they'd just give him a break and a little time. In a week and a half what they gave him was an undesirable discharge, a section eight; and Claire took that, a duffel bag full of clothes, and a case of diaper rash on back home to Cocke County with him.

And making a living? A lifted leg. A fart. Didn't Beau Jim ever consider the God Damned lilies of the field? Two or three times a month he drove cars for his uncle from used car auctions back to his uncle's lot in Greenville. Made a hundred and fifty, two hundred dollars a month doing that, and took in another two, three hundred a month hustling pool. He'd cut Beau Jim a piece of the pie. It was as easy as that.

Where did you leave off believing him? He was very glad to be going to Greenville to meet Claire's uncle, grateful; although he didn't really believe he would be hired and allowed to make so much money for only two or three days work a month. But they were on their way there, and that seemed a little too much trouble to go to for a bluff. Twenty-five dollars a car, drive one and tow one, and you had fifty. But the big favor Claire seemed to think he was doing him was to cut him in as a pool hustling partner, and that was going too far. He didn't quite believe any of it anymore. It came to him suddenly that he had never, even as a child, quite believed Claire. For some reason he couldn't name, he had always liked him. From the moment he had first laid eyes on him and spied that joke, or whatever it was, at the bottom of Claire's eyes, he had liked him, but there had always been some doubt about what he said that no amount of proof could quite clear up. He thought that if Claire were to show him his discharge, there would be some part of him that wouldn't believe it. But it would not be polite to say so. Beau Jim tried again to explain that he wouldn't be any good as a pool hustler.

"Just rest easy," Claire told him. "Leave it all to me."

"Ole buddy, I'm just not a pool shark," Beau Jim said. He didn't know why Claire refused to understand that one simple point. "I wish I could tell you different," he said apologetically.

"A man doesn't have to be a shark to hustle pool; he just has to be better than the fellow he's playing," Claire said.

Beau Jim waited, but Claire didn't appear to be going to say anything more. Beau Jim picked his nose and looked out the window—*how the Hell can you argue with crap like that,* he thought. *The poor bastard's crazy.* If it weren't for friendship, he wouldn't have gone along with it.

Claire reached into the clever little plastic cooler installed over the differential between them and withdrew his third or fourth bottle of Budweiser—Beau Jim hadn't been keeping a strict count —and opened it one-handed with a church key hung from the side of the cooler. Other than the fact his eyes were constantly bloodshot, drinking seemed to do Claire little harm, and Beau Jim had quit trying to keep up with him.

But he couldn't help puzzling over him. He didn't seem to have any friends, like an old man who had outlived all his contemporaries. But even as a kid, no one seemed to have much to do with him; maybe it was because he was somehow old even then, maybe it was his believability. But there he was, a little gray and paunched at twenty-three, and even the car he drove was an old man's car, a pearl gray 1950 Dodge Coupe he claimed to have bid off the auction block through his uncle for next to nothing. *Believable?* It ran like a watch, and from the slow careful way Claire drove, it was likely to for a long time. His apartment, like his car, was in perfect order; his clothes, only khakis and cheap short sleeved sport shirts, were always clean and sharply pressed. And how did all that fit with the rest? All the beer he drank, the playing head, the farts, hustling pool for a living?

Claire took a pull on his fresh beer, turned his face toward Beau Jim and winked. It was a heavy face with dry, big-pored skin and a very sparse reddish-blond stubble glinting here and there on his round cheeks. "The trick to hustling is not to play anybody you can't beat, Jimbo," he said, as though, at last, he had decided to explain.

"How do you know they can beat you if you ain't played them," Beau Jim said.

"When you've had experience, you can tell. You can watch a man's stroke and tell just about how much trouble he'll be. If he looks too tough, you just don't play him. Hell," he said, "I don't even play a lot of fellers I can beat the shit out of. If I played them, I'd have to show too much, and that would be bad for business. Ever pool hall has got it's local hotshots, and you can't beat them if you want anybody else around to play you." He took another swallow of beer. "It's like rasing chickens," he said, "if you kill em all off, you put yourself out of business. Most hustlers have to keep moving just because of that. There's one that comes through these parts ever now and then, wears a Grey Hound Bus driver's uniform, but he don't drive no bus." He shook his head and laughed his breathy, whiskey laugh. "He takes all the money from the hotshots and then moves on. Maybe he's changed his costume by now, wearing bib overhauls or something," he said. "If you want to stay in one place, you got to be smart and lie in the weeds. Course we're lucky, living in a college town. Ever year a new crop of suckers comes to us."

Beau Jim got a beer out of the cooler for himself. "If you were telling me we were going to try to make a living playing poker or shooting dice, I'd like it better," he said.

Claire gave him a sideways look. "Horse dookie," he said, "I'm not talking about gambling, man."

All the way to Greenville, Claire went very slowly but steadily through bottle after bottle of beer and winged his empties out the window. Beau Jim had two himself and could feel them. They gave him a certain philosophical distance on himself. He was back in Cocke County, he was thinking, and he had begun to be able to take the heat again, but he had no proper feeling of home. Dan was all the time busy. He was up before good light in the

morning and didn't get in from the service station until around
ten thirty in the evening, and there was just no way to break into
his constant labor and get at him. He seemed the same old Dan,
the quiet, slow talking brother he remembered, but he was always just a little out of reach. Charlene, on the other hand, was
testy and made him think that he ought to be looking for another
place to live. He could see himself moving out without ever
having a chance to sit down with Dan and have a good talk; or
even, since Dan was not much of a talker, sit around on the porch,
say, and not talk, but have a smoke and be still for a good long
time and maybe just watch the cars go by up on the highway.
Something of that nature seemed important, but he didn't think
there was going to be a chance for it. And of the pool hustling,
he thought: what the hell, if it didn't work, and of course it
wouldn't, it wasn't like joining the army. All he had to do was
put down his pool cue and walk away.

"You're smart," Claire was saying, "you'll grab right on to it.
If you work it right, you can take a college boy for thirty-five or
forty dollars a month, and he'll never know where his money is
going. He'll be blaming the laundry for overcharging him, the
cost of food, the lousy gas mileage his car gets, or even his room-
mate for stealing from him, but he'll never think of you if you
handle him right. You just have to help him believe what he
wants to believe anyway, which is that he's breaking even, or
maybe even a little ahead of you. I'll tell you, hoss, it's scary."
Claire began to laugh a low gravelly laughter and shake his head.
"I had a kid last year—father owned a mill or something—and
I'd been taking him for a hundred and fifty dollars a month, near
about. And, you know . . ." Claire winged an empty beer bottle
out the window and reached into the cooler and brought out the
last of the beer, and laughed his gravelly laugh again, "I'd lose to
him from time to time as a matter of policy. Well, we were
leaving the pool hall one night, after I'd let him take about ten
dollars from me to sorta keep the pump primed—I used to call
him 'Slick' all the time—and I said, 'Slick, you were way ahead
of me tonight. Damned if I'm not goan have to get me another
job to be able to support you.' And ole slick didn't say anything
for a while, and then he took hold of my elbow and stopped me
and acted embarrassed and tried to give me fifteen dollars, telling
me how he knew he'd been taking too much of my money."

Claire shook his head and laughed on and on, his whiskey voice rasping pleasantly until Beau Jim began to laugh too.

"What did you do?" Beau Jim asked.

"Hell, I took it," Claire said, and he laughed so hard he went into a kind of coughing fit and had to slow down to clear his throat and spit out the window. "I agreed with him and took it," he said after he had gotten himself under control, and began to laugh again.

"Hustling is a matter of psychology, Jimbo. In two weeks I can get your game steadied up where you can beat seventy-five percent of the fish we'll play, and then the rest is psychology."

As they came into Greenville, Claire explained how Beau Jim would be a decoy in one situation and a partner in another, and they'd split the money down the middle. But it didn't sound workable at all. Still, Beau Jim was content to go along with it for a little while and not argue anymore. What harm could it do? He didn't think Claire actually believed it himself.

But Claire's uncle, it turned out, did own one of the biggest used car lots in the state of South Carolina. Beau Jim was shocked at the size of it. There appeared to be four or five acres of cars in neat rows and a whitewashed cinderblock building perhaps two hundred feet long by fifty feet wide with half a dozen bays just for washing cars on the left hand side, a very large garage for mechanical work on the right, and at least ten offices for salesmen in the middle. Around the whole property a string of colored flags the size and shape of school pennants hung suspended ten or twelve feet above the ground with the word, VALUE, printed down the center of each.

"Jesus!" Beau Jim said, "Your uncle owns this whole thing?"

"A fine man too," Claire said, opening the door and swinging his feet around to get out, "a fine man. You see those niggers over there washing cars?" He flicked his hand in their direction. "Pays em by the car, and they have to work like niggers to make twenty-five cents an hour more than the minimum federal wage. If he paid them by the hour, he wouldn't get half the work out of them. Plus he'll make em do a car over, if they don't do a first rate job, and he couldn't stand to do that if he was paying them by the hour." He winked at Beau Jim and gave his elbow a little nudge, and they started toward the building. "You'll love working for him, Hoss. Prince of a fellow. Pays his salesmen a straight commission. A whopping five percent. Don't know what he does about his mechanics, probably loses a lot of sleep over them. Come on," he said, "Let's get this over with. This place makes my ass suck putty."

They found Claire's uncle in the doorway between the salesmen's cubicles and the service department. He was talking to a mechanic, his head moving in jerky, impatient nods. He was thin, rather than paunchy, as Beau Jim had somehow expected, but he did have a cigar in the corner of his mouth. When he turned toward them, Claire said:

"Brought you a new driver." Claire tipped his head toward Beau Jim. "This here is Mad Dog Early."

Claire's uncle kept both hands in his pockets, chewed his cigar and looked at Beau Jim with his small hard eyes. Beau Jim said, "Hydee," and turned a little red.

"All right," Claire's uncle said, "I can use him."

"Good," Claire said. "Old Hit-And-Run here can use a job."

Claire's uncle rolled the cigar from one corner of his mouth to the other with no expression whatever on his face. "How do I call you?" he asked Beau Jim.

Beau Jim thought he was asking him what he really used for a name, but before he could say "Call me Beau Jim," Claire said: "Just call me. If I can get him sober enough to open his eyes, I'll bring him with me."

Beau Jim laughed, but Claire's uncle did not.

"All right," he said, giving Beau Jim one last going over with his unforgiving eyes, "you saved me a call. I can use you both Friday to go to Atlanta." He turned away from them then and started through the door to the service department. "Be here at five-thirty in the God Damned morning," he said and disappeared around the corner.

Neither of them said anything until they got outside again, but once they were in the open, Beau Jim said, "I appreciate the build-up you gave me. You went out on a limb, didn't you, son of a bitch?"

"That rat fucker," Claire said.

"Well, thanks for the recommendation anyway," Beau Jim said. "I mean, Christ, your uncle ain't the friendliest bastard I ever met, but compared to you, he don't seem half bad."

"Come on," Claire said. "I've run out of beer, and we need to put your ass in training."

When they got back in the car, Claire said, "Don't give that asshole another thought. He's my mother's brother, and they ain't nobody on that side of the family worth a shit. My ole man loaned him the money to get started fifteen years ago and never did get it back." Claire swung the Dodge out into the traffic and winked at Beau Jim. "Now, hoss," he said, "we goan get down to real business."

"That's a funny thing," Beau Jim said, "I never thought you had a mother and father. I remember your aunt, but whatever happened to your folks?"

Claire didn't seem to mind talking about it. It seemed less than nothing to him that his mother had left him and his father when he was six years old. She had run off North with another man. Claire's father had gone after her and left him in care of his aunt who lived in Sharaw, and Claire had seen neither of them since. When he was eleven, word had gotten back that his mother had died of an overdose of sleeping pills while she was living with some new man. "Awwh, she was a whore anyway," Claire offered simply.

His father was in Detroit when last heard from, and that was years ago, though he had sent money for Claire's keep until Claire was eighteen. Still, Claire had no bad words for his father or his aunt, who was his father's sister. And even when he had called his mother a whore, it seemed without rancor and even generous, as though he were offering an excuse for her.

"Which side of the family was your uncle Theodore on?" Beau Jim asked.

"I don't have no uncle Theodore except when I'm drunk," Claire said. "He's my best relative. But what do you say we quit turnin over rocks, ain't nuthin under em worth the strain."

They stopped at a bowling alley a few blocks away where there were two pool tables, one covered in gold, and one covered in blue felt. "I don't do any business here, Jimbo, so I can show you a thing or two without revealing my true identity," Claire said. "Shazam!" he yelled and gave a jump toward the bar to get himself a beer. He racked the balls for Beau Jim and told him to knock them all in the holes. When, with many misses, Beau Jim had got that done, Claire bobbed his head and seemed pleased. "You got a good eye," he said. "Sweet Jesus knows you ain't got nuthin else, but you got a good eye."

Surprise again. It appeared that he was serious about this hustling business. For the rest of the day he had Beau Jim work on his bridge and his stroke, making him cradle the butt of the cue very lightly between the thumb and middle finger of his right hand, making him shoot through the cue ball as though it were three or four inches ahead of where it really was. Claire didn't shoot at all himself; he didn't even pick up a cue; he merely watched Beau Jim, occasionally reaching out to adjust the position of Beau Jim's bridge and curse his missing finger, or take him by the right wrist and shake it and tell him to keep it Goddamn loose, Goddamn it. He congratulated Beau Jim, teased him, cursed him, goaded him, repeated over and over again that he had to keep his right wrist loose, that he must not squeeze the butt of the cue, that he must shoot through the cue ball; that he must line up the shot, pick a spot on the object ball and then shoot through the cue ball to that spot.

Beau Jim had never shot very much pool, for some reason, but he found he liked it. He felt he owed Claire for the driving job and was content to go along with him in this business of pool, at least for a while. He wondered, himself, why he had never done more of it. It was pleasure, a good thing, to see a ball plop down into a pocket, and while he shot rack after rack of balls, Claire drank beer after beer. Finally Beau Jim realized that Claire was no longer offering either criticism or advice, but sitting on the adjacent pool table with his chin tucked into his chest, his eyes extremely red and bleared.

"Buddy," Beau Jim said, "I think you're a little drunk."

"You are absolutely right," Claire said. "Absolutely. Absolutely." He wagged his head from side to side and belched. "We goan make one hell-uv-a-team, Amigo. Ha!" he said, and his head tossed as if the laugh had been a little explosion that snapped it back. "In one week," he said and held up a finger, though he was looking at the floor, "in one week, you will be shooting two hundred percent better than you do now. Then we might even take a little of the working classes money. Move around a little. Ha!" he said and his head snapped up, and then he tucked his chin into his chest and belched. "We got em by the short hair, Jimbo. But first," he said and he held up his finger again, "I'm goan give you a little lesson in humility." He slid unsteadily off the pool table and got himself a cue and racked the balls.

Beau Jim allowed himself to feel pretty good. He had half a

dozen times run five or six balls off the table before he missed and that was real improvement. Who was to say, maybe they would win money at it.

"Play you a game of nine ball before we go," Claire said and he motioned for Beau Jim to break, which Beau Jim did, though nothing went down. When he looked at Claire, he found that Claire was leaning against the side of the pool table grinning drunkenly at him and carefully chalking the end of his little finger instead of the tip of the cue. Beau Jim knew immediately that he wasn't so drunk as he appeared, or that, in any case, he was able to get himself under control, for the business of chalking his finger could only be a joke. He looked at Beau Jim and squinted his eyes and pursed his wet lips. "Don't you never do to nobody what I'm fixing to do to you, old friend," he said, and smoothly, without missing a shot, he ran all the balls off the table. The last ball he shot in using the wrong end of the pool cue, after which, he winked, lifted his leg and farted.

Chapter

Ten

Beau Jim flung out his arms and
yelled, "Whooeey," but the pig went right on by him and clattered away through the dry cornstalks. Dan tucked the Copenhagen a little more snugly inside his lower lip and jerked his head
in amusement. "Why didn't ya catch a'holt of em there, Mr.?" he
asked.

"Cause I'm afraid of em, by God," Beau Jim said and laughed.

"Shaww," Dan said softly and deprecatingly, since he could
think of nothing else to say. He had meant no offense, had intended no malice nor condescension, and Beau Jim had understood. But Dan began to fear that he'd caused Beau Jim embarrassment. He was, in fact, very proud of Beau Jim and had begun
to call him "Mr.," not merely out of whimsy, but out of a very
real respect for the fact that very soon, Beau Jim would actually
be attending college.

"Don't you remember Irey?" Beau Jim asked him.

For a moment the name floated free and familiar in his head,
but he could attach to it no man he knew. Then, all at once, he
remembered an old gentleman named Irey Stalkup who used to
hang around the service station when Beau Jim was in grammar
school. He always wore very shiny shoes and a blue work shirt

buttoned primly at the neck, and he liked to argue politics with old Luther Willard who ran the service station in those days, and he loved to pitch horse shoes. Dan gathered moisture in his mouth and spat. *Irey was missing a thumb on his left hand. A pig had bitten it off.* "Awwwh, that was an old sow he was a'messin with," Dan said and chuckled, "wad'nt no little shoats like these here."

"Shoats?" Beau Jim said. "Shoats! You call these half wild, razorbacked . . . Heyuup!" he yelled, but the pig didn't turn and got by him on the right, and a third sprinted almost between his legs. *They got his number,* Dan thought, *They, ever one, goan run by him.* Sure enough, the dozen or so pigs that remained ahead of them had broken into nervous little clumps. They grunted to one another; tested the air with their flat, wet, articulate snouts; bunched; seemed to talk it over; and then strung out along the fence, doubling back toward Beau Jim.

In the beginning they had had no trouble. The three of them —he, Charlene, and Beau Jim—had herded the pigs easily through the corn toward where the pickup was parked and Sheila waited, perched on the left rear fender and ready to slide back the bar over the tail gate. The pickup, with its high wooden sides on, was parked close to the gate, the front bumper pulled right up against the fence. There was a plank laid against the wheels on the right side so the pigs wouldn't be tempted to run under the truck, and the idea was to herd them up next to the pickup, open the gate until it touched the rear bumper of the truck and thereby close them in a kind of temporary pen from which he could extract them one by one and run them up the ramp into the truck —the ramp being two long two-by-tens laid from the tailgate to the ground, supported in the middle by a saw horse. But the closer the pigs got to the fence and the pickup truck, the more suspicious and edgy they became. First, they had tried to flank him by going to the left around Charlene, but Charlene was carrying a handful of clods, and she threw them accurately. "Git, you nasty things!" she shouted and burst a clod of dirt smack on the snout of the closest pig, and when he turned, she hit him dead center as he was going away. She hit another on the shoulder and a third on a foot. There were squeals and startled grunts and a great clattering of retreating pigs through the corn. They did not try to run over Dan.

Now, the three that had got around Beau Jim seemed to pull

the rest like a magnet, and they all began to hump it down the fence line on the right. Beau Jim was moving over to intercept them, but they didn't turn back until Dan faded over behind him, and they caught his scent and faltered. They handled the air with their flat, wet, mobile snouts and then doubled back toward the truck. For a while they were confused, but when they realized that Dan now had the right flank and Beau Jim had the middle, they funneled again toward Beau Jim. Dan came over to head them, and the two or three hindmost pigs seemed immediately to calculate the angle and give up; then another four or five did the same thing. Finally, all except the lead pig, faltered, realized they had been headed, and gave up. But the foremost of them must have felt he could run over Beau Jim before Dan could intercept him because he kept coming. He was coming very fast, but at the last moment, when he and Dan were almost in collision, Dan bent at the knees and caught the pig's left rear foot and allowed its momentum to swing him around on his heels and pull him up into a standing position again. In another second he had both rear feet.

Above the pig's terrific squeals Beau Jim shouted, "Now how the Hell did you do that?"

While the pig kicked desperately with his hind feet and Dan's arms absorbed the shocks, Dan raised his eyebrows and tried to puzzle out what Beau Jim was asking him, but he couldn't quite understand how the question was aimed. "Just catched on to em," he said apologetically.

"Sure," Beau Jim said. He drew his mouth down at the corners and shook his head. "I got it now. All you do is just grab the bastards."

All at once Dan understood that the question had not been a question at all, but a statement of admiration, and it embarrassed him a little. "Git em by the hind feet and they cain't do nuthin," he said. "You can run em around like a wheelbarrow then." He brought the pig up to Beau Jim to demonstrate. The pig walked on its front feet and screamed as if it were being torn apart, murdered, inch by inch.

"You hold onto this'un, and we'll get them others catched up," Dan told him. "Hold em tight but don't fight em."

Beau Jim held the pig, and Dan and Charlene moved the others in by the truck and swung the gate around to pen them.

"If you think you and brother-in-law there can handle it, I'd like to git on back to my kitchen," Charlene said.

"Well," Dan said.

"I got better things to do than mess with pigs," she said.

"Well," Dan said.

But when he took the pig from Beau Jim and called to Sheila to pull back the bar so he could run the pig up the ramp and into the truck, he saw that Sheila had her hands clamped over her ears against the terrible squealing.

"Pull the bar back, Punkin," Dan called to her again, but she kept her hands over her ears, looked at him with her round startled eyes, and didn't move.

"Shoot," Charlene said, who had started out the open gate. She came back into the field and went around to Sheila and pulled her off the fender. "Git on to the house," she said, but Sheila stood where she was, watching her father holding the squealing, screaming pig. Charlene pulled a hand away from her ear and said, "Git on to the house," and Sheila began to run with her hands clamped again to the side of her head. Charlene pulled back the bar and Dan ran the pig up the ramp and off the end into the bed of the truck. "You better get em on loaded if you want any dinner," Charlene said.

"Well," Dan said, and with Beau Jim opening the gate to admit him and closing it quickly on his heels again, and Charlene sliding the bar back and forth, Dan went again and again into the maelstrom of squealing pigs and extracted them one by one until he had ten in the truck, and Beau Jim swung the gate around and closed it, and the two remaining pigs broke for the open cornfield.

"Yawl come on quick as you can," Charlene said and started back to the house.

The two of them lifted the two-by-tens off the tailgate and laid them up next to the fence. Dan cleared the saw horse away, and Beau Jim moved the board propped against the wheels. Finally Dan drew his handkerchief from his back pocket and mopped his face and the back of his neck. He dug his tongue under the roll of snuff inside his lower lip, flipped it out, ran his tongue over his teeth and spat. "Well, Mr. Early," he said, "Less us go on up to the house and git our dinner."

"Boy I'm ready," Beau Jim said. "I'll get the gate and you drive on through."

"Less leave it down here, if you don't care," Dan said. "Sheila don't seem to like that pig squealin much. Less us just walk up," he said.

He drove through the gate and Beau Jim shut it behind him, and the two of them walked the two hundred yards or so to the house. Their feet raised little puffs of pink dust, and Dan felt fine, not even tired, until he glanced toward the house and saw the drilling rig in the side yard. He kept his steady pace up the road, but the empty shrinking sensation came again to his stomach. For minutes, sometimes almost as much as an hour, he could forget its presence, though he could not look toward his house without seeing it. It was bigger than a small fire truck, and it was red; and if he looked in its direction, it was as impossible to ignore as a piece of grit in the eye. *Five dollar a foot*, he repeated to himself, again in despair, *little ole bitty round hole in the ground no bigger around—not even big as a groundhog hole—got no business to cost a man five dollar a foot.* His stomach drew down upon itself in a bitter knot. *They ain't nuthin for it though. Not a thing for it, but to go on ahead and get her dug.*

"Hit's dug, but a goodurn," the man had told him when he'd first come to look at the farm, "Hit's never yet went dry." And it wasn't none of his farm. He only rented it, and that's why it was so run-down likely. Why should he take a pride in a thing that wasn't his own? Out past the barn, a Bob White whistled, and another answered from far down towards the river, though that was only another pleasure, a deep, strong pleasure to be sure, but he had already made up his mind to buy the farm. What with the cool of the evening upon the land, it being Fall, and the dew already making up and lifting the smell of earth and grass the way it does, and on down the road, some man's cows bawling as they will that time of year and day; all he had wanted then was to get hold of that space of earth where the daylight was fading and the quail calling, and the dew had lifted the cool fragrant smell of grass and dirt. So it was not the man's fault for having said the well was good, for, in his mind he had already bought it, and had him back the land that his father had not, after all, robbed him of. And though Charlene would not even get out of the truck to look at the house, he had made up his mind. She would mend. She would see that she was wrong.

They came up into the yard where the rig was scotched and blocked, but idle, since the men were around on the other side of the house in the shade eating their lunch. *He had waited a week and the water didn't come back, and he had spent twenty-four fifty for a rebuilt pump with nothing for it to bring up. So now it was five dollars a foot for drilling, and what if it was two hundred feet before they struck enough to stop? Down already over fifty feet—two hundred and fifty dollars worth of hole and not enough water to make a pot of coffee. Thirty-five dollars a pig at the stock barn in Butler would give him another twenty feet, if they had not already got that while he was catching up the pigs.*

"Go on ahead and wash," he told Beau Jim when they came up the back steps and through the door to the tiny screened-in back porch, and Beau Jim dipped into the milk can full of water and filled the washbasin resting on the rough wooden sideboard. He took the soap from the scummy aqua dish and washed quickly without rolling up his sleeves and got the cuffs of his army shirt wet. He dashed the water through the rusty place in the screen out to the ground where there was an island of lush green grass, dried his hands on the feed sack towel hanging from a nail, and went in the kitchen.

Dan took a dipper of water for himself and rinsed his mouth of the snuff that lingered in it and spat through the rusty place. *What if they went down two hunnert feet and didn't get nuthin?* the grieved voice inside him asked. He made it no answer. He rinsed his mouth again and spat and poured the rest of the dipper into the tin wash-basin. Carefully he poured two more dippers of water into the basin, rolled his sleeves, and washed his hands and wrists and forearms vigorously as if in an effort to raise his spirits. He even dipped up water with his hands and washed his face and the back of his neck. He took the damp feed sack towel and dried his face and neck and hands and arms, rubbing hard enough to make the skin pink, hard enough so that the skin tingled for a long time afterwards.

He was not hungry, but neither did the taste of food offend him, and he ate almost as much as usual, but he did it mechanically, without haste and without pleasure. When he was almost finished, he remembered to tell Charlene what he should have told her the evening before. The business of the well had pushed it out of his mind. She was not sitting at the table with him and Sheila and Beau Jim, but across the kitchen where she had set herself a plate on the sideboard.

"Cass was askin yestidy if there was any doves a'feedin where I was hoggin down my corn," he began.

"Christ, there must be a thousand of em in there," Beau Jim said.

"I told him there was a good many," Dan said, and he looked up toward Charlene. "I told him to come on out tomorrow and bring his gun," he said, and he left the end of the sentence up in the air as if he were asking a question.

Charlene was through eating, and she took a puff of her cigarette and picked a piece of tobacco off her tongue. "It don't make a never mind to me," she said. "What do you think I care about it for?"

"I told him to come on to supper," Dan said.

Charlene let the hand that held the cigarette flop to the sideboard. "I hope to fly, you did!" she said. Her voice was full of both anger and amazement. "No water in this house, and you askin people to supper! I hope you ast his wife and youngins too." She got up suddenly and scraped the remains of her lunch into the slop bucket and almost flung her dish to the back of the sideboard. "Why don't you ast what's his name, your buddy, Claire, to supper tomorrow evenin too?" she said to Beau Jim. "And I'll ast the niggers across the road, and we'll have us a party!" she said.

"Cass ain't expectin no big spread," Dan told her. His face had lost some of its color and he fingered the wiry tufts of hair that grew out of his ears as if they were somehow responsible for what he had heard. "Hit's just a matter of settin another place to the table," Dan said. "He knows we carryin water."

"Better yet," Charlene said, coming forward to pick up Beau Jim's and Sheila's plates, "better yet, why don't we just move in with the niggers and invite everybody over there. We don't live like white folks noway," she said. "Least they got water over there," she said. She took Sheila's plate and plopped it into Beau Jim's; picked up both their glasses, clacking them together; and turned on her heel. "Even if they don't use it, they got it." She dipped a pot into the milkcan of water sitting in front of the sink and slid the pot on the stove to heat for the dishes. "Tell yo daddy how them little niggers teases you cause they got a television and you ain't," Charlene said to Sheila. She wiped her hands on her apron and laughed. "Why doncha tell him that?"

"Whoa now," Dan said. He could feel pin pricks at the back of his neck and at his temples.

"They didn't tease me," Sheila said, "They just ast me did I have one."

"Shoot," Charlene said, "that least girl asked you if you didn't have no new shoes too, didn't she?"

"Yes'um, but she won't teasin me," Sheila said.

"Well, she sure nuff had new shoes, though, didn't she?" Charlene said.

"Whoa now," Dan said. His temples were tingling, and he wanted to frame some statement that would justify him, but he could extract nothing from the place in his throat where his anger bubbled and all his words seemed lodged.

"Whoa?" Charlene said. "Whoa? You think I'm a mule er somethin!"

"Christ, Charlene," Beau Jim said, "the man just said he was going to bring Cass Willard to supper, that's all."

"It's a whole lot of your business too," Charlene said, and scooped up his silverware, a plate with a few sliced tomatoes left on it and a bowl with a rim of grits snuggled along one edge. "What is it you do around here besides eat and sleep?" she asked him.

Beau Jim's jaw went rigid and he looked as though he was going to say something, but Dan spoke instead.

"When Cass comes in tomorrow evenin, you'll set him a plate just like the rest of us," Dan said calmly. He rose from his chair and laid his hand for a moment on Sheila's head, and the anger in him seemed to shake down and become a kind of heavy sadness.

Charlene came back to the table and took a bowl of green beans and a platter with cornbread on it. "Maybe I will, Mr. big britches," she said, "and just maybe I won't."

"I don't want to hear no more," Dan said. "Whatever grub we got, is what you'll lay out, and he'll have to go it just like the rest of us will," he said.

"Is that a fact?" Charlene said.

"You want to ride to Butler with me?" Dan asked Beau Jim, and Beau Jim, a little red in the face, got up.

"You see can you get me some water in this house fore you decide to entertain the county," Charlene said.

"It's a gettin got," Dan said.

"Lemme go too, Poppa," Sheila said plaintively.

"Now Punkin," Dan told her, "you don't want to ride to Butler with no pigs. You stay and hep your Momma."

"Nooooo," Sheila said, her voice, small, but rising up the scale,
"I wanna gooooo."

"We'll be on back directly," Dan said. "You hep your
Momma." He patted her head clumsily, and she stuck her thumb
in her mouth and shook her head *no*, but without any conviction.
She stared at the oil cloth where her plate had been.

When they started the truck and pulled down the dirt road, the
pigs squealed and screamed and fought each other. And when the
pickup wallowed and bounced from the dirt road up onto the
highway, there was such a terrible screaming and commotion in
the bed of the pickup that Beau Jim turned to look through the
rear window and saw two or three of the pigs bite each other
with quick violent motions of the head. Near the tailgate one pig
took another by the ear and shook his head viciously, exactly as
a dog might have done. After they were on the highway for a
while the pigs seemed to settle down a little, but even then there
were occasional outbursts of commotion in the bed of the pickup
which seemed to pass with sudden contagion through every pig
until all had bitten, kicked and squealed.

Dan had said nothing since they had left the house. He had a
fresh pinch of Copenhagen tucked inside his lower lip, and he
probed at it with his tongue, and occasionally his worn down and
yellow teeth cropped, and spat out the window.

After they had driven two or three miles and the pigs had
settled down, Beau Jim shifted his feet and got a Lucky out of a
pack in his shirt pocket. "I've been thinking about my room and
board," he said. "Seems to me a hundred and fifty dollars a month
ought to about cover the damage. How do you read it?"

Dan turned to face him. He tucked the snuff deeper into his
lower lip. "What are you talkin?" he said, and he turned toward
the window and spat.

"A fellow's not supposed to live free," Beau Jim said. "I'm a
grown man. I've got to pay my own way."

"You not going to pay to live at my house," Dan said. "I don't
even want to hear no more about it."

"It would cost me a lot more than a hundred and fifty anywhere else," Beau Jim said. "I won't stay unless you'll let me pull
my part of the load."

Dan spat out the window and blew a little snort of air through his nostrils. "Well I ain't got to where I start chargin my own kin to live with me yet," he said. "You just go to that college and git yore education. That's a'plenty for you to pay for and worry about. Don't let me hear no more about this room and board, now. Yore welcome to stay with us as long as it serves you," he said and probed the snuff with his tongue and spat out the window.

Chapter

Eleven

Dan was on the north side of the field standing in the shade of a locust tree. Claire was far below him on the eastern edge beneath the big dead chestnut snag. Beau Jim was squatting just outside the fence on the southern side of the field. And Cass Willard was on the west in the ditch beside the road.

Though the sun was almost down, it was still hot enough to stick the shirts to their backs; and only occasionally did a breath of air stir to rattle the dry cornstalks, and it did not cool, since it was only a movement in the heat.

There had been many doves, and Dan was watching three more winging up the fence line from the southeast. When it appeared that Beau Jim was not going to see them, he shouted, "Commin'atcha, Jimbo."

Beau Jim came up like a jack-in-the-box, and his shotgun said, "Kapow! Kapow!" But no doves fell. "Moose shit!" Beau Jim said and sat down again.

The doves flared toward Dan, and he tucked the Copenhagen down inside his lower lip and drew the hammer back on his pump gun. It was an old gun and all its bluing had worn away so that it was the color of an old nickel, and around the last inch of the barrel a white piece of adhesive tape had been wrapped. When the gun came up in his big chapped hands, the doves saw the movement and flared toward the west. But even as they shied away, the white piece of adhesive tape caught up with the middle one and bucked, and the dove was slapped askew and began to fall. He pumped the action and caught up with the lead bird just as it was going into the sun and shot again. The dove dropped out of the glare and into sight, and its wings, pulled upward by its descent, trailed it down like rags. He pumped the action again, and the adhesive tape was under the remaining dove, but though it was going dead away from him, it was too far, and he did not shoot. He lowered the gun and eased the hammer back to half cock.

The dove was winging straight for Cass Willard. He came up out of the ditch, and his automatic said, "Kawhung! Kawhung!" Dan could feel the columns of shot winnow the air many feet above his head. Then the dove was past Willard, but he had turned with it. When he fired the third shot, the dove seemed to lose momentum and direction and began a kind of circular and fluttery descent. It landed on the road, and Willard got out of the ditch and went after it. The bird made fumbling, awkward attempts at flight, but Willard overtook it and slapped it down with his baseball cap. He caught it then and pulled its head off and held the body out to the side while the wings beat furiously and the heart pumped the blood out. "By God, this is one them damned razorbacks of yours won't get," he said.

Dan didn't know what to say to that, so he didn't say anything. He found his two doves and brought them back beside the locust tree and dropped them in the shade with the others. He had perhaps fourteen in all.

"I think yore pigs have eat enough of my birds to where you ought to give me at least a ham when you slaughter em," Willard said as he got to his ditch and squatted down again.

Dan could not think how to answer that, either. Some answer was needed and he knew it, and it embarrassed him. He did not want to give Cass Willard a ham. He couldn't quite tell whether or not Willard was kidding.

"Over your head," Beau Jim shouted, and Dan gave his snuff a tuck and looked up, but there were no doves over him. They were wheeling over the road and ditch. Willard shot, and one of the two doves tumbled down into the corn field, and then he shot twice more, but he didn't get the other one.

Willard started across the fence but suddenly he yelled, "Heiii, you son of a bitch!" and stepped down on his side again and picked up a rock and threw it. "Get outta here, God Damn it!" he shouted. "Fastest eater I ever saw. That son of a bitch ate that bird fore it even hit the ground good. Heiii!" he yelled and threw another rock and this time a pig squealed shrilly. "Hah," Willard said, and then more to himself than to anyone else, though Dan could hear, he said, "I ort to shoot the son of a bitch."

"That must be ten those bastards have got off me already!" Willard shouted. "I think you goan owe me a whole pig fore the evenin's over."

Willard had lost only four doves; Dan remembered each of them clearly. It puzzled him why he would want to pretend that he'd lost so many more, but he would not argue with him if it pleased him to say he'd lost ten.

At that moment there was a shot from the other end of the field, and they looked and saw a dove falling from the chestnut snag.

"Don't you ever shoot unless they're sittin, you bastard?" Beau Jim called.

Claire's voice, made thin by the distance, came back to them from beneath the chestnut snag: "Awwh, he had one foot in the air."

"You bushwhackin bastard!" Beau Jim yelled.

Although Beau Jim had shot over two boxes of shells, he only had four doves, and one of those had been sheer accident. There had been four doves flying in a line, and he had aimed at the first one and killed the last. He had also shot a dragon fly. Willard had yelled *commin atcha*, and he had heard the soft wheedling of dove wings and turned. When he saw what he thought was a dove coming toward him from twenty yards out, he snapped Dan's new double to his shoulder and fired. The dragon fly was hovering only about ten feet away, and it simply disappeared. Just as he fired, when it was too late to stop, he had known it wasn't a dove. Though no one had been close enough to see what he had done, his face throbbed with embarrassment for minutes afterwards. "Jesus Christ," he'd muttered to himself, "you're gettin flaky as Hell."

He had almost quit when he shot the dragon fly. He was hot and tired and so thirsty his throat made clicking noises when he tried to swallow. Also his shoulder was very tender. He had unbuttoned his shirt and lifted it away from his shoulder to look, and there were little freckles of blood under the skin where the unyielding plastic buttplate of the shotgun had pounded him over fifty times. He had bought high-powered shells because they were more expensive and he thought, therefore, they would be better; but later Dan told him that the only difference he had ever been able to see in high powered shells was that they kicked harder.

Sitting on the edge of the field, hot, thirsty, and disgusted, Beau Jim had begun to decide that Dan and Cass Willard, and perhaps even Claire, had a certain foolish capacity to endure heat and thirst that he did not have. Also, he could not hit the doves. He'd tried everything. He'd held on them, led them from one to some-thing like ten feet, he'd snap shot; and all with the same result; the shotgun kicked the shit out of his shoulder, and the doves kept right on flying. He wanted a beer, a beer so cold it hurt his throat, and he wanted to be in a beer joint where it was cool and dark. To jump up out of the weeds every time some bird flew by and pull a trigger so that a goddam buttplate pounded his shoulder and a goddam explosion pounded his ears, was crazy; and to wait around in the blazing sun, dying of thirst, in order to do it, was even crazier. Dan and Willard and Claire were not tougher than he was, he decided: they were dumber. He thought he could whip two of the three of them, if it came to that. But he'd had enough of dove hunting. He didn't need it. He was going to be a college man. Live the good life. Wear nice, clean clothes. Drink ex-tremely cold beer. Try to keep from sweating. His head was built wrong for it; somehow the sweat funneled into his eyes and made them sting.

He thought he probably had sun stroke.

"Commin atcha, Jimbo," Dan yelled, and Beau Jim decided immediately that he'd had enough. He jumped up without his gun, swung with them and yelled, "Bang! Bang!" The doves flared away just as if he had shot.

"What the hell are you doin, boy?" Cass Willard called.

"Shit," Beau Jim said, "I done missed again."

"You didn't have no gun," Willard said and laughed.

"Hey, well, I know what I did wrong that time anyway," Beau Jim said. "If you see me doing anything else wrong, tell me. No shit," he said, sitting back down again, "I'd appreciate any advice you got."

"What do you think has gone wrong with yore little brother there, Early," Willard called. "Do you think he's eat too many smart pills or sumthin?"

"I don't know, but I reckon maybe he's just ready to quit," Dan called back.

Beau Jim knew the old bad joke, and he didn't like Willard anyway. He never had. And he didn't like the way Willard had been trying to tease Dan into giving him a ham. "What I need is more practice," he shouted. "Why don't you throw Willard up in the air for me, Dan, and let's see can I hit him on the wing."

"Don't let your mouth overload your ass now, son," Cass said from the ditch.

There was warning and no humor in Cass's voice. Beau Jim could think of things to say, but Willard was Dan's guest, and his boss, so he didn't say any of them. "I'll watch out for it, Mr. Willard," Beau Jim said, trying to put just enough edge in his tone to let Willard suspect that he had been given no apology. Willard didn't say anything else, and Beau Jim's anger eased a little.

What he truly wanted, he realized suddenly, was to be out with a girl.

Claire was no help there. Every time he'd asked Claire what the situation was, Claire seemed generally uninterested. Yancey Tillard was the only girl he could think of from their high school days who had neither married nor moved away. She sold tickets at the Dan-Dee Drive-in-Theater. When Beau Jim had said he'd have to go out there and check into that, Claire had made a face and said, *I'd rather fuck a handful of doughnuts than Yancey Tillard.* Beau Jim had said, *Awwh, she wasn't so bad.* As he remembered her, she was a little big, not fat, just all over big, and maybe a little loud, but she had every thing in the right places. She had red hair, brown eyes, freckles, and big, not overly white teeth, if he remembered, but she was not a bad looking girl. But Claire had said, *I'd rather fuck a ground hog hole if there was a ground hog in it that was breathin hard.* And Beau Jim had said, *you shouldn't talk that way about the girl I'm going to marry,* and Claire said, *You're right, I'm sorry. It don't matter a bit that you'd have to carry a stepladder around in case you wanted to kiss her.* And Beau Jim said, *I wouldn't have to carry no stepladder at all, bastard! I could just ask her to squat.* And Claire had said, *Sure, or you could just climb her like a tree and hook your toes in her garters, or even just ask her to pick you up.* And Beau Jim had said, *Sure I could.* But he was a little hurt that Claire should have talked her down so. Perhaps it was only because she was the only girl they could think of, but in his memory it wasn't hard for him to believe that he and Yancey had always had a deep secret feeling for each other, unexpressed, but there, and ready now, at last, to be admitted.

"Damn you, anyway," he muttered toward where Claire was sitting under the chestnut snag at the far end of the field, though he had no real anger for Claire. It was just that Claire, like everyone else he could think of, seemed for the moment unworthy of him. Charlene, for instance, had taken his seventy-five dollars, which had thrown a pall over the whole day—not so much that she had taken it when Dan wouldn't, but the way she took it. He had gotten her alone that morning when Dan was out in the barn working on the tractor, and he'd told her he wanted to pay for his room and board, but Dan wouldn't take any money from him. In his hand he'd had the seventy-five dollars he'd made driving cars for Claire's uncle—on the first trip back from Atlanta he'd brought two cars, driving one and towing another behind, but he'd had only one the second trip, though Claire and another driver had two both trips. Charlene told him to put the money down on the sideboard and she would see to it that it got used. She didn't even thank him.

All in all, he was in such a bad and solitary mood that it put the army in a certain nostalgic light for a moment, although he didn't quite allow himself to think about re-enlisting. In his mind's eye he could see himself sitting hunched over his beer, hash marks running up the sleeve of his jacket, his wits soured by army routine, his eyes bleared, his temper short and peevish. No, he told himself, he didn't want back in the army. He had it made where he was. Absolutely had it made.

There wasn't anything the matter with him except he couldn't hit any doves, and Charlene had taken his money without thanking him; or maybe, more important, he was hot and thirsty, and he needed a girl to be with. "Hey Claire!" he yelled down the field, "get up outta there and let's quit this shit!"

Just at that moment Willard shot three times and dropped two doves that were wheeling in over the western edge of the corn-field. There were five in the bunch, and the other three flew the length of the field, ducking and dodging just over the tops of the corn, but at the eastern edge, they began to climb, and all three fluffed to the top of the chestnut snag and lit. Immediately one toppled out and the other two took wing, and an instant later the report of Claire's shotgun reached them.

"I hear you talkin," Claire called.

Willard was in the cornfield and had found his doves. He pitched them over the fence. "You quittin just at the wrong time," he called. "It always gets the best about ten, fifteen minutes after the sun goes down."

"If it was any better, I couldn't stand it," Beau Jim said. He stood up and broke his double barrel down and gathered up his remaining shells.

"We got a'plenty, I guess," Dan said from his position beneath the locust tree, "and I got to git on and milk."

The three of them met on the road in the slanting light of the sun. Dan had already cleaned his doves and was carrying them in an old shoebox he'd brought out to the field for that purpose. The shoebox was full of the small, dark red breasts. "I got a plenty here for supper," Dan said to Willard. "You carry yores on home, why don'tcha?"

"You ain't got enough to feed us all," Willard said.

"Me and Claire are going on into town," Beau Jim explained.

"Show me how you clean em out, and I'll add these four to yours," Beau Jim said to Dan.

"Just hull em like a nut," Dan said and took one of Beau Jim's doves and showed him how to press down and apart with his thumbs on the center of the breast which broke the tender skin and pulled it away from the meat; then, with his thumb and forefinger hooked around the bottom and the top of the breast, he broke the bird and twisted the wing sockets loose and dropped the heart shaped breast into Beau Jim's hand. It was cool and sticky and soft. "You just hull em out," Dan said. "I'll take these on to Charlene so she can get to cookin em. Yawl go on ahead and shoot you some more if you want to. When you clean em, just throw the offal to the hogs so's it don't commence to stink."

Beau Jim dropped the breast into the shoebox and tried Dan's cleaning method, but he couldn't seem to get the wing joints broken loose. He twisted and pulled and tore the tender breast meat. Finally Willard offered him a knife.

"I got a gracious plenty here," Dan said. "Why don'cha give yourn to Cass and let me get on to my milkin."

Beau Jim said all right, though he didn't want to give his doves to Cass, and Dan started up the road.

Beau Jim could see Claire skirting the bottom of the field and coming up the rise toward the house and barn, carrying his shotgun over his shoulder, holding it by the barrel with the stock sticking up behind. No hunter would carry a shotgun that way, and Beau Jim felt affection for him. He was a no good drunken, lazy bastard, was what he was, and Beau Jim liked him better for it. In a moment Claire's grey coupe backed around and came down the road for them. When he drew up beside them, he was holding two open bottles of beer out the window and had one for himself in the hand draped over the steering wheel. "You killers thirsty?" he asked.

"Shitass," Willard said, dropping the dove he'd half cleaned and giving his hands a wipe up and down his britches to clean the bloody feathers from his fingers, "Give it here, son." He took both bottles and handed one to Beau Jim.

"How'd you do?" Beau Jim asked Claire.

"Oh, after I learned to let em light in the tree fore I shot at em, I did alright," Claire said. "I got eleven."

"What you goan do with them bushwhacked doves, now that you got em, you bastard?" he asked.

"Hell, you can eat em, cain'tcha?" Claire asked. "I'm goan eat the boogers."

"Why don't you give em to Willard and we can get on to town?"

"Don't want em," Willard said. "Never did like the taste, but the wife makes up a barbecue sauce for em that'll let ya keep em swallered."

"Shit, I'm goanna eat em," Claire said. "I bushwhacked the bastards fair and square." He began picking doves up from the floorboard by the feet and dropping them out the window. "Help me clean em and we'll go on."

Willard put his cleaned birds in a plastic bag, and he had an extra bag which he gave to Claire. They all had another beer apiece out of Claire's cooler and finished cleaning the doves. And sure enough, while they worked, doves came in twos and threes and sometimes more and circled and wheeled and dropped down into the field to feed on the corn the hogs had trampled and scattered. While the three of them cleaned their birds, their ears were seldom without the soft whistling, wheedling sound of wings, and as often as they looked up they could see the doves flaring and wheeling over the field and fluffing down among the cornstalks.

"Look at the sons a bitches," Willard said. "What did I tell you? Right now is the best time of the whole God Damned day."

When they were through cleaning and had thrown the broken and breastless remains of the birds to the hogs, Beau Jim said, "Ride me on back up to the house so I can get my car."

"What for?" Claire said. "Come on in this one."

"I got a little business I need to attend to at the Dan-Dee Drive-in Theater," Beau Jim said.

"Awwh for Christ's sake," Claire said, "We got better things to do than that."

"Maybe you have," Beau Jim said, "But I ain't."

"Awwh for Christ's sake," Claire said.

Chapter
Twelve

She had homefries, snapbeans, fried apples, slaw, biscuits, and for dessert, pineapple upside-down cake; and the kitchen was already hot as an oven from the cooking when Dan brought in the doves.

He put the shoebox on the sideboard, and Charlene wiped her hands on her apron, tipped the box toward her to look inside, and then gave it a little shove away. "Nasty things," she said. "How do you want em fixed?"

"I wanna see the birds," Sheila said, running in from the living room. "I wanna see em," she said, and she took hold of one of her father's fingers and stood on tiptoe. She looked solemnly at the small bloody pieces of meat, sucking her thumb.

"Fix em how ever you choose," Dan said. "They need rinsen off, and it may be some shot in some of em." He moved to get his milking buckets, and Sheila, still gazing into the shoebox, released his finger absently. "Cass and them is down at the field dressin out theirn. I expect he'll be on up in a little," he said and dipped water to wash the cow's teats from the fifty gallon milk can by the sink into one of the buckets and went out the back door and down the steps.

"Wait on me, Poppa," Sheila said and ran to catch him.

"Don't you squirt that chile with no milk now, you hear me?" Charlene called after them. "She's goan wear that dress to school tomorrow!"

If they answered, she did not hear them. She went to the back door and saw the black and white cat coming around the corner of the barn to meet them. "You hear me?" she shouted.

"Well," Dan said in a voice just loud enough to carry back to her.

Charlene turned back into the kitchen. "Well, nuthin, she'll just go to school stinkin if you do," she said to herself.

Weeks ago she had caught them at their game. She had been out getting some cucumbers from her garden, and she had heard a great meowing and giggling from the barn, and when she went to see what was causing all the fuss, she found Sheila and the cat sitting side by side waiting for a stream of milk which Dan, every now and again, would lean back and give them. One expert stream of milk shot into each open mouth. Sheila would giggle and mimic the cat who would be cleaning the milk from its face and whiskers, and then they would both begin to mew again, Sheila, loud and plaintively and with occasional fits of giggling, and the cat softly. Then, after a certain period of time, Dan would give them each another squirt, the cat catching the first hint of motion and opening its jaws as wide as if it were yawning —the white teeth and ridged roof of its mouth somehow hideous in the soft light of the barn. Charlene thought the game was disgusting, but she seemed unable to make them quit.

"Awwh, twon't hurt her a bit," Dan had insisted.

"She kin just go to school tomorrow smellin like soured milk for all I care," Charlene said to herself and dipped water into a dishpan to rinse the doves. She stopped and listened for any tell-tale sounds from the barn, but she couldn't hear anything. She began to go over the doves in a hasty, irritated, slap-bang manner, washing them off and flipping them into a cornbread pan until she discovered a black spot beneath the skin of one breast and cut into it and found a bloody feather and a piece of shot snuggled deep into the meat. After that she looked them over much more slowly and carefully. "Nasty things," she muttered.

When she got them dipped in bacon fat, salted and peppered and put in the oven, she went into the bedroom to take off her apron and put on her good shoes, which seemed suddenly not nearly so good as she remembered. Then she went into the bathroom to look at herself and pluck at her hair. At the last minute, though she never intended to, she got out her mascara and touched the brush to her tongue and began hastily to make up her eyes. She even got out her rouge and put a little in the palm of each hand and put her palms on her cheek bones and wiped hard toward each temple. She looked for her lipstick and then remembered that Sheila had got into it and ruined it months ago. She had given her a spanking for it. For a moment the sense of loss over the ruined lipstick came back to her again. "I'll teach that chile to ruin what little I've got," she said softly, but all at once she grew even more angry with herself and threw the rouge back into the small rusty shelves with the curtain over them that served as a medicine cabinet and stamped out of the bathroom. In the hall she turned her ankle painfully, but not seriously, in the unfamiliar high heels.

The minute she stepped back into the kitchen, Cass Willard came through the door from the living room. It irritated her that he hadn't knocked.

"Hydee, Charlene, you wouldn't want to stick these in the refrigerator for me would you?" he asked cheerfully and handed her a plastic bag of dove breasts. "Dan still out squeezin cow tits, is he?" Cass said and winked.

She put his doves in the refrigerator and didn't answer, and very oddly and without preponderation, the thought shot across her mind: *I'd fuck yore ears off Cass Willard!* The thought came bitterly, as if she had cursed him, and it made her blink her eyes.

"Well, how do you like livin on the farm?" Cass asked her.

"If yore a hermit, it ain't bad," she said. "It's got its good points I reckon." She got a cigarette and tapped it on the counter and lit it. "It ain't noisy like town, and in the mornin and evenin it's right purty sometimes." For some reason it gave her intense pleasure to lie to him. He was an arrogant man, and that made her mad. She didn't like the way he walked, as though he owned whatever he put his foot on, and she didn't like the way he stood either, all reared back as if he were a king. Black hair boiled out of his shirt collar, and he didn't seem to have a chin at all, though his adams apple stood out like a broken joint. It was an insolent thing somehow, that appeared about to break the skin.

"How'd you like those snakes this summer?" he asked and

made his eyes big and moved his head to the side as though he were dodging a blow.

"Well I sure don't go down to the river to see em," Charlene said, "and as long as they don't come up to the house to see me, I guess I can make out."

"Just teasin," Cass said. "Man, it's been a scorcher, ain't it?" He picked up a salt shaker from the table, licked the back of his hand, poured some salt on the wet spot and licked it off. "I'd like to have me a place in the country sometime where I could get out and do a little quail huntin. Deeda wouldn't put up with it though, so it would have to be an extra place that I'd rent out or somethin."

"Would you like a glass of ice tea?" Charlene asked him.

"I guess not," he said. He put down the salt shaker, fished a cigar out of his breast pocket, took his pocket knife out, cut the cigar in two, and stuck half of it between his teeth, but he didn't light it. "There was a place over by Senneca I looked at back in the early part of the summer—man raised horses—had a nice white fence all around, nice big house." He rolled his cigar from one corner of his mouth to the other. "Deeda wouldn't even look at it," he said.

Charlene made herself a glass of iced tea. "Let's go in the living room; it's hot as an oven in here," she said.

"She's got to be in town where she can play bridge and visit and gossip," Willard said.

"How is Deeda?" Charlene said. She didn't like Deeda any better than she liked Cass. Spent half her life at the beauty parlor, had a butt like a washtub and little bitty skinny legs, and acted like she thought she was the queen of England.

"Spendin money and gettin fat," Cass said, and sat down in Dan's easy chair and laughed.

From where she sat she could see the fins on Cass's fancy white and Pepto Bismol colored DeSoto, and again the thought, as harsh as a curse, shot across her mind: *I'd fuck yore God Damned ears off.* And for the second time it surprised and repulsed her.

After Dan and Sheila came in from milking and Dan had strained and put away the milk, she felt relieved, though all through supper she was very irritable. She scolded Sheila for getting her dress dirty, for picking her nose, and for not eating. And she scolded Dan too: He should have made certain that this place had, anyway, a decent well before he bought it, she told him. It for sure and certain didn't have anything else. And there was no reason for not buying one of those big square window fans to put in the kitchen to draw out the unmerciful heat; they didn't cost that much, and even if they did, there were some things a man ought to have the decency to provide.

Dan didn't say a word back to her, but a peculiar flush came to his temples, and once his eyes flicked to her face, and there was a very cold and forbidding light in them. For a little while that kept her quiet, but her frustration with him was like a terrible itch that needed scratching, and she seemed unable to quit scolding him, though she didn't want to, particularly before Cass Willard. She felt out of control, as though she could no longer select what thoughts were going to come into her mind, or what words were going to come out of her mouth.

She decided she had better busy herself, and she got up from the table and began to pick up the kitchen though she had eaten very little. She served Dan and Cass and Sheila their pineapple upside-down cake, and ate hers from the sideboard while she worked. But by the time she had finished the dishes and joined them in the living room, her frustration was again upon her.

"If there wasn't nigger one in this country, you wouldn't recognize it," Cass was saying. "And it wouldn't be just not havin no nigger shacks and trash all over everthing. Hell, ninety percent of em live on welfare or handouts or some such nonsense as that. We wouldn't have to have half the police we got. Most of the trouble in the country comes from the niggers in one way or another. They're immoral, they're shiftless, they're sneaky, they'll lie to you, cheat you, steal; they'll stab you in the back if they get the chancet. They'll work for nuthin, which is twice what they're worth, and keep a good white man out of a job, or if he gets it, he's got to work for nuthin too." Cass leaned toward Dan and shook his finger. "I'll tell you the truth," he said, "the honest to God truth, they've ruint the economy and the moral fiber of the white people in this country, and it's goan get a Hell of a lot worse if somethin idn't done." He leaned back in his chair and crossed his legs. "But, Hell, I don't have to tell you nuthin, you got yore baby girl goin to school with em." He paused as if waiting for Dan to say something, but Dan didn't say anything. Sheila sat on his lap and blinked sleepily against his chest.

"Tell him that again," Charlene said, "I don't think he heard ya. He don't hear me when I tell him."

"What I don't see," Cass said, "is why you don't tar and feather that Haggerman and them school board troublemakers too and run em right out of the county."

"What I don't see," Charlene said, "is why the town school ain't got no niggers in it."

"Cause we wouldn't put up with it, that's why," Cass said. "We not lettin some damned Washington moron that don't know a thing in the world about it, tell us what to do. Your Foscoe school board folks have done outsmarted themselves. They trying to ease into it. They taken the notion that if you push a thorn in a little at a time it twon't hurt," Cass said. "That damned Haggerman is a lot to blame; he ort to have shot the first nigger that put his foot on school property."

"Why don'cha put little punkin here to bed?" Dan said to Charlene.

"You can stick her in," Charlene said. "You the one holdin her."

"Well," Dan said, and he got up carefully and carried her into her room.

"The Registrar over at Senneca was in the other day," Cass said. "And he told me there was five of them damned stove-lids trying to get in over there. Five! Hot Damn!" he said and shook his head and forced a laugh. "I don't know what they're thinkin of. They ain't got no more business in college than a coon dog; Hell, no where near as much!" He clamped his teeth together, pulled his lips away from them and gave his head a jerk as if he'd just had a very sharp pain. "Black niggers in a white man's college. Ha!" he said. "I ort to shoot them damned monkeys myself. Imagine tryin to teach em in a college," he said. "Why, if you had one with enough white blood in him to learn anything, why he'd up and use it against the very folks that was good enough to teach it to him. You can't trust no nigger."

Dan came in from the bedroom then, and Cass said, "Hell, I can't even teach Sammy to grease a car and trust him to do it right, and he's as smart a nigger as I ever saw. Ain't that right, Dan?"

"He's purty likely," Dan said.

"But he still don't remember to check the rear end but about half the time, does he?" Cass insisted.

"That's right," Dan said.

"I'm tellin ya, if it won't one stovelid in this country, the white folks could make it a garden of Eden. It'll tell you right in the Bible where they're a cursed race, and they're cursing this country to Hell." He rolled his unlit cigar from one corner of his mouth to the other and back again. "You tell me this," he said, "if the Lord don't love em, how the Hell am I supposed to? Tell me that! Hmm!" he snorted and rolled the cigar to the opposite corner of his mouth. "It's ever white man in this country is carrying two or three lazy niggers on his back, whether he knows it or not, and that's half the reason he can't make a decent livin for his own family, cause he's having to support some nigger's family who has run off from it, or too lazy to work. And oncet they get in the white schools the poor little white children won't even be able to get a decent education."

He uncrossed his legs and slapped his hands down on his knees and rose out of his chair. "Well," he said, "well, I got to get on back to town." He felt of his front pockets and patted his hip pocket as though he were checking for his change and his billfold. "I fooled around here and let thinkin about them damned black niggers ruin a good time," he said, "and I'm sorry." He bobbed his head at Charlene. "I sure do appreciate that supper," he said. "I can see Deeda even pretendin to have somebody in to eat when she didn't have no water in the house."

"It's some of us gets use to not having things," Charlene said and wiped the corners of her mouth with her thumb and looked at Dan as though she expected him to respond, but Dan had risen to see Cass out and didn't say anything.

"You be sure and remember that ham you owe me now for all my doves them razorbacks of yores swallered," Cass said to Dan and smiled hugely and slapped him on the back. "I did enjoy myself," he said. "Yawl come by and see us." He gave Charlene a final wave and went out, and Dan went out behind him to stand on the porch while the DeSoto started up and pulled away.

Chapter
Thirteen

He sat parked in the crescent of gravel just past the Dan Dee Drive-in-Theater sign, feeling a little like he'd set a time and place to fight a bully. Yancey Tillard wouldn't even recognize him, and even if she did, he had never dated her in high school, and there was no reason to think she would even give him the time of day. He should have gone to Bolivar with Claire and tried his hand at hustling pool. With a little burn of regret he imagined himself making cool precise shots, Claire keeping the suckers laughing, himself straightening the wrinkles out of dollar bills and folding them thickly into his pocket.

"Less us just ease on over to Bolivar, and see if you are ready to begin separating some of these old boys from their money," Claire had said. "You don't want to be sniffin around after Yancey Tillard. It's time we got a look at you when the greenback dollars are on the table. You may be a candy-ass when the chips are down."

"Well, I guess I may be," he'd said, "but I'druther try and show my stroke to Miss Yancey Tillard tonight, I believe." In a deep and superstitious chamber of his mind, he told Yancey he was only teasing and meant no offense. Still, he felt guilty and jinxed.

"Awh, come on, for Christ's sake." Claire scratched his belly, "Ain't you got over that high school crap yet?"

"Lord no, have you?" Beau Jim asked.

Claire had been preparing their dinner—he was a damned fine cook—and he stopped turning homefries and onions and gave Beau Jim a look. "My uncle Theodore used to say that there wasn't nothing so overestimated as a piece of ass and nothing so underestimated as a good healthy shit," he said.

"Well it's no wonder the poor sucker ran around hittin himself on the head with a tire tool," Beau Jim said.

Claire opened the oven door, peered in at the doves and shut it again.

"It's not but two things a man has really got to have in this life, old buddy," Beau Jim said and took a swallow of his beer. "One of em's a woman," he said. He laid the nub of his finger under a nostril so it looked as if he had shoved it almost out of sight up his nose, and when Claire turned around to face him, he made his eyes big and rotated the nub. They both laughed. "Quick as I find out what the other one is," Beau Jim said and smiled hugely, "I'll be all set."

"No use arguing about it," Claire said. "If it won't nuthin else do you, go ahead. Sneak up behind her, grab her like a bowling ball, drag her off in the weeds and get it over with, for Christ's sake!"

"Well I thank you," Beau Jim said, "I was just this minute trying to think me up a smooth approach." *Jinxed again. Don't listen. I was just kidding,* he told the image of Yancey in his head, but he couldn't help imagining her angry with him and hurt.

Claire was quiet and sulky while they ate. Once or twice he sucked his teeth and said something insulting about Yancey, but he didn't mention Bolivar again.

When they were through eating and Beau Jim got up to leave, Claire said, "Well, I hope you catch a dose of the clap," and looked off at some idle corner of the room and patted himself on the stomach.

Crickets grating in the ditch along the road. Sporadic cars arriving for the late show. About the size of a golfball somewhere inside him he could feel the total of his human worth and wisdom. He seemed to know its size, if not its exact location. It felt small, private, serious, and lonely, and no trip to a pool hall in

Bolivar was relevant to it. He didn't know why he thought Yancey would be. Still he seemed to remember her in a special way, as though she might look at him and not see just a nine-fingered veteran. His palms were misty. He accused himself of bad planning. If he drove up to the ticket booth and tried to talk to her, cars would likely pull in behind him, and he'd have to get out of their way, and he wouldn't get a chance to say much of anything. If his first encounter with her was awkward, the second would only be worse. He lit a cigarette and thought it over. She wouldn't remember him anyway. He made up his mind to give it up and started the car, and then drove slowly right for the ticket booth, against his will and better judgement.

Inside the nimbus of light, he could see that it was, beyond doubt, Yancey, though she looked older. He stretched a dollar bill toward her, and she took it with no more than a glance at him and into his car. Just as he remembered, her face was sequined with rust freckles exactly the same color as her hair. She handed him back a torn ticket and his change, and her red nailed hands were almost as big as his own. "Yancey," he said, feeling that portion of himself he cared so much about grow warm and dangerously light, more like, say, a ping-pong ball. "Yancey, how you doin?"

She ducked her head to squint at him through the semicircle cut in the glass, and since she was sitting a little sideways, the counter before her pushed one large breast up with grotesque beauty.

"How've you been," he asked to fill up the silence.

"Who's that?" she said, squinting at him, her red-brown eyes ready, it seemed, to take offense. But then something happened to her expression as though she were reaching back through layers of time. "Theey," she said, "is that Beau Jim Early?"

He hadn't allowed himself to hope for so much.

"Well, I'll Swannee," she said. "I thought you wuz dead and in Hades, or way off in the navy and gone for good and always."

"How you doin?" he asked again, hoping immediately he could work a little more variety into his conversation.

"Oh, gettin prematurely ugly," she said and laughed a kind of yodeling laughter that ended on a high and fading note like a sad echo.

"You look good to me," he said.

"Jesus, would you listen to him," she said. "Don't run off. I'goan come out there and hug you till you holler," and she laughed again. And as if she had practiced it, the last note was once more like an echo, or maybe like a sigh.

"How you doin?" he asked for the fourth time.

"Oh, I'm hanging on, I guess. What are you up to, back in these parts?"

"Fixing to start college over in Senneca."

"Are you kiddin me? Is that a fact?" she asked.

Was she excited, or surprised that someone like him was going to go to college? For a moment it damaged his confidence.

"Well, what'cha goan make out of yourself, Mr. Early?" she asked.

"Well, I don't know just yet," he said. He almost asked her how she was doing again, but he managed to shut his mouth on the question just in time. Someone gave a very light toot on his horn, and Beau Jim glanced in his mirror and saw that there were two cars behind him. "Look," he said, "I sure would like to see you sometime."

"Saints alive," she said, and cupped her hand behind her ear and rolled her eyes, "I'bleve you askin me for a date, or did I misunderstand?" she laughed her musical and practiced laugh, but cut it short. "When, for goodness sake?"

"I was hopin we could maybe go somewhere tonight?" he said and felt afraid.

"Well, I don't know," Yancey said gravely. She appeared to ponder the question and then she bent even lower to the circle cut in the glass, and her generous breast, pushed up by the counter, swelled round and freckled into the V neck of her blouse, and he could see the upper half of her brassiere, and he had a hard time trying to look at her face. "Keep your motor runnin, Sugar, and I'll be right with you," she said and laughed hugely and slapped her hand down on the counter top. A car horn sounded behind him, and she said in a loud and brassy voice, "I'll come back there in a minute and put a kink in your tooter you'll never forget." She had straightened to say that, but in the next moment she had bent toward him again, and the counter lifted her breast, and his throat thickened. "A lady needs a little more notice than this, Mr. Beau Jim Early," she said, "but why don't you park up close to the concession stand, and when I get done, I'll come over and we can have us a talk, anyway. Can't afford to let you get away," she said and laughed her practiced laugh.

He raised his hand, Indian fashion, in a salute and pulled away, the Studebaker grumbling along the dim marker lights, and then into the forest of speakers. The theater was not crowded, and it was easy to choose a speaker right next to the concession stand.

Even though it was over half an hour until Yancey appeared, he had no notion what the movie was about. One moment he would feel ready to lean his head back and let out a cry of pure joy, and the next he would not feel joyful at all but uneasy as though talking to Yancey might somehow do him damage. It wasn't so much Yancey, any girl who had known him when he was a kid in school would have made him just as uneasy. Six years had gone by since then, and what had he become? Then all at once, the image of the trapper was upon him. *Awwwh, you doin all right,* he told himself, *the God Damned Indians ain't got you yet,* and he wondered what in hell, exactly, he was worried about. Women did funny things to a man.

Gravel stirring beside the car and Yancey calling, "Open up!"

He reached across the seat, opened the door for her and said, "Come on in the house," and Yancey lifted one heavy but shapely leg in, and then sat down too quickly and spilled some of the coffee from the plastic cups she held in her hands.

"Oh dodo," she said. "Here take your coffee," and when he had taken it, she brushed at her skirt. "Messy as a hog," she said, but then she was smiling at him with what seemed great happiness and warmth. "Well, here you are, been around the world two or three times and just had to come back and see me, right?" She laughed and gave him a push on the shoulder.

He held on to his coffee cup, but a little wave licked over the rim and basted the inside of his thigh with scalding coffee. "That's right," he said in a tight voice that served him instead of a grunt of pure pain. But the heat faded very quickly.

"So," she said, "you goan go to college and get yore knowledge, huh?"

"Well, I got the G.I. bill," he said, "and there's no sense in lettin it go to waste. Anyhow, if I didn't go to school, I'd have to go to work."

"Ain't that the truth," she said. She was a lot of girl, maybe five-eight, maybe a hundred and fifty pounds. Her perfume filled the car. Stirred him. "I get so tired of this ole job. Velma," she said and tipped her head toward the concession stand and took a sip of her coffee, "works behind the counter there—Velma had her boyfriend ask her to marry him the other day. Got a good job at Bond Chemical Co., and do you think she would give him a simple yes? Why no. The silly thing." She tipped her head back and laughed. "I came in from the ticket booth and caught them right at it," she said.

"At what?" he asked bravely but in a husky voice.

She laughed again and gave his shoulder a shove. "Holdin hands across the counter," she said. "He was proposin. I told her if any man ever took ahold of my hand and asked me a thing like that, I'd be just like a mud turtle, I wouldn't let go till it thundered." She went into a fit of laughter which sounded genuine until the very ending sigh, and Beau Jim laughed with her.

"Lord," she said, "Lord, Lord . . . so you came on back home didja? They's sometimes I think I'd do anything in the world to get away from this ole place. Makes me so blue I could cry some days, but then I think, Hades, Yancey, wouldn't any other place be any better. Least I know what I'm up against here. Lord, I guess when I die, I'll want to go straight up and not get off even five degrees in any direction." She crossed her legs and flung her arm over the back of the seat, which caused the far lapel of her blouse to pucker open, and he could see again the swell of her breast and this time even a white ellipse of flesh, not having had enough of the sun to freckle and therefore even whiter than the undergarment, and though he'd had something to say before she made that motion, he couldn't remember what it was. "Course if I'd been all over the world like you have, I'd probably know better. I bet you were in Paris, France and places like that weren't you?"

"No," he said, "no I wasn't ever in Paris, but I was in London once and Rome twice and maybe one or two other places."

"They Lord Have Mercy," she said, "I been known to brag about gettin to go to Atlanta which is as far as I've ever been away from where we're sittin this minute."

"You ought to be glad," he said. "Travelin around isn't any good for you. Make you homesick all the time, even when you get back home." He grew a little embarrassed with himself. She was looking at him and not saying anything, and he scratched the hair behind his ear, wiped his forefinger back and forth under his nose, and tried to drink from his empty cup of coffee.

"Well, you're a regular philosopher," she said.

He ran his forefinger back and forth under his nose again. He couldn't think of any response.

"You seldom catch a man talking about anything but money, or whose wagon he claims he's goan fix for good and proper, or some gal whose after him, he'll tell you, or who he's goan straighten out and teach a lesson."

The compliment made him bold. "Hell, Yancey, less get outta here and go somewhere," he said.

"Awwwh, I can't," she said.

"Why?" he asked her.

"Oh, I'd like to, but Mr. Wynette, the manager, always gives me a ride home."

"Tell him you've got a ride this evenin," he said. "Hell, that ain't any trouble is it?"

"I better not," she said.

"Why not?" he asked, and then he began to sense why not. Of course if it was only a matter of a ride, the boss wouldn't care. He wondered if Mr. Wynette was married. Hoped he was. Hoped he wasn't. Didn't know what he hoped. She was sitting with her hands folded in her lap now, and no white ellipse of flesh showed, but he remembered it, and his heart shriveled. He asked himself what he had expected. "Sure," he said, "all right." He thought of trying to find Claire and going over to Bolivar, of going on back home to his brother's house. "Couldn't you tell him your cousin just came back from overseas and dropped by to see you?"

She raised her head and stroked her throat with her finger-tips and then turned to look at him. She drew the corners of her mouth into a funny curl of a smile and gave her head a jerky little nod. "Why not?" she said, although she sounded as if she knew why not.

"I'd sure be proud if you would," he said.

"I haven't seen anybody from school in a coon's age," she said.

"That's the way!" he said. "Take off, Miss Yancey and tell that man about your cousin!"

"Why not," she said, sounding a little more determined. "Keep your motor runnin, and I'll be back in a jiffy."

She wasn't back in a jiffy, in fact it was more like twenty minutes before she came back, carrying her purse, an electric fan, and a rather flat aqua sofa pillow. She looked angry and a little pale. "Less us get outta here," she said, and they did.

Proud, but with his fingers cold and clammy on the steering wheel, he drove randomly around the countryside, and they talked. They never shut up. They laughed over things that weren't particularly funny. They remembered themselves in situations they weren't really ever in. They remembered good times they hadn't had. But there was something in it somewhere that was true, even though all the facts were wrong, and he began to feel very nervously tender about this big, not quite pretty red-headed girl who was working so hard for the good old days.

When they passed a honky-tonk where the Bear Creek Pike met the road to Foscoe, he asked her if she'd like something to eat or maybe a beer, and she said she would.

A Negro boy, maybe fifteen, wearing a soiled white jacket and a white paper hat came out to wait on them, and Beau Jim ordered a hamburger and a beer, and she ordered a cheeseburger, but at the last minute, decided a beer was too fattening. She was in a kind of celebrating mood though, she said, although to Beau Jim there seemed something just a little wrong somewhere. He asked the boy if he could buy a drink, and the boy said, "Nawh suh," and shifted his feet. Yancey explained that the county was dry except for beer, but, she told him coyly, the boy would bring him a pint if he didn't mind being overcharged. He didn't mind, and he ordered a pint, and the Negro doffed his white paper cap. Yancey called out after him that she wanted a ginger ale too, and he flung an okay sign over his shoulder and gave his head a couple of nods and moved his feet as if he were dancing. He returned with the hamburger, the cheeseburger, his beer, her ginger ale, two plastic cups filled with ice, and a pint of Bonded Beam in a paper bag. Beau Jim paid for the food and legal drinks, and for the whiskey separately. The whiskey was four dollars.

"Bonded Beam, huh," Beau Jim said, "must be Jim Beam's brother."

The boy snapped his head to the side, made a kind of hissing laughter and took the four dollar bills out of Beau Jim's hand with a kind of gentle slap, as though they were musicians greeting each other.

Yancey said drinking was a sin, and she was going to have to go to church next Sunday to make up for it, but she'd like a light one if he didn't mind. He filled the cup of crushed ice half way up with Bonded Beam and leveled it off with ginger ale, and from that moment she changed. She slipped a foot or two closer to him on the seat and seemed to get somehow cuddly, and once again he got the feeling that something was wrong somewhere. Something was going on he knew he hadn't altogether provoked. *Well,* he thought, *the world is full of strange and crazy things.* He decided to have a drink from the bottle himself and chase with beer, but when he swallowed the Beam, he couldn't stop a nasty shiver, and it took his voice away like surgery. Still, it didn't matter, for though she asked him a question, she answered it herself.

"What on earth will you think of a girl that would have a drink with you on the first date? You must think I'm pretty naughty," she said.

Then she tucked her chin into her chest and spoke in a lower voice: "No, Miss Yancey, but I can't help hopin," and she giggled and gave him a poke in the side with her elbow that hurt more than he wanted to admit. He decided there had to be trouble between her and this Wynette fellow, and the old lonesome traveler had come along in the middle of it probably. It made him feel sorry for her. He noticed that her drink was gone, and he suggested that she go to Sunday School as well as church next Sunday, and have a second. She swung her cup over for him to pour, and he poured four fingers of Bonded Beam into the bottom of the cup and added enough ginger ale to pale it a couple of shades. She took a sip and snuggled up next to him, having a large girl's mysterious ability to make herself small. "Yes sir," she said, "I'll go to Sunday School, and I promise not to sass my Momma for a month."

She straightened up then and moved just a little away and said, "I really am ashamed of my behavior." She sipped her drink and appeared to think about that, her lips in a pout. He had another drink from the bottle. It wasn't one whit smoother. It peeled the inside of his throat and brought tears to his eyes.

"Tell me the truth Beau Jim Early," she said suddenly and very seriously, "do you think I'm too plump?"

He would have told her that he didn't think she was too plump at all, if she had given him the chance, but she answered for him again: "Well, Lord no, Miss Yancey, your charms are only more generous than most," and she laughed her long practiced laughter and gave him a shove on the shoulder that bounced him against the door. "But I am I guess," she said and sighed. "And I know for a fact I'm too generous in every dadgummed way."

The world is full of misery, he thought. He saw himself as the trapper, the very brother of hard times. *Poor ole red-headed beaver,* he said to himself.

"Yancey," he said, "If you was to sign up for summer Bible School, me and you could get serious with the Bonded Beam."

"Have mercy on me, Mr. Man," she said and giggled, "but that's a fact."

Neither of them touched their food, and before long the pint bottle was empty. They signed Yancey up for a two year tour as a foreign missionary, and Beau Jim blew the horn for the carhop and another bottle. "What'cha got besides Bonded Beam?" Beau Jim asked him.

The carhop looked off toward the honky-tonk. "What'cha want?" he asked.

"Got any Early Times?" Beau Jim asked him.

"I'll look see," he said.

He brought them a pint of Fairfax County. At least Beau Jim had heard of that. The alcohol motor in his head was warm and purring, and he was feeling fine. Loose. Happy. He paid the Negro carhop and told him to take the food tray away.

"But you ain't eat it," he said.

"How do you know?" Beam Jim asked him, and the boy snapped his head around and made his hissing laughter and slapped the palm of Beau Jim's hand again. But when he turned back to Yancey, she was stiff as a board and looking straight ahead through the windshield. He couldn't believe what he'd said. *Ignorant hick. Filthy-mouthed drunk,* he said to himself, and very tenderly he poured her a drink, but she wouldn't take it.

"I've had way more than plenty, thank you," she said.

"Awwh, Yancey, I don't know how to act," he said, and shame screwed his eyes shut.

"I've been a fool all my life," Yancey said. "I'd make somebody a good wife in spite of what anybody says, and I'd make a good Momma too, and a good Grandmomma. In spite of what anybody will tell you, I would." She turned her face away from him and looked out of the opposite window.

*No wonder you're a trapper and live out in the goddamned woods by
your big-mouthed-self,* he told himself, *you're too damned dumb to live
with anybody.* "Yancey," he said, "you got to forgive me. I been
in the army around old nasty soldiers so long, I don't know how
to act."

"It's not your fault, it's mine," she said. "You'd know how to
act if I did."

He felt very bad. He took a pull on the Fairfax County and
didn't even blink. And pretty soon she began to tell him about
Mr. Wynette, how she knew it was wrong, how there wasn't even
much to him, and she didn't even really care for him, but still it
had been going on for almost two years. Did he think that was
awful, she wanted to know. Lord no, he said and meant it, he
didn't think it was any worse than the sun coming up in the
morning or the snow falling in the winter time. He knew he had
been right about her. How was it that he had come along at such
a time?

She was just looking for anything that resembled a man to be
good to, she told him. Hell, she could be good to a dadgummed
posthole digger if it gave her the chance, she said.

She said she thought she would have another drink if he
wouldn't think any the worse of her. Said she was, By God, going
back to the Dan-Dee Monday and get her space heater that she
kept out there for the winter time.

"You're a fine woman," he told her and gave her the cup of
bourbon. When she had taken a swallow of it, he put his arm
around her and squeezed her. His head buzzed pleasantly. "I'll
tell you what your trouble is," he told her.

She raised her freckled face, and he looked into her astonishing
foxy brown eyes. "I wish you would," she said.

"Your titties are too little," he said.

Her brown eyes glowed for a minute, and he thought she was
angry, but then she giggled and her fist banged his ribs, and pain
as thin as a knife blade reached up toward his heart.

He closed his eyes and put his face against her hair. "Lord, the
world is full of misery," he said, meaning it, and took her right
breast in his hand, half the size of a football and twice as heavy,
and she gave him another shot in the ribs with the point of her
elbow and pain went around him like a girdle. "Less us get out
of here," he said.

She didn't say anything so he reached through the steering

wheel with his left hand and turned the ignition key. He was very careful to give the Studebaker only enough gas to move it. He didn't want a backfire. It rumbled and chortled, and he backed around and started down the Bear Creek Pike, not having any idea where he might park. He was caressing her breast, stoking it up from the bottom and across the nipple and down again, very gently, hoping she wouldn't hit him. "Oh Lord, oh Lord," she said.

He pulled out the tail of her blouse, and she leaned forward just a little and pulled her shoulders back to help him with the hooks, but he could not undo them one-handed. She slipped back a hand and helped him there, and they were unholstered. He caressed them very gently. "Oh Gawwwd," she said. He tried for even tenderer parts, but with his arm around her the way it was, he couldn't reach far enough down, even though she tilted her hips upward to help him. But at that very moment she seized upon the root of him and squeezed so hard he had to set his jaw. Was she going to tear it out by the roots, reduce it to jelly? He tried to steer, he gritted his teeth. *Jesus-Christwhatagrip. Turn her loose and fuck yore hat*, the trapper said. *Cover yoself with leaves and play dead.*

"Turn left," she said.

He didn't see any place to turn left, but he was fixing to turn anyway. There was nothing in the way but a ditch, a rickety fence and some six foot loblolly pines. He left the lower reaches of her belly alone and went back to her breasts, and she eased her grip. *Thank you, Jesus.* He saw a dirt road to the left and took it. Unbuttoned the ole blouse and out of the corner of his eye he could see them in the faint lights from the dashboard. Turned and gave the nigh one an appreciative kiss and drove, looking through the fur of his left eyebrow.

"Turn right at the top of the hill," she whispered and strained her breast upward.

"Stop the car," she said, and he reined the Studebaker in and pulled up the emergency brake. She caught his head and mashed his face into her breast and then went up and over the back of the front seat as easily as a goat. He cut off the lights and followed, creasing his skull on the dome light.

The body of the Studebaker wracked and jounced while she bucked and tossed. *Rollin for my point, fawh!* He felt like a man trying to hang on to a life raft in rough seas. Then he was sitting in one corner of the back seat, and she was sitting in the middle, and for a long time nobody did anything but breathe. A head with the chicken cut off. The moon was only a sickle, and the night was pitch black. The crickets were going at it, and there were other unidentifiable night sounds as he caught his breath and rested. But after a moment or two she began to giggle and get friendly and make jokes. She felt for and took hold of his exhausted dick.

"Who dat?" she said.

"Who dat?!" he answered.

"Who dat who say dat last 'who dat'?" she asked.

He wasn't up to another round quite so quick. He thought he'd rather play. He felt around on the floor and found her step-ins. "Yancey," he said, "I'm goan get in your britches."

"Have mercy, Mr. Man," she said. But then she discovered with her hands what he was doing. "Don't you silly thing," she said, "I can't go home without those."

But he already had a leg in. "Ain't this what they mean when they say that?" he asked.

"Stop, you silly thing," she said, and she began to struggle to put them on too and got her leg in as well. "Stop it," she giggled, "you stretchin the dodo out of em."

For a second he didn't know what had happened. The car was flooded with light, and there was a terrible loud noise. A car had sneaked up behind them, thrown on the headlights, and was laying on the horn. *God Damned Cocke County rednecks from the honky-tonk? Cops?* He tried to jump over the front seat, but they each had a leg in her britches, and the nylon was very strong, and he couldn't make it. *Mercy.* She was struggling to get over the front seat too, and there was a terrible confusion of arms and legs, elbows, knees and titties, and he had a momentary image of what it must look like from the rear, and then they were both over the seat like Siamese twins, and he landed right, but the nylon gave, and she rolled to the floorboard. He had the Studebaker cranked in an instant, raced the motor, popped the clutch, and with a backfire like a thunderclap, they were off. Dirt and gravel spraying. He saw through his rear view mirror that the car behind him only had one headlight. A rock flung from his rear wheel must have taken out the other. He didn't know who to hope it was, but whoever, he had no intention of being caught by anybody without his pants on.

Yancey was back up on the seat before he'd gone fifty yards, holding on to the dashboard with both hands. "Go left at the bottom of the hill! The other way's dead end!" she yelled.

Mercy. It was a ninety degree turn, but he never let up, and the Studebaker went into a four-wheel drift and slid right across the intersecting road and into the right hand ditch, but still he kept it on the floor and got out of the right hand ditch only to get in the left hand ditch before he could straighten out; then he was back in the right hand ditch again; still, he never let up on the gas and when he fought back into the road a third time he was able to keep it there. Fishtails diminishing, he roared down the road, pink dust boiling out so thickly behind him he could see nothing of the other car, which meant, he was satisfied, that the other car couldn't see anything at all, and therefore couldn't catch him, not if they were rednecks, cops, boyfriends, fathers or Indians.

Chapter
Fourteen

Dan had stood with his hands in his pockets and watched the tail lights of Cass Willard's DeSoto recede down the dirt road and jounce up onto the highway. And even after they had disappeared down the pike toward town, he looked after them and did not go in. He sat on the edge of the porch with his feet on the steps, his forearms resting on his knees, and his big hands loosely knitted. He could hear Charlene in the kitchen washing the dishes, and he didn't want to go inside for fear she would speak to him, and if she spoke to him, he didn't know what he would do then. He didn't think he would hurt her, but he didn't trust himself. His anger had turned inward toward weariness and despair, but still he did not trust himself to go back inside. If he could just sit still and quiet for a while, he thought he'd be okay; the cool and the dark would do him good. But if he weren't left alone, he knew he might get mad again, and that would serve no purpose.

Across the highway, one of Sammy's hounds began to bark and then the other joined in, but they quit after a minute, having given whatever scared them only a half-hearted bluff. He could tell by the way they sounded they were under the house. *One of em's stomach probly growled and spooked em*, he thought. *But they done clamped their tails back around their butts again by now and courtin sleep with one eye open,* he thought and tried to laugh, but he couldn't. His depression remained. The window fan Charlene had spoken about oppressed him. Like so many other things, he had no money for it. He was lucky to put food on the table and clothes on their backs. As far as he could see in the future there wouldn't even be money for window fans and things of that order, and how could that be, he asked himself, when he worked all the time? He was doing the best he could. He didn't know how to do any better. And every time something wore out or went bad, he seemed to be losing ground. At that very moment, behind him in the side yard, he could feel the presence of the well drilling rig. Blocked up and monstrously still by the mimosa tree, it threatened him, put as much fear into him as a shotgun aimed at his back. It was even worse, for a shotgun, hit or miss, was clean and quick and understandable, but debt and failure hounded a man through all his days and nights and ground him down; he was satisfied that no shotgun could make him crawl, but he wasn't sure about failure. He wasn't sure that failure couldn't break him. It was still hard for him to believe that something like the well could hit him when he was already not getting by. He was going to have to take a second mortgage; he knew he was. If they would consent to give it to him. And that would mire him down even deeper. Even with the drought and having to buy his stock and fence and feed, he could have come close to breaking even, when he sold his pigs, if it hadn't been for the well. He wouldn't have broken even, but he would have come close, and he would have had a jump on next year.

And if it had been his own Momma in the house, or a woman like her, he wouldn't be so bad off as he was. There would have been enough canning done to get them a good ways through the winter, but Charlene hadn't put up one can. Not even a can of beans. *If a frog had wings, he wouldn't bump his ass on the ground ever time he jumped neither,* he told himself. He shifted his feet slightly on the steps and rubbed his hands together. *But I'm just like an ole tractor in the mud,* he told himself, *I'm goan grind on up out of it one day.* He wiped his mouth with his hand, and as though he might have been attempting to start a conversation with another, thought to himself, *Hit's a gettin almost cool, the breeze musta turned around and be comin off the mountains,* but the pretense of it made him feel ill. Willard had put a fear and despair in him that he couldn't shake off. Willard just might know what he was talking about. He owned himself a service station and was smart enough to run it and had himself pretty much what he wanted. He had acquired property and things of value, and therefore knew how things worked, and when he said the niggers were being allowed to ruin it all from top to bottom, well then, a fellow had to listen, didn't he? He could not remember all that Willard had said, nor properly get his mind around what he did remember, but the very idea that the niggers could ruin what little he had, that they were already doing it, that somehow, in ways he did not understand, he was already being made to pay for their sloth, all that made him suddenly so mad that anger bubbled in his throat, and he all but growled.

A moment later Charlene came to the door behind him and said, "Hit's near ten o'clock, you plannin to come to bed tonight?" But he was stiff with anger and could not speak.

"Well, set out there like a hoot owl then," she said, "I'm a'goin to bed."

On the fringe of his consciousness, he heard her walking away and saying more to herself than him: "I'm tired, even if you ain't."

He sat a long time while the anger drained away again, and it left him feeling frail and weak, as though the fierce rage, when it eased, had taken his strength along with it. He asked himself if it was his own foolishness after all, as Charlene claimed, that had brought them to such a state, and he could not absolve himself. But he hadn't fooled anybody, nor tricked them. He'd told her right off that he was going to have him a farm. Maybe she had thought it was only talk and hadn't believed him, but he hadn't fooled her about it. He had worked for seventeen years and saved every spare nickel for that end. The hope and anticipation of it had kept him. He was, and always had been, a farmer, no matter what he'd had to do for a living. He could not be like Cass Willard. He couldn't even envy him. How could he want to be like someone he couldn't understand, and he couldn't understand Cass Willard. He could not, he knew, read, nor write, nor figure well enough to operate the service station and face the obligations and responsibilities that Willard had to face every day.

He couldn't believe that getting himself a piece of land was wrong. It was the one thing he could put his head and hand to hour after hour and day after day. A piece of land could not be so traitorous as to break him and bring him to ruin. He couldn't believe it. No piece of earth could be so poor, so past reclaiming. Nothing he'd planned on so long and worked on so hard could turn right around and hurt his daughter, say. *A man's got to take hold of what he can do and stick by it,* he told himself. *I'm goan grind on up out of it. Hit won't be a well to dig ever year, nor no drought. When I put up a fence hit'll stay fer as long as I'll need her; maybe the next man will have to put hit up again, but I won't need her when she falls. I'm goan grind on up out of it. If I kin just stick it for the first little while till I get a good grip and purchase on her, I'll make her flower.* But he could feel specters around him in the dark, and they seemed not simply constituted of his own ignorance and bad luck, but of another quality too, symptomatic of the times and willfully destructive.

He rubbed his huge hands together slowly and pressed them down on his knees to rise, and he felt almost infirm. His joints seemed rusty and old, his knees too weak to hold him, but he went on inside to go to bed.

Charlene was sunk into sleep and didn't move when he sat down on the bed to take off his shoes. He took off his socks and his overalls, but nothing more. He lay on his back and looked at the ceiling and eased from memory to dream and back again, all through the night.

Sam stands in the traces, patient as summer, still as a tree, not so much as shuddering his hide to show he is awake until, trying to bluff a man's voice, he says to him, "Come up!" and strains to keep the plow point deep and straight, the handles being yet too high for him. He stumbles down the furrow, wrestling the plow through every foot of soil. "Haw!" he calls out at the end of the furrow, and Sam obediently turns left, and he rears down and back on the handles for all he is worth, but his feet clear the ground again and again, and he cannot get the plow point up, and he plows off in a left hand tangent. "Hoe!" he calls, and Sam stops and stands patiently, turning a long and sensitive ear curiously back toward him from time to time while he struggles to lift and right and turn the plow. "Come up!" he says again, straining to make the plow point bite in and the furrow lie more or less parallel to the last one. "Gee!" he says at the far end, so worn out, his voice is almost a sob. But he gets the plow turned around in good order and clears his throat of its unmanly tendency, and

*even ducks his head to one shoulder to wipe the sweat from his eyes before
the plow goes over on its left side and gets dragged uselessly. And in his
bed he strains and twists to right it before his eyes come open and he blinks
stupidly at the dark. After a moment he lets his left hip sink back to the
bed, lets out his held breath, and after a little longer, he closes his eyes
again. He thinks of better times: the loamy earth rolling slowly back from
the moldboard in a time when he didn't have to reach up to the plowhan-
dles and could follow a plow without stumbling every second step. The
furrows didn't look like worm tracks then, but ran straight and deep, and
he could get a day's work done in the morning, and another in the evening.
And what he planted would grow and he could harvest it.*

*He tries to keep that thought, but he thinks instead about the red clay.
It would not crumble in a man's hand the way it ought. It was either rock
hard, or dust, or mud. Left a glazed stain on a man's fingers if he tried
to feel it, and didn't even smell right. "Wore out patch of misery," says
she, "soak up yore last penny, yore last drop of sweat and not give you
nuthin back in return." "If hit'll grow loblolly and kudzu, hit'll grow
food for the table if you give it the proper hep," says he.*

*He shifts and sighs, his muscles harboring an unhealthy ache as though
he were catching flu. He courts a vision of himself making a go of things,
sees himself riding on his tractor, cutting hay. Beef cattle out to pasture
on his right. Down the slope a field of corn with every stalk already
shoulder high. Back of the barn behind him, shoats roaming the pen while
three or four sows doze. The kitchen garden getting ready to bear early
peas and sweet corn; and squash and okra, green beans, tomatoes, turnips
and potatoes all coming on. All around him fence posts set firm, and wire
tight enough to play a tune on. A new silo at the end of the barn, and
new corn cribs too, still a third full from last year's harvest. Such rewards
everywhere from his labor, they begin to confound his ability to count and
appreciate them. He can see so much bounty, he grows uneasy, begins to
feel glutted and unhappy. He does not want so much, but when he admits
that, the vision alters peevishly, and he can see fields as barren as if they
had been salted, his fences down, his barn, broken-backed and sagging
toward collapse. He can see himself wandering through its empty stalls,
and nothing there at all save chaff and ancient dung, dry and stringent
as dust. On the broken hinged barn door there is a sign with words too
large for him to cipher, though he knows he should try, for he knows
immediately the sign would tell him what has transpired, but he has no
patience for it and hurries away. He can see no one has lived in his house
for a long time for the windows are broken and the screens torn, and there*

are no steps up to the front porch, which is rotten and silvery gray and has a hole in it through which he can see cans, old catalogues, and human feces littering the ground beneath. And though there was not one living thing in sight the moment before, he has only to turn his head to find two nigger boys playing mumblety-peg in the dust beneath the pecan trees. And where his pickup had always stood, there is a black cadillac car with a broken windshield and one of its white sidewall tires, flat and wrung half off the rim. When he turns back toward the porch, a young, very thin Negro woman is sitting on the edge, nursing a baby on a pap no bigger than his thumb and looking far off to the west. She pays not the slightest attention to him, nor do the boys who laugh and curse and flip the knife from chin, or nose, or elbow. None of them notice or heed him save one small ragged black girl who squats shyly behind the nursing woman and watches him, her wrinkled thumb in her mouth and her broad nostrils jeweled with green snot. But he is afraid. Fear, like hot coals, is inside him, and some ancient and perfectly familiar grief is upon him as though he has suffered this many times before. He cannot think what to do until it occurs to him that his one small chance to understand is to go back to the barn and try to read what is posted there. If he cannot decipher what is written, he cannot name what he has lost, nor learn its specific gravity. But there is no barn. Nor can he find the spot where it might have stood. The whole topography and configuration of the land has changed. He can almost recognize it as Watauga County, North Carolina, but there are houses and roads where none had been before, and the earth does not remember him the way it should. He begins to fear that he has lost his way, and he cannot understand how he has traveled so far. But it comes to him that, not moments, but years have passed, and because he had never once forgotten his home, he had deceived himself that it was only steps behind him. Still it surprises him to see how stooped and frail he has become. His hands are so crooked and warped with arthritis, he can do nothing with them, and his sight is filmy. It comes to him that he is dying, and he frets over it inconsolably, for he does not wish to die in such a strange place. As if he were a child with a child's inability to accept fate, he refuses to believe what has come to pass. He has been misused and cheated, and he feels his loss keenly and cannot forgive it, and over and over again he weighs his memory of what he has done in an effort to prove he should not have been brought to this. He should not have to die in a strange country with nothing familiar to rest his eyes upon, with none of his own work to see and take comfort in. No man laboring his whole life on his land should have to die as a trespasser. "Forgive me my trespasses," says he, but the moment it is out of his mouth, he realizes his guilt and is frozen by the horror of it. One hundred times his punishment would be merciful, for he has abandoned her. The knowledge scoops at his heart. He cannot believe he could have mistaken her for only another of the niggers when she had been right there before him, her sweet eyes upon him, the spray of freckles across her nose, her little arms and legs, pale and thin. She was there on the porch waiting for him to take her up, and he had gone away. Her face had been full of faith and trust in him, and he had given her no sign, nor even recognized her as his child, his daughter, flesh of his flesh, blood of his blood. And all down the years she must have waited, he had not thought of her until this moment, though she had been somehow as much with him as the beat of his heart. He can not bear the knowledge that he has betrayed her. He cannot bear to imagine her patience and suffering, and he is filled with such grief that he can neither move nor speak. And even after he is awake and sitting up in bed, the terrible regret and guilt of it will not leave him, and he holds himself to blame even for having dreamed that he could have abandoned her.

He cannot sleep after his dream and does not want to try, for he has grown afraid and suspicious of himself. There is a stranger in him he has glimpsed and does not wish to see again. After a little he allows himself to stretch out on the bed once more, but he does not close his eyes. He waits anxiously for morning.

Much later he hears Beau Jim's car coming, hears it stop beneath the pecan trees, and can tell both, that Beau Jim is a little drunk, and that he is trying very hard to be quiet. Charlene stirs when Beau Jim, shoeless, stumbles softly in the hall beside their door, but she does not wake; and he hears Beau Jim feeling the wall with his hands and sliding his feet along the floor to his room. He hears him, at last, sit on his bed and begin to undress.

Sounds of fire popping and cracking in the rest of the house like muffled pistol reports. He and Beau Jim are sleeping in a room over the kitchen wing, and he listens only for a moment before he knows what he is hearing and swings his feet down to a floor already hot. He snatches on his britches, sticks his feet in his shoes, but does not lace them, grabs up his jumper, and drags Beau Jim from his cot. He opens the window and lifts Beau Jim out on the roof and climbs out behind him and slides down the roof and off the eaves to the ground, but when he turns to catch Beau Jim, he is not ready to jump, but, never fully awake, has curled back into sleep against the windowjam. He yells at him, and with horror, sees that Beau Jim appears to be about to climb back through the window into the burning house. He picks up a piece of stovewood and throws it accurately and yells, "Come awn youngin! Jimbo! Come awn!" and his brother, roused at last from his deep child's sleep, begins to cry and crawl toward the eaves.

The roof beam over the single story section where Vernon and Bernice sleep and where the fire must have started, collapses at once. He wraps Beau Jim in his jumper, and the two of them stand by the woodpile and do not speak. There is a ridge of old snow in the lee of the woodpile. It is flecked with bark and chicken droppings. It reflects the fire. The March wind blusters among the flames and ascending sparks, and neither of them move, or speak, or notice Gaither when he comes up from his place, down the road toward Boone.

In less than a month he and Beau Jim leave North Carolina for Cocke County, Georgia. He has become twenty-one. Beau Jim is not seven. Rumor says that, in this Georgia place, a chemical company has moved in to mine phosphate and is paying big wages, and since the war is on, they cannot find enough men. He will not hear Gaither's advice to stay in Deep Gap. He will not leave Beau Jim for Gaither to raise.

They have some clothes the neighbors have given them. They have eleven dollars and fifty cents in cash. They have Vernon's Model A which yet consents to run.

They even have a little over three dollars left when they get to Sharaw and find that, though Bond Chemical Co. has tested the area and found it rich in phosphates, they will not begin their mining operations for almost a year. And not until that first night, when he has driven a little outside Sharaw to pull off the road and sleep, did grief catch up with him. Beau Jim, noisy with asthma, asleep on the seat of the Model A, and him stretched on the ground beside it. And he does not grieve for Bernice and Vernon and the fire, but for all that went before it. The farm was lost anyway, and it couldn't have been much longer until they would have had to get off, and he is glad Bernice did not have to find a way to live with that too. Just as surely as if he had witnessed it, he knows what happened: Vernon reaching into his shirt pocket and withdrawing a cigarette pinched between his thumb and forefinger, laying it into the corner of his mouth where it droops, stuck to his damp lower lip. Reaching into the pocket on the other side and bringing out a match which he strikes on his thumbnail. Reeling his head drunkenly back from the flash. Lights it. Puffs. The cigarette flipping up and down. Thinking of a new scheme to make money, he fumbles it and goes to sleep. But of all Vernon's misdeeds, this last seems the easiest to forgive. He decides that he will not go back to North Carolina, no matter what he finds in this new place, and once he decides that, it makes it easier.

Chapter

Fifteen

A little over an hour after Dan left
for Sharaw, the well was capped and covered, the plumbing
connected, and the well drilling rig was gone. The well was
down one hundred and sixty-three feet, but they were getting a
good twelve gallons a minute.

By fifteen minutes after one, Charlene had finished the dishes,
mopped and cleaned the kitchen, and made her decision. She was
going to get a television set. All morning she had thought about
the seventy-five dollars and what to do with it, and some of her
notions, she knew herself, were wildly foolish. She thought of
taking the money and running away to Atlanta or Chattanooga,
and silly as the prospect was, she had a hard time dismissing it.
She thought of hiding the money too, saving it, and the next
seventy-five dollars Beau Jim should give her, and the next, until
she did have enough to leave Sheila and Dan and go off to some
big town like Chattanooga or maybe even Nashville. But she was
afraid to try to save it, for Dan would surely find out about it
sooner or later. Beau Jim couldn't keep a thing like that secret,
he wouldn't want to, and when Dan found out about it, he might
make her give the money back. She suspected that Beau Jim
would be moving as soon as his school started anyway; he

wouldn't want to be so far away from everything; even as it was, he hardly came home. The more she thought about the money, the more she could see how urgent it was that she get the money safely spent before Dan took it from her and gave it back to Beau Jim, or applied it to the cost of the well, where, like any money spent on the farm, it would simply disappear without trace, or any noticeable benefit.

There were lots of things she wanted: an electric churn, for instance—she was certain she was the last woman anywhere to make butter with an old wooden churn—and she wanted a window fan, and she thought she could probably get them both for seventy-five dollars. They seemed very wise choices, but the more she thought about them, the less satisfactory they became. Getting them was the same as admitting she was going to spend her days on the farm and never get away. If they moved back to Sharaw, they wouldn't need them; even so shoddy an apartment as the one over Judge Taylor's Hardware Store was air-conditioned, and they would need no churn if they didn't have a cow. And even if they should stay where they were, and she couldn't stand for one moment to admit the possibility, she would only use the fan six months out of the year. Finally, even the television set seemed a sad choice after her flirtation with the idea of running away, but at least it would keep her company the year around, and when they went back to Sharaw, once Dan had finally learned his lesson, the television could go right along with them.

Still, she knew the moment she made up her mind, Dan was not going to like it one bit when he came home and found a television set. It made her both afraid and angry to imagine what he might do, but ultimately the knowledge that Dan would disapprove only made the television set more appealing, and she began to compose things to say which would justify her purchase. How he got to go into town at least five days a week, while she seldom ever got to set her foot off the place. How a television set was a very common article that almost everybody had, or ought to, anyway, and how no one should kick up a fuss over one. But she did not wish to tell him how absolutely unhappy she was, or how lonely, or how often she thought of running away, for those things spoke of grievances ultimately deeper than just being stuck on the farm. Instead she refined and polished her few retorts until they had the proper bite and repeated them to herself until she felt justified, and even a little righteous; and having got that far, she became suddenly anxious to have the television in the house and decided to wake Beau Jim up and get him to take her into town so she could buy it right then, that very afternoon.

She went into the bedroom and put on her best dress and best shoes and fixed her hair. But just as she was ready and tucking the seventy-five dollars importantly into her purse, Beau Jim shuffled from his room without her having to wake him. Not until that moment did she think about his breakfast, and she took up her apron, put it on, and tied the sash with an impatient jerk.

"So, you decided to get up, didja?" she called, though she tried to make her voice sound cheerful. She came out of the bedroom and met him in the hall. "The water's back runnin," she told him, but he only groaned and smacked his lips sleepily.

His face puckered disagreeably and he shivered. "Oh me," he said, and went past her into the bathroom.

She asked through the door what he wanted for breakfast, but he thanked her and said he didn't want anything. She told him she would be happy to fix eggs or anything he'd like. She could hear him brushing his teeth and gagging. "No thanks," he said in a funny voice as though he were imitating a duck, and she heard him gag again. "How about coffee?" she asked him. "Good," he said in a duck's voice.

She warmed up some biscuits for him anyway and buttered them and set out some jelly. When he came into the kitchen, he looked very pale and let himself down slowly into his chair. She waited until he'd drunk a swallow or two of his coffee before she said, "Reckon you could carry me into town and back in a little while?" She took off her apron and rolled it up and laid it on the sideboard and plucked nervously at the hair over her ears. "I want to go over to the shopping center there by the Senneca pike."

He wiped his eyes and rubbed his forehead. "Sure," he said, "whatcha after?"

"You'll see when the time comes," she said, unable to keep the edge of indignation out of her voice, but she got herself in hand. He was giving her a ride after all, and he had even given her the money, though she assured herself it was her due. "Want your coffee warmed up?" she asked him, trying to sound as nice as she could.

"Just a tad, I guess," he said.

She filled his cup back up to the brim and gave the saucer with the buttered biscuits a little shove toward him. Then, waiting for him to finish, she got a cigarette from her pack and lit it and lifted one buttock and hung it on the edge of the counter and half leaned and half sat on the sideboard. "You look a little red-eyed and hung over this mornin," she said.

He had his mouth full of biscuit and he let his eyelids slide down over his eyes and shook his head slowly and said, "Mmmmh." But then, as though he realized she was being more friendly than usual, he looked at her with a little puzzled interest in his face and even let his eyes stray down the length of her until she realized that her position was not altogether lady-like and let her fanny slide off the sideboard. Somehow it angered her that she had sat on the counter with her dress a little hiked up and that he had noticed. "Huh," she said, "it must be nice to be able to run around and do whatever you please, and not have anything worse ahead of you than having the government getting ready to pay your way to college." Bitterness had crept into her voice again, but she didn't care and wasn't sorry. It wasn't right that some people had things so good while others were caught and penned like geese. She waited but he didn't say anything.

"Well, you finish your coffee. Gimme a minute in the bathroom, and I'll be ready to go," she said and left him, aware that, no matter what sort of favor he was doing her, she could not keep sweetness in her voice. She decided to give up on it.

He got in the car right before she did and reached across to open her door from the inside. He appeared to notice the torn panties on the floorboard just at the same moment she did. His neck and ears turned a deep red, and he tried, as though he wasn't aware of what he was doing, to kick them under the seat as she was getting in. All the way to town neither of them spoke a word, and Charlene wouldn't have mentioned it if, when they parked at the shopping center in Sharaw, he hadn't tried again to scrape them under the seat with his foot; but somehow that got the best of her and she said, "Great God! Quit pawing at the damned things, what the Hell do you think I care!"

She opened the door and got out. "You comin in or waitin?" she asked him.

"No, I'll uh, stay." He was red in the face. He tried to laugh.

"Good," she said and shut the door on his nonsense.

She walked toward the building, plucking at the hair over her ear and thinking to herself, *must be proud of hisself or somethin, a'pawin at em the whole time.* Suddenly then, it occurred to her to wonder why they were on the floorboard of his car instead of on the girl where they belonged, and why they were so torn up, and she hesitated and glanced back over her shoulder at Beau Jim, but one look at his face made her dismiss the possibility that had just come to her mind; he wasn't going to rape anybody. She snorted in contempt at the thought.

Still, torn step-ins on the floorboard of his car was a thing to puzzle about, and it distracted her so much that she wandered in a kind of aimless huff through the luggage, jewelry and clothing sections of the store before she came to herself enough to look for a sign that said appliances, or to ask someone where the televisions were.

She found them in the basement and was stunned to see the prices. She knew that, ten years before when television sets were just starting to appear around Sharaw, they were expensive, but she thought that had all changed, she thought—now that they were common and the factories had learned how to make them easier—they were much cheaper; but the tags she saw went from almost five hundred dollars down to one hundred and fifty-nine dollars for a little bitty one with a screen no bigger than a hotplate, and nowhere did she see a set even close to seventy-five dollars. She couldn't believe it. *How could them niggers across the road have one?* she asked herself. She looked at the tags and shook her head and snorted. *They lyin, is what,* she told herself, *they ain't got one a'tall.* But somehow she knew they were not lying. It mystified her how they could afford one, made her angry, and finally even scared her; and when a salesman showed up and asked if he could help her, she was in no mood to be friendly.

She blinked her eyes angrily at him and told him that she'd thought to buy a television set, but she could see that there wasn't anything there for a person who didn't happen to be rich. She asked him what his sets were made of: Was it gold or silver? She asked him how many of them he had to sell before he could retire and move to Florida. She pointed a finger at him and told him she had come with seventy-five dollars, prepared to pay cash on the line, but she could see she was going to have to do her trading somewhere else. But the longer she talked, the more she suspected his prices were not really out of line. She had simply forgotten for a moment who she was, the nature of her fate. Of course the mistake was hers. What did she know about the cost of things like that? She didn't know the proper price of anything that cost more than a dollar or two, and of course it was not her lot simply to walk up, like a regular person, and buy something she wanted. She let what she was saying to the salesman trail off, and waved her hand vaguely in front of her face as if she were clearing away a cobwebb. Her shoulders sagged, and she looked at the television sets and blew softly through her nose and shook her head.

She only meant to stand there a minute, just until her disappointment eased a little. She was only waiting for her resignation —her special talent—to grow like a frost flower over the whole miserable business until she could convince herself that she hadn't truly wanted a television set in the first place and she could turn on her heel and walk away—she was only waiting for that to happen and not really looking at or listening to the salesman, though she could both see and hear him. He still had the smile he had greeted her with, stuck on his face, and absently, she marveled that he could wear such a stale and betrayed expression and speak to her about the store's low profit margin and long guarantees. He explained to her that almost no one just walked in and paid cash for a thing as expensive as a television set; most people only made a down payment and then paid them off a little each month. At that, she came a little way out of her own private thoughts and said to him, "Is that so?" Then she thought immediately to herself with deep relief and satisfaction, *sure, that's what them niggers do. Sure. They ain't goan have no four hundred dollars, no more than me. Not for a minute. They just give somebody a dollar or two down and then owe for the rest.* But the moment she realized that, she realized too, as much as she wanted a television set, she could not allow herself to do what they did.

"Well, I thank you," she said to the salesman, as though, since he had solved the problem for her, she had decided to be courteous, "but I don't reckon I'll buy anything I can't pay cash for."

She gave him again her distant and preoccupied admiration when he nodded to her and told her, obviously lying, that it was a pleasure to talk to her and he hoped she'd come back. "It's just that we haven't got anything for seventy-five dollars," he said, "unless you'd be interested in a used set. We take in an old set from time to time on trade," he offered, "and I think we might have one or two back in the stockroom that are in your price range."

She had turned to walk away before he made his final confession, and though it surprised her, when she turned back toward him, she was already wearing a smug smile. Her faith in his basic dishonesty was renewed. He had tried to get the price of a new set out of her until the very last moment, but he was not going to let her get away with seventy-five dollars, if he could help it.

Of the ten sets in the stockroom, four needed repairs and didn't work, and three were too expensive. Of the three that remained, the best by far, according to the salesman, was a portable with a handle on top like a suitcase and a screen not much larger than a common postcard. But Charlene picked out a set with a nineteen inch screen. The metal cabinet, painted to look like cherry, was scratched and dented, and the gold paint that bordered the smoky screen had begun to flake away, but she had them hook it up, and though the picture wasn't as good as the new ones, she was more than satisfied.

Her guarantee had been explained, such as it was (no charge for labor and wholesale on parts for thirty days), sixty-five dollars had been counted out and wrung up in the cash register, and the stockroom man had dusted the set with a rag and was preparing to carry it to the car, when the subject of the antenna came up. She knew there were such things, for they were everywhere, even on Sammy's house across the road, but she had forgotten them altogether. When she found that it would cost an additional twenty-five dollars to buy the antenna and have it installed, she seemed suddenly to turn hollow. She couldn't even get mad. She almost cried. The impulse only made her eyes wet for an instant and did not in the slightest change her expression, but it seemed to hurt something in her chest, and she listened docilely while the salesman explained that the rabbit ears on the set might pick up Greenville, and maybe even Atlanta, but that without an antenna, she wouldn't get much of a picture and couldn't hope even to pick up Asheville or Chattanooga. She listened without moving or speaking and didn't even think of asking for her money back. The seventy-five dollars simply ceased to interest her any longer. It had lost its value; it had caused her too much excitement and too much disappointment, and she was weary of it, as though it were only a false hope she had decided, at last, to give up.

The stockroom man carried the set to the car, and Beau Jim drove her home, and when they hooked it up and could get nothing but vague outlines on the snowy screen, she was not surprised. She sat with her hands folded in her lap while Beau Jim struggled with the dials on the side of the set and in the back. Nor was she disturbed when one of the rabbit ears broke off in his hand while he was trying to turn it around in another direction. She simply nodded her head when he explained that it had been already cracked and just about to fall apart.

He spent at least an hour after that trying to get a decent picture for her. Finally, he used a metal coathanger to replace the broken antenna and got the Greenville channel almost clearly. He backed away from the set with his hands held up and his fingers spread less the picture dissolve into snow again, but the image held.

He left her then, and she watched the whole afternoon. And when Sheila came home from school, she watched too. Both of them sitting on the couch, watching whatever appeared, without preference, and without the slightest diminution of attention. And a little at a time, the thin ache inside Charlene's chest began to dissolve as though it were a piece of ice caught low in her throat from the time in the store when she had almost cried.

Chapter

Sixteen

It was around ten o'clock Tuesday morning and he'd just gotten out of bed when Yancey called and asked if he could drop her fan and cushion by. She seemed so proper over the phone, it took him a little by surprise and didn't leave him much to say. Several times he was on the verge of making a joke about Sunday night, but there didn't ever seem to be a place for it. Anyone listening in would have heard absolutely nothing out of the way from him, and nothing from Yancey beyond an innocent, friendly apology for being so much trouble and asking such a favor.

Still, before he got out of the car at her house, he took her torn and trampled step-ins from the glove pocket where he'd kept them and stuffed them into his hip pocket, thinking it would be fun to return them along with her fan and cushion, but the girl who met him at the door was again like the phone call, and nothing like the Yancey in the back seat of his Studebaker. She was polite, friendly, scrubbed, shiny, dressed in a white blouse, a white skirt with daisies and green leaves on it, and had bright green ballerina slippers on her feet. She invited him in, led him into the kitchen, took her things from him, and told him how sweet he was to bring them by. He began to feel a little strange.

He hadn't gotten to see much of her house when he'd taken her home. They hadn't sat parked at the curb telling each other what a good time they'd had. There had been no good nights. She had rushed inside and left him sitting in the car. And so, even the house bothered him a little. It seemed a big respectable place even if the paint was peeling, the floors sagging. Dim and cool it was and full of the vibrations of an air conditioner somewhere at work. He felt the lump of her underwear against his hip, but he left it where it was.

She served him a cup of coffee and a fried pie she had just made, seated herself sweetly across from him, and asked him to tell her just everything he could think of about what he had been doing and about all those foreign countries he had visited.

Then, all at once, he figured it out. Her mother was somewhere in the house out of sight, listening. Probably in the next room. And Yancey's behavior was for her. He gave Yancey a wink to let her know he understood, but her face, sweet-smiling, didn't change a whit. Still, he wouldn't give her away. If she wanted to be a big red-headed Miss Muffet, he'd help her all he could. He tried to make conversation about Europe, but although he had been there better than five years, he couldn't think of much to say. He felt like he'd buried a coffee can full of money in his backyard and then couldn't find it again. He told her there was no speed limit on the open road over there, that there were lots of big churches, that the beer was very strong, and that a lot of German girls didn't shave their legs or armpits. The last piece of information out of his mouth took him by surprise. It caused his ears to heat up, and he made a face of apology to Yancey. God knew what her mother thought, but Yancey took him in stride. She asked him to tell her about his plans for college, and how it was to be back in Cocke County after all his broadening travels, and he struggled with that for a while. *Poor, big, ole gal, I'm trying not to let you down*, he thought.

But not until it was clear that he couldn't offer another word, did she rescue him by telling him what she had done the six years he had been away, which, she insisted, was practically nothing. She told him about Howard, to whom she had been engaged for almost a year. But she told it in a funny sort of a way, as though it weren't very important. He had a hard time remembering any Howard, even after she described him and explained that he had been a year behind them in high school. He thought he could remember a big, tall, tow-headed boy with a face as innocent as a lump of dough, but he couldn't be certain he was the one she meant. For her mother's sake he pretended: *Sure, Howard! A heck of a nice fellow!*

Howard had joined the merchant marines, she told him, and had probably found himself a native girl somewhere. Laughter from her. Silence from him. Should he continue to brag on Howard, or not? He wagged his head in sympathy and decided to eat his pie. But even that wasn't going to be easy for him. The first bite was so hot his eyes welled instantly with tears. His teeth clattered like a popcorn popper as he wallowed it around in his mouth, and it burned all the way down when he swallowed it. *Mercy.* Sweat sprung to his forehead, and for some reason he reached back with his hand and checked her step-ins to make sure they were safely tucked out of sight. *Mercy.*

Yancey had moved on to other things. She toyed with a paper napkin and told him about how her poor father had died of a heart attack four years before. He remembered Jerry Tillard better. A big red-headed, red-faced carpenter who liked his whiskey and good times. He had been a kind of local hero when Beau Jim was in school. People liked him because, with all the rest, he had been a good man and a hard worker. Her father had called her his "Dollbaby," his "Sweet Little Strawberry," and she laughed and confessed that when she was little, she planned to marry him. She had made up her mind absolutely and wouldn't hear any arguments to the contrary. It seemed only right and proper to her, and she had thought herself very generous for telling Hilda, her mother, that she could stay when the time came, and even play with her toys and sleep in her room. There was to be no misunderstanding about who was really Daddy's girl, but she wasn't going to throw her mother out in the cold, and giving her the consolation prize of toys and room, made her feel very proud of herself and generous. Yancey laughed her high, fading laughter at the memory and sighed. Well, she told Beau Jim, good a man as he was, he wasn't the sort to save his money, but he'd had an insurance policy that paid for the house when he died, so she and her mother had that free and clear, and what with them both working, they got along well enough. Of course her mother had to work much too hard. Six days a week in the Cafeteria of Bond Chemical Company. The poor thing. But since she, herself, worked seven nights a week at the Dan-Dee Theater, at least they didn't see enough of each other to ever have many arguments, she told him.

The discovery that they were alone, after all, put her behavior in a different light and took away what little ability for conversation he had. All at once it made him feel somehow ashamed of himself. He pulled his ear, rolled his shoulders, patted his foot against the floor, ran his finger back and forth under his nose and told her what a dynamite fried pie she made. It was the only thing he could think of to say, although he saw his mistake immediately, for it caused her to try to press another on him. He told her he had to be going, but he couldn't quite seem to get his feet under him or find just exactly what he wanted to say in parting. Even Yancey was reduced to unattached sighs and *wells* and *sos*, and all he could think to do was smack his lips over the pie he'd eaten to fill up the silences. Finally he got himself up and she saw him to the door.

"Well, Mr. Beau Jim Early, I want you to know I expect to see just a whole lot of you now that you're back home," she said. "I'm here all alone every day with not one single, solitary thing to do but push dust around this house," she said and gave him, one last time, her high, musical imitation of laughter.

Strange though, that when he drove away, his guilt and embarrassment seemed accompanied by another stronger feeling of being somehow gratified. It made his throat thicken. And even when he told Claire how he had spent his morning—a mistake he regretted—and endured a few of Claire's ruthless jokes, the gratified feeling still didn't go away.

When Yancey called the very next day, what he felt inside his chest was, very distinctly, joy. He was on to her long before she finished talking, but it didn't matter. She begged his pardon for being such an awful bother. She was really very embarrassed by it, she explained. She knew she shouldn't tell her troubles to someone she had only just renewed acquaintances with; but she had a very complicated problem. She needed advice, and he was the only person she could think of to turn to. Could he come over, she wanted to know. She felt silly for asking, but could he?

This time when he arrived, she was wearing peach colored pedal pushers and a skimpy halter, and the sight of her made his eyes water. She wasn't a skinny girl, no one could argue that, but he didn't know where he'd gotten the idea that she was fat. If that was fat, he told himself, then, by God, he'd pay for it by the pound, and to hell with Claire Buckner. Big, healthy, red-headed girls probably scared most fellows, he thought. Sure they did. He knew it was so, because she scared him a little. There wasn't anything small and defenseless about her to make a man feel like the boss. But he decided to listen to any and all problems she had. He could already think of some pretty cagey advice.

But it wasn't that easy. Her problem seemed so difficult she couldn't even explain to him what it was. He drank cup after cup of her coffee and ate three of her delicious fried pies while she sighed, skirted, flanked and side-stepped whatever was bothering her. Often she got suddenly and unaccountably gay, as though, periodically, she had made up her mind to forget the whole thing and not ask his advice after all. And it wasn't until the middle of the afternoon that she began to talk about Mr. Wynette and hung her head like a sunflower on her freckled neck. *Big ole gal, if you looked close at her, she was nearly as pretty as a gal could get without actually being pretty.* Inside his chest he felt vital machinery sag with honest pity for her. She'd had to quit her job in order to go out with him Sunday night, she explained. But she told him not to worry about it for a minute because it was a mess she had brought on herself, and he hadn't done anything but show up when she was ripe for trouble: Velma's boyfriend proposing and all. Well, she told him and laughed, she and her boss had had themselves a nasty little fight all right; but that wasn't the worst of it. The worst of it was that Mr. Wynette had called her Monday morning to apologize and hire her back, and positively the worst of all, was that she had gone back. She needed the job, and God knows what else, she said. She hadn't even missed one miserable night's work.

She got quiet, wouldn't look at him, and he thought for a moment she was going to cry. He was sad for her. The small teeth of jealousy even gnawed a little. But he didn't know what sort of advice he could give. He tasted the inside of his mouth speculatively, squinted his eyes and tried to think. "Awwh, Yancey," he said, "Miss Yancey, it'll turn out." He was moved to say more and was thinking of how to put it when, out of the blue, she turned very gay again. She called herself silly. Thanked him for help he hadn't given. Even gave him a quick hug for it. It made him wonder if he'd said something he hadn't heard himself say. He didn't think so. Whatever—she wouldn't discuss the subject further.

The third morning when she called, she said she wanted to make up for the bad time she had given him the day before and wouldn't ask him anything except whether the peach pies she had just made were up to the apple he'd been eating. She called herself a goose for pulling him into her troubles and acting so blue the day before. And she laughed a lot and sounded extremely happy.

He didn't know exactly what to think of her. And when he got to her house and found her in a black lace nightgown and a gauzy black negligee, he was surprised again. Anyway, he thought he was surprised. But before he could sift back through her behavior to see if he was finally and after all, truly surprised, she began to talk:

"I was just too triflin to get dressed this morning," she explained. "I guess it's time you knew the worst about me," she said and pointed a finger at her bosom and gave it a shame on you rub. "Half the time, to tell the tacky ole truth, I just don't pull myself together until noon. Honest to God, though, if I didn't work late, I wouldn't be so lazy. But, this once you'll excuse me and let me off, won't you?"

He nodded his head.

"Well come on in here for goodness sake, fore the neighbor's get their eyes full," she said, and she pulled him through the door.

He wondered if she knew that in certain lights you could see right through all that gauzy stuff. Half the time she was between him and some strong source of light, and she insisted on acting, for the longest time, as though she had on plenty of clothes, as though butter wouldn't melt in her mouth, and his ears weren't red, and his conversation wasn't stupid, even for him. But then, by God, all confusion went away, and it was late that afternoon, just before her mother got home, before she turned him out, sweaty, rug-burned, and almost too exhausted to drive away in his car.

All the way over to Senneca to find Claire he roused periodically out of a stupor to giggle and say, "Hot Damn!" in an excited, strangled voice only to lapse immediately back into an incredulous daze again. Once, half way to Senneca, he kicked the gas pedal to the floor and the Studebaker sputtered and nearly stalled and then cut in again with a terrific backfire, and he slapped his leg and shook his head and felt on the verge of some very wise thought, but the only thing that came to his lips was, "Hot Damn!"

He didn't say a word to Claire about where he had been. He didn't have to. He came through the kitchen door from the outside third floor landing, calling, "Hey ugly, where you at?"

Claire was sitting on the living-room couch dangling a can of beer from his hand and giving his head a tiny and continuous bob. "What?" he said at last, "did the line get so long outside her door, you had to get out of the saddle?"

Beau Jim pointed at Claire and squinted, although he couldn't keep a smile from stretching his mouth, "You can't make me mad, ugly. You just can't do it!" he said and laughed. He did a little jig, flapping his elbows and grinning. "Fawh!"

Claire watched with his eyelids drooping. "About two hours ago I was supposed to be teachin you how to draw a cue ball," he said.

Beau Jim stopped still and wiped his hands on his thighs reflectively. "I apologize to you there, Amigo. Time sort of got away from me."

"Well, Slick," Claire said, taking a huge breath and letting it out, "if you ain't fucked yore brains out, do you want to get to work, or not?"

"Sure," Beau Jim said. He began to grin and flap his elbows again. "Sure. Hell yes."

What was it that made his eyes snap open in the mornings, instantly so clear he felt he could see the tiniest leaf on the most far away tree? All things, great and small, had begun to seem right and proper. He found he had even made peace with Dan's constant, tight circle of labor. With Charlene's mouth. Claire's mouth. The mechanical quirks and rumblings of the Studebaker. He could even almost forget the fear he had of college, which would start in little more than a week. And if he'd stopped to think about it, he would have wondered if the Indians hadn't somehow lost his trail.

Friday and Saturday, without any phone call for an excuse, he was over at Yancey's. She owned half the wrinkles of his brain.

Big, dumb ole sweet gal, full of freckles and corny tricks she could somehow make work—why somebody hadn't married her for her cooking, smooth sad shoulders, and foxy eyes, he didn't quite understand. Probably, he thought, if that was all she'd had going for her, they would have. But she had way too much to give away. She piled it on so hard and fast, it was scary. Now and again he felt he ought to explain to Yancey that the world was full of foolish men, and that if you gave them just what they'd always wanted and dreamed about, you'd scare the shit out of them every time. The poor old gal didn't seem to know that, and it was shaking her loose in the head. But he couldn't tell her that. You couldn't tell somebody a thing like that, not when it was already too late anyway.

Friday and Saturday were good days. Sunday he hung out with Claire because her mother would be home. But Monday he was back on her doorstep, bright and early.

Surprise. She met him at the door in pedal pushers and a man's shirt and didn't even say hello; simply left the door standing open and went on back down the hall. There wasn't any breakfast waiting on him in the kitchen. "Say, what's up?" he asked her, but she didn't answer. She ignored him and went through the house cleaning and dusting and picking up, and he followed her, smiling good-naturedly and trying to get in front of her to look into her face. Finally, in the living room he trapped her in his arms and said, "Gotcha!" but she stood as still and lifeless as a department store dummy, which, very quickly, made him so nervous he turned her loose again.

"Hey, Miss Yancey," he said, and sat nervously down on the couch, "how come you're so chapped with me?"

"As if you didn't know," she said.

Although he didn't know, he felt completely guilty. "Gimme a hint," he said.

Yancey stood still in the middle of the floor holding a dustmop. Across her stiff, squared shoulders seemed to be written: *MAD*. But then she bent and began to dust. "Where were you yesterday?" she asked.

"I couldn't make it," he said. "Besides, your mother's home on a Sunday, I thought."

"That's right, and I aggravated poor momma until she washed her hair and put on her best dress to meet you in," Yancey said, and she moved the dust mop around with great speed and determination. "And Sunday her only day of the week to rest and lie around."

"Shitass, Yancey," he said, "how was I supposed to know that? Why didn't you give me a call?"

"You don't have to talk nasty," Yancey said. "I'm not a girl you can talk nasty to." She dusted as though dust had the ability to dodge her mop unless she was quick enough to catch it and mash out its life. "I didn't call you Friday or Saturday, and you were here pecking on my door."

She went out of the room and down the hall, and he followed, trying to think of something to say, but nothing came to mind. She went through the back door and out on the small sagging back porch and shook out her dust mop. He noticed that she jiggled all over, even her rump.

"I'm sorry," he said when she came back through the door and passed him in the hall, but she didn't answer him. She stowed the dust mop in the kitchen pantry and passed him again at the kitchen door and went down the steps into the basement. He followed behind.

The basement was cool and damp and smelled of earth and soap. The floor was of hard-packed dirt except for a wooden platform by another set of stairs leading up to the outside bulkhead. Yancey stood on it, sorting clothes into a washing machine. Oddly there was something about being in the basement while Yancey worked and sulked that made him very uneasy, as though some significant, dangerous milestone had been passed.

"Hey Yancey, I'm sorry," he said. "I'll show up next Sunday."

She did not reply. She continued to sort clothes and stuff them into the washer. He sat on the stairs, aware that it had got beyond a simple apology or a promise to come by next Sunday. She wanted more than that. She wanted some sort of commitment from him, something extravagant and binding. He could see it in the very curve of her back, tilt of her head, line of her jaw. She stuffed in the last of a load of clothes, poured in a cup of soap, and slammed the lid. She turned the ratchety dial. The machine groaned and began to whinny and fill with water, and without a word she passed him where he sat and went upstairs again. After a moment he got up and left by the bulkhead door.

Tuesday Claire said, "You know I'll bet ole Yancey was having a hard time balancing on them round heels of hers, but since you've been good enough to give her a couple of days to stand up, Jimbo, they might be getting damned near flat enough to walk on again, whattaya think?"

Beau Jim looked into Claire's blue eyes. "What I think is that if brains was pistol powder, you couldn't shoot your mouth off enough to say, 'Hydee.' "

Claire looked steadily back, his mouth closed but moving as though he were chewing something, sparks of humor glowing at the bottoms of his irises, as unquenchable as phosphorous. From somewhere to the rear of him came a vibrant, *blaaaattt.*

That evening in the pool hall in Senneca, there were one or two new faces. Early arrivals to the campus. He and Claire shot eight ball, Claire being very subtle with his coaching. But Beau Jim was strangely restless and itchy, and when Claire went to the toilet and a fat kid in a shiny indigo blue shirt came up and asked him if he wanted to shoot a little nine ball, he said, "Okey doke." By the time Claire came out of the toilet again, they were at it. Claire watched a few moments, puffed his upper lip full of air, and went up to the counter for a beer.

After every game the fat kid put Beau Jim's money in a different pocket, his pudgy hands tucking it quickly out of sight in his shiny shirt with the collar turned up as though against the wind, or in his soiled, shiny, grey trousers. It was as though he thought that if he got it quickly out of sight, Beau Jim wouldn't know he'd lost it. But scattering the money through all his pockets was some sort of strange precaution Beau Jim couldn't understand. Still by the time he had lost thirty-five dollars, he understood he was outclassed and quit.

Claire made a motion with his head and went out the door and across the street to Tuckers, and Beau Jim followed. When Beau Jim got over there, Claire had a table and two bottles of beer. "That pusselgutted, sweaty, toad fucker you got glommed onto when my back was turned was a Goddamned hotshot, God Damn it!" he said reasonably when Beau Jim sat down. "He ain't that good, but he's a hotshot. How come you did it?"

"Ahhh," Beau Jim said vaguely and waved his hand as though to wave it away.

"You feel better?" Claire said.

Beau Jim waved his hand again and took a swallow of beer. He didn't say that, in some small part, he did feel just a little better.

"There ain't no percentage in it this way, Hoss. Till you get the hang of it, you got to let me pick em for you."

Beau Jim drained his bottle of beer thirstily and set it down. Claire looked at him a moment and puffed his upper lip full of air. "Ahh, you'll get on to it," he said and stuck his middle finger in Beau Jim's empty. He took a swallow of his own beer. "You'll get on to it," he said again and began to play "All Around The Water Tank," on his head, keeping excellent time and adding all the grace notes and bass runs that a good guitarist might have included. Beau Jim didn't mind that he'd lost money. He listened to Claire and told himself that he wasn't even giving Yancey a thought.

The next night they played in the pool hall in Sharaw. Claire gave him the nod to shoot nine ball with a kid who couldn't have been more than fifteen. The kid was thin and grim and had a purple scar on his upper lip that turned white each time he concentrated for a shot. He was almost but not quite, harelipped, had practically nothing to say; and it took Beau Jim almost two hours to take six dollars from him. Six dollars was all the boy had. Beau Jim had seen into his billfold when he took the last dollar out. Claire, meantime, was playing a farmer in overalls.

But then Beau Jim and Claire got to be partners in a snooker game with two electricians, and that took the bad taste of the kid's six dollars out of his mouth. For the first time, Beau Jim actually enjoyed shooting pool for money. They took the two construction electricians for fifteen, maybe sixteen dollars apiece, and he could tell they enjoyed every minute of it. Claire joked constantly, changed cues every third or fourth shot as if they were to blame for balls he'd missed, and stuck his head practically into the pockets to say insulting things to the balls the construction men made. Claire, himself, made very few balls. With what appeared to be pure chance and artlessness, he left the man who followed him almost impossible shots, and that man in turn, often snookered, and having to use all his skill even to hit the proper object ball, or lose points, often left Beau Jim relatively easy shots. It was clear from the way the electricians talked, they thought Beau Jim was much better than Claire. Just before the pool hall closed, the four of them had a beer together, and showed themselves all around to be anxious for a rematch.

Back in Claire's car when all the money was added up and divided, Beau Jim showed a loss, over the two nights, of five dollars and a quarter, if he didn't count the beer he'd drunk. "Stick with me," Claire said, "and you'll never go hungry. When you get to shootin twice as good as you do now, which isn't more than five times better than you shot two weeks ago; then you can begin to learn how to behave." He got a cold beer out of the cooler over the differential hump between them. "You won't be nuthin a'tall like that fat hotshot that clipped you for thirty-five dollars the other night, cause he's too damned dumb to hustle. He won't never be good enough to look bad, and he ain't smart enough to keep from being clipped near as often as he clips somebody else." Claire took a contented pull on his beer. "But what's worst of all about the pusselgut is that there ain't no joy in him. No joy at all." Beau Jim looked at Claire, at his red-rimmed eyes, his round, somehow womanish cheeks, despite their blond stubble; and he began to believe, for the first time, that he actually might be telling the truth.

Thursday, they went to a used car auction in Atlanta. Oddly, he was more grateful for the distraction than the money he would make, although he needed the money too. Friday was registration day and that made him nervous. He didn't want to think about it, and part of his mind was braced against considering it. Then there was Yancey. For some reason, walking out of the basement door Monday no longer seemed quite justifiable to him, and he was trying not to consider that either. It helped to be on the road going somewhere and to think about moving into Claire's apartment in Senneca. It had been Claire's idea, but he didn't have to give it a thought before he accepted. They would split the seventy-five dollars a month rent right down the middle, and even with Beau Jim sleeping on the fold-out couch, it was a hell of a deal. The air-conditioner and all the furniture belonged to Claire, even the refrigerator. Only the stove came with the place, and Beau Jim had no such investments. It would cost him more than thirty-seven fifty a month just to drive back and forth from the farm to the campus. But as much as the convenience, it pleased him, made him feel like somebody to have an apartment in the huge old white Victorian, right there in the center of town. And even if Claire was taking only one course, he would be handy, knew the ropes, and was in it with him. It was good to have somebody in it with you.

But even when he got back to the farm that evening with a hundred dollars in his pocket, he was nervous and uneasy. He had been lucky enough to make two trips with two cars a trip, but the hundred dollars didn't seem to mean very much. He gave Charlene fifty for board and room, even though he would be gone next day and didn't owe that much. Somehow, since he was leaving, he couldn't resist trying to buy into her good graces, once more. Without a moment's hesitation she took it, and as though it had paid for his right to the information, as she tucked it away, she told him that Yancey had called. He would have called her back, right then and there, if she hadn't been at work.

And the next day, although he could have called her, he did not. The strain of being, at last, on the campus and the confusion of registration were so great, he had no thoughts for Yancey.

He never even found Claire.

He spent the morning filling out endless forms in the field house where registration was held. He met with his advisor—a busy, friendly, inefficient man, who, with his hasty directions and scraps of information, left him more confused than ever. He spent hours wandering from table to table, feeling ignorant, angry and like a goat among the sheep. Finally when he got what he could only hope was a proper assortment of courses, he hunted down the appropriate office in the basement of the Administration building and signed up for the G.I. bill. Last of all, he bucked the crowds at the bookstore for his textbooks.

He felt his books, like his courses, might be wrong. Carrying them back to his car, he gave himself over to the feeling that had stalked him every moment of the day: the sure and certain knowledge that he was nothing like the rest of the students who swarmed all over the campus. It was an empty, cold, lonely feeling in the pit of his stomach. Twice, driving out to the farm to pick up his things so he could move in with Claire, he almost ran off the road, as though he had lapsed into a coma of anxiety and confusion.

But once he got back to Senneca and pulled into the gravel parking lot behind the white Victorian house, his spirits rose a little. God, it was a handsome house. It had green and gray striped awnings over every single window and even over the large front porch. It looked to him like the kind of place where a doctor or a lawyer might live; and when he climbed the outside rear steps up to their third floor landing, he felt, momentarily at least, like a man who just might conceivably handle college, since he too, lived in such a place.

It took him only two trips to move in, one with his books and another with his duffel bag over one shoulder and a few hangers with shirts and britches on them, over the other. He left his textbooks on the kitchen table, and gave them as much room, until he and Claire went out to the pool hall, as if they were a nest of rattlesnakes.

Early next morning, while Claire was still asleep, he drove to Sharaw. In the Rexall Drug Store he bought a huge box of candy, had it wrapped, and by eight thirty he was knocking at Yancey's door.

When she finally opened up, he was surprised to see her in pajamas and a faded aqua robe, and she looked so pale, he thought for a moment she might be sick. A second later he realized he had never before seen her without make-up, that all those mornings when he had thought she was just barely up and warm from her bed, she had actually gone to a lot of trouble to fix herself up. Somehow looking at her pajamas, faded robe, and her pale, broad, puffy face, it struck him as very funny and gratifying.

"Mornin Glory," he said and laughed, but she went back down the hall and turned into the kitchen. When he followed, he found her sitting at the chipped wooden table by the window. Some time ago the table had been painted white, but where the paint had chipped away, a dull mossy green showed through; and she sat there, in her faded robe and sipped her coffee.

"Mercy," she said, not looking at him, "You must have lost your way."

"I'm honest-to-God-sorry, Yancey," he said and sat down at the table, putting her box of candy before her. "Day before yesterday I had to go to Atlanta, and all day yesterday I was trying to make out like I was a student." He ran his finger back and forth under his nose. "I wore myself out just trying to look smart. Haven't saved nothin for my actual teachers Monday." He smiled and leaned back in his chair and crossed his legs. "It might be a week or two before I can work up a half-smart face again."

Yancey blew a little jet of air through her nose and looked out the window. He couldn't help noticing that her hair shone like copper in the light from the window and was thick as a horse's mane, and though it was a little tangled, it was almost too thick and clean to get really mussed.

"Aren't you goan look at the present I brought you?" he asked her, but she kept her face turned toward the window. He couldn't think what she reminded him of, the way her eyelashes and eyebrows, usually dark with make-up, were now the same color as her hair and freckles. She was all pink and rust colored, even her lips, without lipstick, were freckled. "Come on, Yancey," he said, "don't hold on to your mad so tight."

She had her face so completely turned away from him that a tendon stood out from her jaw to her collarbone. "And you probably didn't shoot any pool with Claire Buckner either didja?" she said.

"Well I had to make a little money so I could buy you a present," he said cheerfully.

"I'm sorry I can't put out so you could get your money's worth," Yancey said, "but it's my time of month."

"Hey, don't talk like that," he said, feeling himself go pale. "It's no need to say a thing like that."

"Yeah," she said and stood up, "and you'd a been comin over to play checkers or rummy, right?" She turned her foxy brown eyes on him, and they were full of water and fire and pinned him to his chair.

He couldn't muster an answer, and to his surprise and terrible discomfort, she began to cry.

She covered her face with her hands. "Maybe I could give you a hand job," she said. "Got to do something so you'll come back."

She took him so by surprise, he had nothing to say to her; and as if to protect him against the spectacle of her unhappiness, his mind offered up a capricious thought: What she reminded him of, he realized suddenly, was gingerbread. The color of her hair, freckles, face, lips all pink and cinnamon—reminded him of gingerbread, and with the notion that it might somehow distract and comfort her, he said, "By God Yancey, you know something? You remind me of gingerbread," and he gave a half-hearted laugh, hoping she might laugh too.

But she slapped him so hard the chair he was sitting in rocked up on two legs, and his ears rang long after she had run out of the room and slammed the door to her bedroom down the hall. With the tip of his tongue he explored the inside of his cheek, cut slightly against a crooked tooth, and supposed, after all, it hadn't been a very clever thing to say. He blinked his left eye, which was watering, and sniffed at the moisture which had sprung up inside his nose. *Well, anyway, it's a good thing she didn't ball up her fist*, he thought, trying to tease himself out of feeling bad. He took a deep breath and let it escape through his pursed lips, gave the five pound box of candy a pat as though to comfort it, and left.

The Studebaker was still making popping, cooling sounds when he got back in and remembered that he hadn't even got to tell her he'd moved in with Claire. But it occurred to him that it was probably information she would have no use for, and he cranked up the Studebaker and made a U-turn in order to hit the highway back to Senneca. But the farther he got from Yancey, the more he realized how unhappy he was. Only minutes before he'd had such high hopes, and it was hard for him to believe that things had turned out as they had. Still, a tingling cheek and a very empty feeling in his chest went a long way toward convincing him. "Fuck it," he muttered, hoping suddenly that Claire would be home and ready to go to the pool hall over in Bolivar, say, for he didn't even want to see a college student, much less play pool with one.

When he got back to Senneca, he was glad to see Claire's Dodge still parked in the lot behind the apartment house, and he took the back zigzagging stairs two at a time until he got to the third floor landing and came through the kitchen door.

Claire, dressed only in a pair of clean blue shorts, his hair still wet from the shower, was standing in front of the refrigerator opening a can of beer. He pointed with the bottle opener toward the living room. "Yore frogjaw just called you on the phone," he said.

"Yancey?" Beau Jim said.

Claire raised his shoulders and let his eyelids droop. "She sounded red-headed and fat to me."

"She musta called out to the house and Charlene told her I was here," Beau Jim said, not even thinking to try to control the relief in his voice. "What did she say?"

"She said, 'Bleeeah, whaaa whaaa boohoo,' or something along that line," Claire said and went past him through the living room and took a pair of clean, light blue seersucker pants from a hanger flung across the bed in his bedroom.

Beau Jim couldn't even get mad, in fact, he couldn't keep a smile off his face. "Come on, Slick, what did she say?"

Claire drew his pants on, ran his belt through the loops and buckled it over his round, hairy, self-satisfied, and somehow muscular looking gut and sat down on the bed to pull socks on over his feet. "The gist of it seemed to be that she was just all shook up and sorry as Hell about something and wanted to thank you for her present." He stood up and retrieved his beer from the top of the dresser, took a pull and smacked his lips. "I always thought them big-tittied girls was cheerful," he said. He opened a drawer and got out a clean, faded golf shirt and put it on. He gave his short, colorless hair a half-dozen strokes with a military hair brush, which didn't change its looks in the slightest. "Maybe you been fuckin a wrinkle," he said.

"Awh, shut up, for Christ's sake," Beau Jim said, but he could not get angry. He wondered whether or not to call her back and decided he would, but not in Claire's presence.

"I understand that on a fat girl it can be a problem," Claire said, "I can see how if you got crosswise in the dark, you'd never find it." He was sitting on the bed again, putting on a pair of newly shined shoes. He was always very neat. "But it's gotta be one of them that runs up and down even with Yancey, ain't it Jimbo?"

Chapter Seventeen

Charlene was fixing breakfast when it came over the radio. She slid the half done biscuits out of the oven and hurried out to the barn where Dan was milking. Chickens, flopping a wing now and again for balance, ran clumsily out of her way, and she began to speak at the very moment she entered the gloom of the barn. "Ha, you won't never guess what I just heard over the radio," she said. She stopped halfway to the stall and threw her head back and put her hands on her hips as though she dared him to try. He turned his head to look at her out of the corner of his eye, but did not take his forehead from the cow's swelled side. "Saaawwh, saawwh now," he said softly to the cow who had begun to shift her hind feet.

"They done blowed up Foscoe Grammar School!" Charlene said. "Done it in the night!"

When he came in for lunch, it was on the midday television news, and he watched with Charlene and Sheila. But he watched dubiously as though he doubted that things of the real world would actually translate to that small, glowing screen.

Still, there was Sheriff Tate Newcome coming down the county courthouse steps in Sharaw, and a man stepping up to him, extending a microphone.

"Sheriff Newcome?" the man asked.

The sheriff was dressed the way he always was: in a pair of suit pants and a white short-sleeved shirt without a tie, and neither visible gun nor badge, but he looked at the newsman as though he should have known who he was and did not answer. He rolled a toothpick from one corner of his mouth to the other. It was Deputy Earl Wagner, standing directly behind the sheriff on the steps, and as completely in uniform as the sheriff was out, who answered for him. "That's him," he said. He had a toothpick in his mouth as well.

The newsman recited the call sign of his television station and asked what time the explosion had occurred.

"Early this mornin," the sheriff said.

He was built like a pear, had a very small head, and small hooded eyes. He stood about five feet six inches tall. Wagner, however, was six feet four or five, and everybody in Cocke County called them Mutt and Jeff, though never in their hearing. Wagner was the sheriff's brother-in-law.

The sheriff rolled the toothpick to the opposite corner of his mouth and looked at the newsman out of his small, hooded eyes.

"We interviewed Mr. Haggerman earlier, and he said the explosion woke him just after two, and that there was another almost immediately, sheriff," the newsman said and held the microphone toward him.

"I bleve that's early in the mornin," the sheriff said with no expression whatever on his face.

The newsman took the censure, if that's what it was, in stride. "How extensive is the damage, would you say sir?" the newsman asked.

"I'm not a building contractor," the sheriff said, "I couldn't tell you."

"Do you know what caused the explosions?" the newsman asked, and deferentially extended the microphone again.

The sheriff took out his toothpick at that, and he seemed almost amused. He held the toothpick up in his unusually small hand and said, "Dynamite," and replaced it. Since he was on a higher step than the newsman, he looked down on him, as if he were a child and rolled the toothpick to the opposite corner of his mouth.

"I understand there was a charge in the first grade school-room and one in the principal's office," the newsman said.

"That's correct," the sheriff said, "looked like maybe eight, ten sticks in each spot."

"Do you have any comment at this time on who might have been responsible?" the newsman asked and held the microphone for the sheriff to speak.

The sheriff looked at him for a long moment and pursed his lips around the toothpick. It wasn't a thoughtful look. It was the expression of a man who had been asked an obvious question. Again, apparently amused, he said, "I'm satisfied about who is responsible. But as to who set off the dynamite, is something I don't know as of yet. It's still under investigation of my office." There seemed suddenly good humored wrinkles around the sheriff's eyes, although the expression appeared no where else on his face, and was gone so quickly, it was hard to be sure it had ever been there. "I suspicion just about ever white man in Cocke County. Wasn't you, was it son?" the sheriff asked and began to move down the steps.

"Would you tell us who, in your opinion, is responsible then, sir?" the newsman asked, rushing his question, for the sheriff was walking away.

The sheriff did not answer. He didn't even appear to notice the newsman any longer.

"Would you tell us who is responsible, sir?" the newsman asked again, doing his best to follow the sheriff and keep the microphone before him. The sheriff did not answer.

"Sheriff Newcome . . ." the newsman said, but he was interrupted by the deputy who put out an arm and pushed him slowly but firmly to the side as a man might push back a drapery. "Excuse me," the deputy said and followed the sheriff down the steps and across the sidewalk to the special place where their patrol car was parked.

Chapter

Eighteen

"Tate ain't goan catch no damned
dynamiters, not if he wants to serve his second term. Him and
Earl can swap off being sheriff till Kingdom Come if they got a
good eye for color when it comes time to put somebody in the
jailhouse. Him borned and raised right out on the Bear Creek
Pike, he knows that better'n anybody," Cass said. He was squatting at the edge of the grease pit talking to Dan. "What gripes my
ass, is that they blew up a good school house instead of shootin
em some niggers. But they separated the white children and them
God Damned little stovelids, you gotta give em that."

Dan stuck his finger in the rear end, struck oil and replaced the
plug.

"The onlyiest thing was, they shoulda waited till Haggerman
was in his office fore they touched it off."

Dan went forward and replaced the plug in the oil pan, and his
right foot slipped three or four inches where the dirty oil had
missed the drain a little.

"Sammy, God Dammit, chuck a little sawdust down in the pit,
so the man don't break his neck!" Cass shouted. Sammy dropped
his hose where he was washing a car in the next bay over, and
when Dan came out to change the filter and put in new oil,

Sammy went down with a grain scoop full of sawdust and spread it around the drain.

"Sammy here, don't want his pickeninnies shoved into no white school, do you Sammy?" Cass said.

There was no answer from beneath the car.

"What's that?" Cass asked him in his loud boss man's voice.

"They goes where they gets sent," Sammy said, coming out of the grease pit with his empty scoop.

"That's right," Cass said. "You ain't pushin no intergration, are you Sam? Sprinkle a little more sawdust down there! That stuff ain't gold dust."

Sam got another scoop of sawdust.

Dan finished putting in the oil, checked the oil stick, the transmission oil, the brake fluid, and the water in the radiator and battery.

"What gets my ass is that stovelid trying to get in over to Senneca. Done got the NAACP behind him, made all the papers, even a couple of big New York Magazines! Did you read where he claimed to have beat out seventy-five percent of the whites on them college board examinations? Now you know that's a bunch a shit. Bet they coached that son of a bitch for four or five years for them tests. He's twenty-three years old, you know. You been readin about him?" he asked Dan.

"No, I reckon I haven't," Dan said. He went back down into the pit to grease the car. They got a paper, but it was Charlene who read what little of it that got read, searching through it to find a name she knew, and trying to keep up a little with what was going on in Sharaw. It was slow and painful work for him to try to read the paper, and he had no need for it, other than to try to find out what farm prices were, but even that was difficult and he got the information wrong more often than he got it right. But he couldn't help hearing about the Negro trying to get into Senneca and that he had lawyers helping him. It had hurt something in him to think that a Negro might just get in where Beau Jim was going. It seemed wrong. It confused the natural and proper order of things. And the notion that the Negro was being helped by lawyers who were also Negroes baffled him. He supposed he had known that there were Negro lawyers in the world, but he assigned them to a special category of freaks and wonders. They were like two-headed chickens, and circus people who swallowed swords and fire. They were things to marvel at, but nothing a man would expect to have to deal with in the natural world.

All the same it bothered him the way Cass had been riding Sammy for the last few days. Cass had told Sammy that he wasn't going to grease no more white men's cars, except Haggerman's; and then when he forgot to put a filter in, or missed half the grease joints, it wouldn't matter since it would be all in the family. Cass had never been careful about what he said around Sammy, but what with the grammar school getting blown up and the Negro about to get in at Senneca, he went out of his way to keep Sammy in his place.

Dan didn't like it. There wasn't any call for it to his mind. There was never any call for torment. Even when the ground hog got in the kitchen garden and ate himself right through the early peas and nipped off half the okra, and he'd found the ground hog's den, and front and back doors, and could have trapped or poisoned him, he had not done it. He'd waited patiently with his shotgun, not moving a muscle or flickering an eyelash until the ground hog got in such good range, he could cut him in half. And he'd done so. He'd blown him apart behind the front shoulders, the shot pattern knocking the animal back, maybe two yards, and, save for a momentary, senseless crawling of guts, and the tiniest, briefest quiver of one hind foot, it was instant death. And even then he'd had pity. The ground hog was only out for something to eat after all. There was no meanness in him. The ground hog was only doing what it was his nature and his fate to do. It was just that Dan could not allow it. Sometimes a man had to step in and protect what he had. But he did not have to devil or torment. And there was no call for Cass to devil Sammy, although Dan did not even consider calling his hand on it, anymore than he would have considered objecting to a particular job Cass told him to do, or complaining about his wages. He never thought of making any suggestions whatever about how Cass should behave, or think, or run his business. When you came right down to it, it would be like asking the ground hog to stay out of his garden. It was Cass's nature to devil folks, like a cat with a mouse; and although he did not think it into words, Dan saw little difference between a man and an animal. They both did what it was their natures to do, and you either lived with it, or you didn't. But he felt in his bones that a man shouldn't torture, nor argue, nor beg, for none of those seemed ever to yield a proper crop. Had he got Sheila into the second grade, the one time he had tried to persuade somebody with talk to do the right thing? Well, he had not. No, he had not. All he had got from it was mixed up for a little while. It had come to nothing, and he'd had to see if he could live with it. It was just that, before he'd had a chance to see if he could live with it, somebody else had decided they couldn't and had dynamited Foscoe Grammar School. And now, for a few days at least, there wouldn't be any school at all for Sheila. The nigger youngins would go back to their own school, Haggerman had said as much. But the white school was part blown up, and they wouldn't let any little children in it until they could tell whether what was left was safe or not. It looked like they were going to use the Baptist Church over in Foscoe for the first and second grades when they got things sorted out.

He greased the car and the compressor said, "Stanta, tanta, tanta," and Cass said he'd bet the ring around his asshole that that nigger had been coached for the five years he'd been out of high school so he could make such a high score. He asked Dan how many niggers he'd reckon they'd started with before they found one who could memorize the examination in just five years, and he vowed it was gettin on toward time when a man was going to have to take down his shotgun and clean a little God Damned house. He said it all in a voice twice loud enough for Sammy to hear. But Sammy washed his car and didn't say anything, and Dan greased his and didn't say anything either.

One of the nipples on the front end wouldn't accept any grease, and that worried him, but by bouncing the car up and down with his left hand and operating the grease gun with his right, he finally got the nipple to accept its proper quotient, and the amber grease bloomed like a flower from the joint. That eased his mind, for he was beginning to worry that he was going to have to put in a new nipple, and though it would be a small expense to the owner, it fretted him.

He came up out of the pit and got his squirt can and oiled the door hinges, trunk and hood latches, and finally, got a sticker and carefully copied the numbers from the speedometer, drawing them as big and round as a child's and wetting the pencil lead on his tongue after each number he drew. He put the sticker on the inside of the door facing, and Cass backed the car off the pit so Dan wouldn't get the seat dirty.

Cass brought in another car, and Dan started all over again, and Cass began to talk about how the niggers had absolutely ruined the economy and moral fiber of the country and how the Bible even spoke out against them. Dan couldn't quite get his mind around it, but it sent the beginning tendrils of the empty feeling through his stomach. A feeling, which at its worst, sapped the strength from him; and a feeling, which, save for the last months, had never afflicted him at all, except in the most discrete and isolated moments when something took him completely by surprise, like when he woke to the fire in his parent's house, or slammed the pickup door on Sheila's fingers, or something of that sudden nature and magnitude. Still, what Cass said was mysterious and complicated and hard to understand. His wits strained at it, and he wanted to catch hold of the matter somehow, get a grip on it, and not let go until he understood. But it slipped away from him, and he could not. Somehow, he thought his best chance lay through the Bible, and he meant to get hold of one and ask Cass where it was that the Bible talked about the niggers. He thought he would understand the Bible although he'd never had the time to look into it much. His mother had been religious and a church going woman, and she had told him some of the things it said. He even remembered going to church with her some when he was little, and before she had given it up. She had never given up praying and reading the Bible, but she had given up going to church because of Vernon. Everyone in Deep Gap knew what a drinker and heller Vernon was, and finally, in order to save them and her the embarrassment of having her show up every Sunday morning, she began to take her religion at home. She hadn't made a fuss about it, nor worried Vernon with it. She just did her Bible reading, and things of that order, at home, and she had read to Dan. He still remembered some of the commandments, and he remembered that although a man shouldn't work on Sunday, it was all right if his ox was in the ditch. He remembered that the sins of the fathers would be visited upon the sons to the third and fourth generations. He remembered quite a lot, it seemed to him. *But I don't remember nuthin bout no niggers*, he told himself. *I need to get aholt of a Bible and find out where them nigger things is set down.* He began to think of all the things he remembered from the Bible. He remembered how Adam and Eve had eaten of the tree of knowledge and got run out of the garden because of it—that story had always given him a deep and secret comfort. And he remembered there was a part where it said that a man would have to earn his bread by the sweat of his brow, and that was all right with him too, since he was up for that. God had made him stout, and all his life, it had seemed to him that he and God had a kind of understanding. He had recognized God right off, and what his mother had read him, bore him out. God didn't waste himself on pity, and he didn't give one single solitary thing away without asking a price, nor did he spare man or beast the trouble that came. You didn't have to do more than drive home of an evening to prove that, for what day was it that he could not see some farm cat knocked dead and drawing flies in the rank weeds of the roadside—dog, rabbit, snake, didn't matter. If you fell in water over your head, and couldn't swim, you drown. Man or youngin, it didn't matter, and he imagined God looking on, without pity. If he hadn't awakened when the fire came, he and Beau Jim would have burned just like Vernon and Bernice had. He knew that. God didn't stop him from getting out, but he didn't help him either, past giving him ears to hear the crackle, and a nose to smell the smoke. But what bothered him was that he had always thought it was just going to be one on one, so to speak, a matter of whether he, himself, could root hog or not. But things, these days, seemed to be happening that he'd had no crack at. No, nor any say-so in. Things that had nothing to do with whether or not he, himself, could cut it. He knew that God dealt in larger orders of things than just one man, and that was where the confusion came. There were things common to all, like the seasons and drought, but at least they were understandable and a man could take steps. A man could see what was happening and fight it, but if there were forces out to rob him that were kept from him and he couldn't even understand; that didn't seem right.

He got to thinking about the story of the flood that Bernice had read to him. It had drowned everybody in the world but Noah and his family, because Noah had got a warning and directions to build a boat. Still, at least a flood was a thing a man could see and understand, and he couldn't help thinking that it would still have to come back down to one on one: *If I'd been a 'livin back there, when the water started comin up, why I wouldn 'ta just sat on my thumbs.*

*I'da tore me some timbers off the barn and made me somethin that would
float. I'da set Charlene and Sheila on it, and we'duv ate drownt chicken
or whatever it was come floatin by, and what would God have done then?
Would he have knocked us off the raft? He'da had to pick hit up and shake
it.* It hurt his head to puzzle over the designs of God when he'd
thought for so long he'd had it sorted out, and it was just one on
one. He was going to have to get him a Bible and ask Cass to tell
him where to look in it in order to understand about the niggers.

He couldn't see, right off, where they were hurting him unless
Sammy's television set was runing the moral fiber of Charlene.
It was a fact that Charlene had taken Beau Jim's money and
bought herself one; and that, probably, at this very moment there
were men putting an aerial on their roof like Sammy's; but it
wasn't any of his money. It was money Beau Jim had given to
Charlene that she'd used for the set and the aerial too, so anyway
it wasn't her economy that was suffering. He didn't like it, he
knew that, but he didn't see what he could do but keep his peace.
Beau Jim had said it was nothing more than a present, and not
rent money he had given her. He didn't like it, but it seemed to
him he had no proper say-so in a present Beau Jim wanted to give,
or how Charlene wanted to use the money, once it was hers. He,
himself, couldn't see why anybody would want to look at the
thing. There wasn't ever anything on it that had the slightest
thing to do with the way he lived his life, or the work he had to
do. Though Charlene liked it well enough, and even Sheila was
seldom to be found more than ten feet away from it. But it was
an offense to him, and he was likely to go out on the porch to sit
in order to get away from the fuss of it. A man couldn't think
with it going all the time, and he needed to think about how he
was going to pay the bank back on the money he had borrowed
for the well. It came to forty-five dollars and forty-nine cents
extra that had to go to the bank every month for a year. It was
more than half a week's pay extra, a good deal more than half, and
he didn't see how he could do it. But if a man had to do it, then
he had to. He had the two sows and two pigs from their litters
left, if it came to that. But he didn't like to think on it, for it would
start him out next year worse off than he'd started out the past
spring. A year's work, and he would have lost ground. He would
owe the bank still some money, and he would have lost the sows
he'd bought and paid cash for.

He didn't know when Cass had left the edge of the grease pit and begun talking to the customer by the cash register. It was just that, all at once, he came to himself and realized Cass was gone. He hoped Cass hadn't asked him any questions that he hadn't heard. Probably not, usually Cass didn't depend a whole lot on the other fellow, but he had no wish to be rude.

Still, when he went over by the door to the office where the cases of oil were stacked, he felt better. Cass was talking about a short-haired pointer he'd bought once that had been used to getting the heads of quail as a reward for retrieving, and had got in the habit of taking the head off himself instead of waiting for the hunter to throw it to him; and how, as time went on, the damned son of a bitch seemed to think the head went further and further back on the bird until he was taking half the breast with his head.

"But I ever more broke his skanky ass of that," Cass said. "I cut me a pissellum stick a little bigger round that a broom handle and run it through that sucker's collar and stood on both ends of it to hold that sucker's head right down on the ground, and then I taken off my belt . . ."

Dan did not hear what happened next since he had gotten his oil and was back under the hood of the car, nor was he thinking about it, but about how, if he could get Charlene to do the milking in the evening, it would save him a dollar and a quarter a week that he paid Sammy's boy to do it. Twenty-five cents an evening just for milking one cow, was a lot of money to give out, though the boy did a good job, strained the milk nice, and put it up, and cleaned up nice after himself.

Chapter

Nineteen

He'd had his sliced barbecue sand-
wich and his beer to wash it down with, but he was still not ready
to leave Tucker's and go to his biology lab. Over the past three
and a half weeks, going to class had seemed to cost him more
effort each time, and he was not ready to leave Tucker's yet and
face it again. Tucker's was a place of great comfort. Safe. Quiet.
Earthy as a cave. And there were no students there. Those who
were old enough to drink, drank their beer at the Lion's Den, a
parlour that catered to them and was right across the street from
the campus. Let them be there. Here there were only working
men, and even they didn't begin to arrive until 4:00 or 4:30.

In Tucker's he could feel like himself without having the notion that he ought to apologize for it. It was a sad admission to
make, and it grieved him, but there it was. He had thought for
a long time it would be his ignorance that would give him trouble
and make him unhappy in the classroom, but it wasn't quite as
easy as that. With the exception of English, where he was carrying a C, he was making good grades in every class. It was something more than the subject matter. He could study that. But
studying wouldn't change the shape of his long lantern jaw, or
make him younger, or keep him from feeling insanely out of

place. It did not help that, more often than not, it was he, himself, who had the right answers; but when he gave them, both the professor and the students were inclined to smile, as though, even with the right answer, there was something a little wrong about him. He could feel it, as though he was a man in an airplane trying to hang around with the birds. It didn't make any difference if he could fly faster and higher, he wasn't ever going to be a bird. There was something wrong between him and the rest. They didn't quite speak the same sort of language. In fact, there was something so basically different between him and the others, he got the feeling that somehow, one day, through wrong answers they would be right, and through right ones, he would be wrong.

That made no sense, and, at the same moment, seemed true. It shamed him to think about it, as though it were unmanly of him. He ordered himself another beer. Tucker, the paper hat cocked forward on his head like a sailor's cap, got off his stool and got it for him, his little flourishes of exaggerated motion somehow endlessly gratifying. He set Beau Jim's beer before him, drew his hand away in an ascending circle, and held it cupped, waiting for Beau Jim to put his money down. There was a cross entwined with a lily tattooed on his spindly, withered, right forearm.

"Mr. Tucker, do you know I've learned that ontogeny recapitulates phylogeny?" Beau Jim said sadly and out of nowhere. He had no intention to brag or be condescending.

And Tucker inclined his head to listen, his face attentive, even to his eyes, which seemed somehow sore, the bottom eyelids turned, as they were, slightly wrong side out.

"Ontogeny is the development of an organism from an embryo to an adult, and phylogeny is sorta like the development of its whole family tree, don'tcha know? Now ain't that a dude?" Beau Jim said, and Tucker cocked his head and smiled as though it were, indeed, a dude, and scooped the money off the table the moment Beau Jim put it down.

Beau Jim drank his beer and thought about ontogeny recapitulating phylogeny. He had thought it a fantastic thing to know. He still thought so. The whole history of a creature printed into it. Telescoped. Millions of years crammed into a few weeks or months. He had embarrassed his teacher with his enthusiasm over it. He embarrassed them often, one way or another, with his manner. And when he saw what he was doing, he embarrassed himself.

How was he to know that college, in some strange way, was a matter of style. But there it was. He felt it in his bones where maybe his history was printed too, long-time history, recent history: too many years in the army, too much time spent playing poker, shooting dice, sitting in places like Tucker's. This business of college was not right for him. It was not his way. Still, he did not wish to give up on it, painful as it was. Even if the future he'd imagined hadn't ever really been his, but borrowed from someone else, Johnny Reisen, say, who was somewhere becoming a doctor. Or maybe he hadn't borrowed it from Johnny, but absorbed it, a particle at a time, from a thousand sources. Glimpsed like pretty girls on street corners. He thought bitterly of the time he had invested in studying, every day, even on Sunday afternoons at Yancey's house, with Yancey helping, and even Hilda, her poor mother, scooting snacks in front of them and taking some sort of pride in what she didn't know was a dancing bear act, a fucking elephant doing the rumba, a goddamn gorilla parsing sentences.

Now just hold on, he told himself. He wasn't any gorilla. A redneck, six-year army veteran, maybe, who was having trouble with the manners of the thing, maybe, but no animal. He tried to convince himself of that, but something in his guts told him it amounted to the same thing. And all at once he could not imagine going on with it for four years, or becoming, when that time was done, whatever one became after having earned a college degree. The style of the thing would never be his. He would be twisted out of shape for the rest of his life. But who was to say he wouldn't be anyway. He drained his beer off and got himself another, having to set his jaw against the knowledge that, if he drank it, he would not get to his biology lab.

All right Trapper, he thought to himself, what about that Negro fellow? Talk about being an outsider, that poor bastard had to get himself in with a crowbar. *If that black boy can stick it, why can't you? All eyes on him everywhere he goes as if any minute he's going to whip out a straight razor and cut somebody, hump the nearest white girl, roll back his lips like Cheetah and eat a truck load of watermelons. If that son of a bitch can stick it, how come it breaks your back?* He couldn't answer that. He thought about it and decided he couldn't answer it. He didn't know why he wasn't Jesus Christ, either, if it came to that.

Lester Flat and Earl Scruggs and the Foggy Mountain Boys appeared on the television screen, and Tucker was off his stool. He got his broom with the notch cut in the handle to fit the volume knob, cut the sound on, and caught the Foggy Mountain Boys in full stride. Earl Scruggs, standing there like a pile of wet wash—slope-shouldered, horse-faced—played the living shit out of his banjo, and Lester Flat sang:

> You bake rite
> With Martha White
> . . .

Beau Jim had never seen anything move Tucker to turn the sound on, but there he was, absolutely still, the paper hat cocked forward on his head, his eyes pouched reverently, listing to Lester Flat's voice rise high as the Blue Ridge:

> Bake the finest biscuits, cakes and pies
> Cause Martha White's self-rising flour
> The one all-purpose flour
> Martha White's self-rising flour
> Has got hot rise.

Flat's voice left no doubt that Martha White's flour would puff up biscuits, and Scruggs banjo picking made that flour sound like it would somehow make the hens lay, the corn grow, and the sun come up in the morning. Quick as the final note faded, Tucker reached up with his broom handle, cut the sound off, and sat down on his stool again, his face once more composed, giving nothing away, watching the quiz show the commercial had interrupted. But Beau Jim was moved, stirred so much that, for a moment, his eyes misted over. He felt he had reached some sort of decision, he, himself, did not even understand. He intended to trace the matter through all its ins and outs, to think about Beau Jim Early, ole redneck, lonesome traveler. But somehow, he didn't get very far. His thoughts had grown warm, purred over by the little alcohol burning motor in his head, and by imperceptible degrees, he was not, somehow, thinking about himself at all, but about Yancey.

How she tried to help him with his English and math, although she wasn't very good at them. How she had taken over his laundry altogether. Said it wasn't any trouble to do his with hers. Ironed his shirts and khaki trousers and hung them in her closet, and wouldn't ever let him take them all home. It was such an odd stubbornness, that from time to time he'd sweep all his clothes together and start out with them just to test, once more, what she would do. How in her dogged, embarrassed way, she'd take hold of a hanger with a shirt or a pair of trousers on it and hang on until he yielded it to her and she could hang it again among her things. It wasn't like her. And she would not explain the strange superstition which was at work. He would have liked to hear it, but she would do no more—when he started out with all his clothes—than grab on to some silly article or other and say, "uh uh, uhuh now." She was not like herself. She had grown strangely mild, and it raised a half grateful, half scared lump in his throat to sit in Tucker's, drink beer, and think about her. Even, tall, tired, big-boned Hilda—a woman made of angles and joints, whose dresses hung on her as if she were no more than a clothes hanger herself—even Hilda had adopted him. It was almost as if he had become a son and brother in that house. No, that was not quite it. But while he was trying to sort it out, Claire came in, stopped, took one look at him, and said:

"Biology my ass. You're shit-faced."

"Hello there, friend," Beau Jim said and swung around on his stool. He had been supposed to meet Claire after his biology lab at four. He didn't know why Claire was so early, but it pleased him. "Lemme buy you a beer. Play me a little head. 'If I Had The Wings Of An Angel.'"

"It's four-o-fuckin-clock," Claire said, "your eyes are supposed to be run together from looking through a microscope or sumpthin. What are you doin sitting here shit-faced?"

"I'm fine," Beau Jim said.

Claire closed his eyes and pinched the bridge of his nose between his thumb and forefinger. "If it's anything that chaps my ass, it's a drunk. I thought we were going to hit Sharaw for a change and hustle up a few bucks."

"I'm ready to shoot the spots off them balls, buddy," Beau Jim said, wanting to please. A moment later he realized that going to Sharaw to the pool hall would, in fact, suit him as well as anything else. "Hot damn, shit A'mighty, let me at em," he said, feigning more enthusiasm than he felt. He got off his stool, and although the movement of his arms and legs seemed somehow protracted, he felt sure and graceful too.

"Well, come on, for Christ's sake. Maybe you'll air out on the way over there."

When they had pulled up to the curb in Sharaw and Beau Jim had started to get out, Claire said, "Look, Jimbo, some people get loose and shoot all right with a little buzz on, I do, myself; but most of em don't. Now I ain't no fuckin mother hen, but . . ."

Beau Jim raised his palm for silence. "I'm feelin fine," he said.

Claire pressed his lips together and raised his own hand deferentially.

The poolroom, one snooker table and seven pool tables long, seemed a good enough place to be. The pool tables appealed. The dull luster of wood set with mother-of-pearl diamonds, the depthless dark green felt and ivory balls, each table standing in its separate cone of light—they gave him a deep sense of pleasure, humility even, as though to compete upon them was an honor, neither he, nor any of the rest of them, deserved. Even the dirty black and grey squares of rubber tile on the floor seemed expensive and grand and too good for them. The small bar to the left of the door, with Big Poke, the owner, standing behind it; the quiet hubbub of voices; the crisp click of balls—all of it filled him with some strange, sad, pleasure. And it didn't matter that Claire had only just walked in when he hooked up with his old fish in overalls, and the two of them began immediately to joke back and forth and rack eight ball, which the old man liked to play. Beau Jim was altogether content to take a table by himself.

He got a beer and cut the light on over his particular field of green. He chalked his cue, drew a bead on the lovely yellow apex of the equilateral triangle and broke. *Now then, ole Trapper,* he told himself. With a precise, smooth stroke he shot a ball, plop, into a leather pocket and watched the cue ball line up on the next. He felt very cool and sure.

Halfway through his second rack, a blond-headed fellow in a light blue shirt and dark blue trousers—it looked like a uniform except there was no badge or patch—came up to lean against the wall and watch. Beau Jim let his concentration slip, half on purpose; shot a little harder than he ordinarily did; and missed one or two shots he might have made. Two tables down, Claire

stuck his index finger in his ear and wiggled it as though there
were water in there, or an itch, he wanted to get rid of. It was
a signal they had worked out that Beau Jim was about to play
someone too tough. When the blond-headed fellow pushed himself off the wall with his elbow and asked Beau Jim if he wanted
to shoot a little nine ball, Claire gave the signal again, leaning his
head into the wiggling finger earnestly as if a bug in his ear was
doing the buck and wing. But Beau Jim had an almost queru-
lously stubborn desire to play this man. For some reason he
disliked him, although he didn't quite admit that to himself.

If I can't take this bird, we won't split tonight, old friend, he promised Claire silently, and while his competition went away to find
a cue and Claire frowned at him, he walked around the table in
a silly bowlegged squat, emptying the balls out of the pockets. He
was trying to think where he'd seen the blond-headed fellow
before, when it came to him that he remembered him from many
years back, remembered a certain iciness looking out of a much
younger face. It was a quality that still haunted the handsome
features of the man, now, probably twenty, two inches taller, and
maybe fifteen pounds heavier than Beau Jim.

Beau Jim called Little Poke, the rack boy, dropped a dime on
the table and told him to rack nine ball. Like the owner, the
rackboy wore a short apron-like pouch around his waist, and like
the owner, he made change from it and kept all money there.
There was no cash register in the place. Most of the folding
money was kept in a cigar box under the counter.

When his competition got back with a cue, they flipped for the
break, and with three money balls, at fifty cents a ball, it took an
hour and a half for Beau Jim to lose twenty dollars. For the first
hour or so, he shot very well and held his own, but then Wagner
—that's what Claire had called him from his own game two tables
away—began to wear him down and beat him steadily.

Wagner had spoken to Claire first. "Whatayasay there, Claire,
baby?" he'd said.

Claire had answered simply with a name. "Wagner," he'd said.

Whatever might have been hidden in Claire's one word response, Wagner's greeting had had the clear and grating edge of
ridicule, although it hadn't kept Claire from coming over to
watch their game when the old man in overalls finally put away
his cue and left. Still, none of that interested Beau Jim a great

deal. He had discovered something about the storeroom that caused him to lose all enthusiasm for pool. The door to the storeroom opened off the back end of the pool hall, and once or twice during the evening, Big Poke had gone through it and returned with a case of beer to put in the cooler; but the interesting part was that, from time to time, someone would come out of the storeroom and get a half-dozen open beers and carry them back through the door, and Beau Jim could see a light back there and men sitting around a table. Right before Claire had come over to watch them, Beau Jim had said to Wagner, "You know, I think there's a poker game behind that door back yonder."

"That's right," Wagner had said matter-of-factly and without even lifting his cold arrogant eyes from the shot he was about to make.

That's me, said the Trapper, *that's us, ich. That is I'm!* All at once pool seemed a poor substitute for the needs of his soul, for all his sad surprises and griefs. "If you don't mind my asking, what's the stakes?" Beau Jim said.

"Two and four, table stakes. Let you pot once; then you got to leave, or go get yourself pumped up."

"Is that a fact?" Beau Jim said. He had been trying to chalk his cue, turning the little cube of chalk absently over and over in his fingers trying to find the indentation. Finally he found it and chalked his cue with a perfunctory twist. His mind was in another place and he put down only one money ball in the next two racks.

If he hadn't been wanting to get in the poker game, it might have made him mad when Wagner looked up at Claire and said, "What about you, ole baby? Want to shoot a little nine for a buck on the three, five and nine?"

Wagner had twenty dollars of his money, and he shouldn't have been asking another man for a game unless Beau Jim had said he'd had enough. It was true that Wagner had twice wanted to go up to a dollar on the money balls, but the principle still held. "It's all right," Beau Jim said agreeably and gave his hand a little wave, although no one had asked him if it was all right.

Claire sat on the next pool table, picked his nose and looked at Beau Jim. "All right," he said in a strange calm voice, still looking at Beau Jim out of his doleful, bloodshot blue eyes.

"Reckon they'd let me sit in that game back there?" Beau Jim asked.

"Yore money's good ain't it?" Wagner said, motioning with his head for the rack boy who came over, picked up the dime Beau Jim tossed on the table, and racked nine ball. Beau Jim gave Wagner the dollar and a half he owed him, and in a loud voice, Wagner said over his shoulder: "Big Poke, here's some fresh meat for the grinder back there, if they got an empty chair."

The bartender looked at Beau Jim, took a puff on his cigarette and gave his head an almost invisible shake. Beau Jim went up to the counter. "I'll take a Millers with me," he said.

The bartender opened a beer and walked with him to the storeroom. At the door he handed Beau Jim his beer and said: "House takes fifty cents from every pot; if you cain't lay fifty dollars on the table, don't set down; no loud talkin; no fightin; if you do up and lock assholes with somebody, don't never come back." Big Poke had recited it all in one breath; then he turned and went away.

What with two twenty dollar bills he kept carefully folded behind his driver's license, he still had almost eighty dollars, and when he sat down with the five men already playing around the felt top table, the Trapper said, *Fawh, have mercy on my soul and hallelujah! Now we've got to the heart of it.*

"New man deals," said the winner of the stud hand, who appeared not to notice a small rat-faced man sitting on a stack of beer cases, reach into the pot, take a dollar and leave a half.

The small man, who dipped for the house, was the one Beau Jim had seen come out for beer. "Nobody antes but the dealer," he said, "Keeps down arguments about who anted and who didn't. It'll cost you two dollars to ante."

"Good idea," Beau Jim said and flipped a twenty to the man who had won the last hand and who made change without being asked.

"Ain't it?" the little rat-faced man said. "I'se the one that thought of it."

"Shut up, Birdy," a man with a striped carpenter's cap on, said around the stump of his cigar, "the only God Damned people who talk are the God Damned people who play God Damned poker!" The little man fidgeted on his cases of beer, but he didn't say anything. "What's the game?" the man in the striped cap asked.

"Seven stud," Beau Jim said, "if that's agreeable."

"It's dealer's choice," said the player across from Beau Jim. He was straightening a stack of bills with a hand missing the middle three fingers. Half his forearm appeared to have been somehow blasted away, and there was nothing left of his hand but the thumb and little finger which opened and closed, pincer-like. "Cept for wild cards and nigger games. We don't play no tonk, nor red dog, nor no cheap shit like that."

A man in a Panama hat, sitting on Beau Jim's left, said, "We put the deck on the table here and drag em off, one at a time, with the thumb."

Beau Jim dealt as he was instructed, and shocked himself by dealing himself two kings down and one up for the first three cards. *Great God!* the Trapper said, *they goan think you stacked the deck. Pull in yore fuckin eyeballs, they're bugged out so far you could knock em off with a stick.* Pincers was showing an ace of diamonds. "Ace bets," Beau Jim said. Pincers bet two dollars. The man next to him, Beau Jim recognized as the old man in overalls Claire had played. He folded. The winner of the five-card stud game folded. Beau Jim called. Panama called, and so did the man in the striped carpenter's cap. Beau Jim dealt around, and again the two-fingered man bet his ace, and Beau Jim and the two remaining players called him. The third round went the same way. When the fourth card was up, the man in the carpenter's hat was showing three hearts. There were no pairs anywhere. Two Fingers said, "Well, I guess I'll see where it's at," and checked. Beau Jim felt he should lie in the weeds, but bet two dollars in spite of himself. Panama called. The man in the striped carpenter's hat gave his cigar a chew and kicked four. Two Fingers plucked thoughtfully at his lower lip, his thumb and little finger closing on it like the pincers of a crayfish. He looked at Beau Jim's cards, an unsuspicious king, four, six and ten; Panama's cards, equally unsuspicious; and the three suspicious hearts of the kicker.

"Shit or get off the pot," the kicker said, rolling his cigar to the opposite corner of his mouth and giving it a chomp on that side.

"I'll shit, I reckon," Pincers said and laid six dollars in the pot.

Aces over, said the Trapper. *Big Mouth might have hisself a heart flush, but Pincers don't believe it, and Pincers is far from broke, which probably means he's far from stupid. Kick both their asses.* Beau Jim called. Panama sighed and folded.

"Deal em," said Big Mouth.

Beau Jim dealt them, shuffled his hole cards. *Squeeze the piss outta em,* said the Trapper, *come on kabangee!* Pincers checked his ace, Beau Jim checked before he squeezed out his last card, and Big Mouth bet four dollars. Pincers called. The full house wasn't there. *Buffalo piss!* said the Trapper. *Big Mouth ain't got it anyhow; kick his ass all the way into the poolroom.* Beau Jim called.

"Call!" Big Mouth said. "Call! Didn't you bastards see them hearts? Two little pair," he said in disgust.

"Aces over," Pincers said.

"Three kings," Beau Jim said.

"Some fuckers don't pay enough attention to get scared," Big Mouth said.

Get up and shake your britches, the Trapper said. Beau Jim stood up and shook his britches, plucked at the seat of his pants with finicky fingers, shook one leg, and sat down again. the poker players smiled, Big Mouth turned red, Birdy reached into the pot and laughed out loud. "You can't win em all if you don't win the first one," he said.

"I done told you," Big Mouth said, "you just dip your four bits from the pot and keep yore God Damned mouth shut. I don't want to lose my ass and listen to you at the same time!"

"Mr. Birdy," Beau Jim said—he didn't know what else to call him—"would you get us some beer?" Beau Jim bought a beer for everyone who wanted it, even Big Mouth.

But after the first hand, the best was over. He won a hand now and again, but his cards were sulky. He won one big hand he shouldn't have won, making two pair on the sixth card and filling on the seventh, but it only seemed to make him more reluctant to fold. He played badly, mulishly staying in hands when it was almost certain that he was beaten, as if stubborness was a virtue to be rewarded. Although he drank a great many beers, his high was gone, and the little alcohol motor in his head seemed to grind out only a low level pain. The Trapper had nothing to say, as though the two of them had merged so completely, there was no longer any possibility for dialogue, and no possibility for any good end. Nor was one desired. In some strange way, what he desired, was to lose everything, to be reduced to a minimum from which nothing more could be taken away, and thereby reach a kind of peace. That was what he was wishing for when Claire came through the stockroom door: he wanted to lose his last few dollars, and have done with it.

"You bout ready to haul ass?" Claire asked him.

"In a little," Beau Jim said.

The five-card stud hand he was in promised to break him. He was facing a pair of jacks, and he had a pair of threes, one of them down. Panama had the jacks and every card, he bet four dollars, and Beau Jim doggedly called. But he caught a three on the last card and won the hand.

"How about it?" Claire asked when he scooped in the pot and Birdy scooped his fifty cents.

"Hold on," Beau Jim said, "I think you brought me luck." But he didn't mean it; in fact, he wanted nothing to do with luck that was so capricious.

Still, even he could not play the next hand. The old man in overalls started right off with a pair of queens, and there were two other people in, not counting Big Mouth, who, like Beau Jim, played practically every hand. Big Mouth had lost so much, he'd even grown quiet for the most part, and the only noise he made was slapping down his worthless cards at the end of a hand. Once, about an hour earlier, Big Mouth had sent Birdy out to Big Poke with what looked like a payroll check and even that had dwindled to almost nothing.

The next hand Beau Jim dealt, and he won again, filling out a flush on the last two cards, when he should have lost and been free of it; he had been three dollars short of being potted on the seventh card and couldn't even kick.

"Come on, Jimbo," Claire said, "If you're winnin, you can come back tomorrow night and give these fellers another crack at'cha."

At that Big Mouth threw his cards across the table. "What the God Damned Hell is this?" he demanded. "If it's past your God Damned bedtime, take your mother and go home! Christ!" he said, "deal the God Damned cards!"

Beau Jim winked at Claire, "Why don't you grab a beer and I'll be out in just a little," he said.

"God Damn!" Big Mouth said in an agonized voice and screwed his eyes shut, "deal the God Damned cards!"

Beau Jim had cut, Panama had started to deal and Claire had opened the door to leave when it filled up with Deputy Earl Wagner who said, "Hup now, Rosemary," and gave Claire a little shove with his fingertips back into the storeroom. No one at the table moved. Panama stopped dead, his right thumb having dragged the next card half off the deck. Beau Jim could see Big Poke through the door, who was looking back into the storeroom and making a patting motion with his hand as though he were dribbling a basketball: it's nothing, don't get excited, the motion said.

"Earl," Panama said, finally, cordially, as though by way of greeting.

"See you fellers are playing a little setback, or bridge, or somethin," the deputy said. "Expect I don't see no money since gamblin ain't what's known as legal. But I don't take to bein run over by no sweet pea who thinks he's goan get away with somthin," the deputy said, looking straight at Claire.

"I don't play cards," Claire said.

"I expect I'll decide that, Rosemary," the deputy said.

"Ask them," Claire said, giving his head a jerk toward the men sitting at the table.

Beau Jim had the feeling he had missed something essential, although he had been sitting there the whole time. The deputy was after Claire, and Claire seemed to know it, to have expected it. His jaws were knotty and his fists were balled at his sides.

"I don't take to being told my business either," the deputy said.

What happened next, happened so fast, it was like an old-time movie. None of it made proper sense, seemed justified, or was believable. Claire only started to walk around Wagner. That's all. But Wagner took him by the shirt front and said, "Hup, God Dammit, you leave when I . . ."

But he never finished what he was going to say, for Claire tried to twist the deputy's hand away from his shirt, and Wagner reached back to his hip pocket and yanked out a sap, and all in one motion, hit Claire over the ear with it. It made a pop like someone touching a penny balloon with a cigarette. And he hit Claire at least four more times with horizontal blows, connecting on the forward, as well as the backward swings, before Beau Jim could get around the table and catch his arm. In the instant before the deputy shook him off, he could have sworn Wagner gave a snort of laughter right in his face.

He'd often heard that people saw stars when they were hit in the head, and he satisfied his mind about that, anyway, for when the sap struck him across the bridge of his nose, he did, in fact,

get to see a real explosion, with all sorts of little lingering flashes
and pinwheels that lasted even after everybody in the storeroom
was gone but him, and Wagner, and Claire. He was sitting on the
floor. Claire, unbelievably, was still standing up.

The deputy had turned away from Claire and was talking to
him, but it still didn't make sense, as though he had come in late
and missed just exactly what all this was about.

"Since you travelin in tandem with Rosemary here, the same
goes for you," the deputy told him.

Beau Jim felt as though someone had taken hold of the bridge
of his nose with ice tongs and hung a fifty pound weight on them.
What the fuck are you talking about? he thought, at least he thought
he thought it; but Wagner kicked his foot and spun him a quarter
turn around on his butt and said, "You don't talk, you listen,
cause I'm lettin you off this time." He'd thought he was listening,
but things being what they were, he didn't doubt he had spoken.
He hadn't truly noticed himself getting up from the table to grab
Wagner's arm, now that he considered it.

But Wagner had forgotten about him again. "You know you
done had yore last chanst!" Wagner was telling Claire. "You pull
any more preversions in the pool hall, or any God Damned
where else in Cocke County, and I'll garuntee, you'll think this
was patty-cake. You better hope to Jesus I don't get no more
reports like I heard tonight."

"What you heard was a God Damned lie," Claire said calmly.

Great God, Beau Jim thought and waited for Wagner to reach
back for the loop he could see sticking out of his hip pocket, but
Wagner didn't reach for it. He gave Claire a shove, and this time
he did fall. "Get'chore ass outta here," he said.

When Beau Jim began to struggle to get up, pain from his nose
went through his head; he was instantly sick at his stomach, and
realized all at once that his shirt front was glued to his chest with
blood. Still, the wave of sickness passed quickly and he got to his
feet, but when he bent to help Claire up, Claire shook off his
hand, got to his knees, fell back, and then got all the way up
without assistance. For almost a full minute Claire stared at
Wagner and brushed at his clothes, flicking at his shirt front with
the backs of his fingers and dusting his britches. Wagner said
nothing.

When he and Claire came through the storeroom door, the

poker players were standing around a bench along the rear wall, all carefully not looking at either of them, all anyway, but Pincers who extended some bills between the thumb and little finger of his demolished hand. "Here's what was in front of you," he told Beau Jim.

As the two of them passed the bar, Big Poke said, "I done tole ya. Now don't never come back."

For some reason that made Beau Jim laugh, and the laughing dislodged a gout of blood which landed perversely on the back of his hand. He allowed himself the pleasure of wiping it off on the door facing as he went out.

Chapter
Twenty

When they got in the car, Beau Jim very carefully touched his nose. It didn't feel like a nose at all, but something monstrously large and painful hammered into the center of his face, a rusty bucket full of blood and broken egg shells, say. "Shitass," he said, "I mean, shitass!" He turned his head this way and that, looking all around the inside of the car, from headliner to floorboard, as if his eyes refused to rest on any one thing for more than a fraction of a second. "I want to know what the fuck happened?" His nose hurt him all over, even in his elbow and knee joints and incredulousness was in his head like buzzing in a jar full of bees. "Goan get you a little bell, ole buddy," he said suddenly, "and the next time something like that is fixin to happen, I want you to ring it. I'm the kind of fellow that needs a little time to warm up." He looked carefully at Claire. "A chance to figure out which way to run, even if I fucked up and missed out on the why." He glanced all around the car again, and then seemed to relax a little. He took a very deep breath, the first he had taken, it seemed to him, in a very long time. Claire did not speak, and in the lights of an approaching car Beau Jim saw his incredibly lumpy face and head. "Christ, your head looks like a sack full of doorknobs," Beau Jim said. "Let me drive."

Claire looked straight down the road and did not speak, and somehow, in that moment, Beau Jim's memory—his nose seemed to have been driven into the center of it like a wedge and parted it—came together again. It made him blink. "That son of a bitch called us faggots, didn't he?" he asked in amazement, and a little explosion of laughter dislodged a gout of blood from his nose. He wiped at it absently, his innards all at once turning cold. "Hey, Claire, didn't that bastard call us faggots?" Claire didn't say anything. Beau Jim wiped at the blood on his face with the backs and palms of both hands. "You may be a God Damned, crazy, no-good drunk, and not much hand with the women, but you ain't no fairy," Beau Jim said. "Right? For Christ's sake?" He managed some sort of laugh again, but in his guts he was turning icy. "Right!" he answered himself.

Claire started the car and pulled away from the curb. "Why didn't you leave Wagner alone like I told you?" he said, "damn ya!" In the lights from the dashboard, Claire's head seemed formed of incredible bone structure, brows above brows; cheek bones below cheek bones; through his almost colorless short hair his skull was almost fluted from the sap.

"But just because you stepped in shit, I didn't have to follow," Claire said, more, it seemed, to himself than Beau Jim. His hand wandered to the cooler between them and fumbled with the top before he got it open and got himself a beer.

"Ahhh, Jimbo, the deputy's little brother, for the love of God." He took a swallow of beer and snuggled the bottle in his crotch.

"I took him eighty-five dollars worth, if it's any consolation."

"Said he was going back to the firehouse, to get more money, but thick as the fucker is, I knew he wasn't that stupid."

"The firehouse, the jail, and the sheriff's office are all down there together, don'tcha see?" He took a swallow of beer, and grimaced and shook his head.

"If you'd just come on when I told ya."

What Beau Jim wanted to say, he couldn't say, but Claire answered as though he had.

"You don't think he was goan go down there and tell his brother I'd taken his ass for eighty-five dollars. Ha," he said humorlessly. "I expected trouble, but I have to admit, he took me by surprise." He drained his beer and flung the bottle viciously out the window.

"I'll tell you somethin true," he said. "You don't never get away from trouble."

"And I'll tell you another thing, just once. Just once and no more. Long time ago, long time ago, the good deputy there, caught me and his little brother Duane sorta wrong. Sorta doin the wrong kinda thing, and I was the oldest one, don'tcha know."

Beau Jim had no words to speak. All his insides had turned to ice.

A car they were meeting once more lit up the unlikely planes of Claire's head. The eye on Beau Jim's side was no more than a slit. "Just one more thing," Claire said. He shifted his hands on the steering wheel as if to seek a better grip. "I don't bother nobody," he said after a moment. "Nobody."

Neither of them said anything more until they got to Senneca. But after they passed through nigger town and came over the bridge onto the short stretch of four-lane highway, Claire said, "There's a doctor over at the Student Health Center you can wake up. Your nose is broke."

"You could use some looking at too," Beau Jim said, quietly.

"Ain't nuthin of mine broke," Claire said. "Just feel like I been playing a little head like my ole uncle Theodore used to." He laughed, but it didn't sound like him. "Did you notice that son of a bitch couldn't carry a tune?" he said. "I don't know what the deputy was trying to play, but he didn't get one good note." He laughed again, but it was not his old, breathy, whiskey laughter.

The doctor was indeed asleep, and the nurse on duty had to wake him, but he came in cheerful, if groggy, and washed his face and hands in the little sink of the treatment room. He looked at Beau Jim's nose and began to hum to himself. He didn't even ask how it happened. He stopped humming long enough to tell Beau Jim it was going to hurt, and then began humming again. He braced his knee against the operating table Beau Jim was sitting on, circled Beau Jim's head with his left arm, seemed to stick a finger in Beau Jim's ear as if it were a hole in a bowling ball; and with terrific pressure of his right thumb, he put Beau Jim's nose back where it belonged. By comparison, the deputy's sap hadn't hurt at all. He was still blind with the pain and fireworks of it when the doctor began to ram gauze up his nostrils with what felt like a baseball bat. When he got done with the gauze, the doctor told the nurse to get Beau Jim's student number and clean him off; and humming to himself, he washed his hands again and went back to bed.

For about a week Beau Jim had a hard time seeing around a large, multicolored piece of meat, mounted, like a hood ornament, in the center of his face. In spite of all the licks he had absorbed, Claire looked only a little worse. Beau Jim did not attend any classes. He spent every day with Yancey, who pampered and petted him. The following Monday, which was October 3rd, he took a job at Bond Chemical Company, driving a truck.

Chapter
Twenty-One

Although usually she watched television at least until Dan came home, and often later, she was unaccountably nervous and couldn't sit still. Perhaps it was the weather. It was almost cool for the first time since early May. Mostly, the wind, if there was any, came out of the east, off the hot lowlands, but this time it seemed to have turned around, to be coming out of the West and off the mountains in Tennessee and the Carolinas. She didn't fool herself that it wouldn't get hot again. There wouldn't be any real relief until almost Thanksgiving, but presently, it didn't seem more than seventy, and she couldn't sit still. Perhaps it was the weather. Perhaps it was that, in two days, on October 9th, she would be thirty-four.

She put Sheila to bed at eight, and a few minutes after, went out the front door and down the steps and walked a good ways up towards the highway, half pretending that she was running off and not coming back. The cool air made her feel like a young girl, and the crickets, grating as they were in the ditches choked with honeysuckle, and the stars spreading over the sky from the east, excited her. Far to the west, the sky was still faintly lit as though from the lights of some big town, and the stars thinned out in that direction, the last sprinkle of them stretching no further than the highway. And faintly, from back toward the house, came music. She had left the television on, and that was where it was coming from, but she couldn't hear it well enough to tell what the song was. Because there was a breeze, because of the beating of her heart, because of her breathing, the music didn't come steadily, but intermittently, like waves rolling faintly in on a shore. She took a deep breath, and the mollypops in the parched fields, and from the river, ragweed, were sweet upon the cool of the evening and made her nostrils flare. Oh, she felt like a young girl waiting for some young fellow to come after her. In a convertible, say. Some young fellow, say, who liked to dance and had some peach brandy in the glovepocket or under the seat; some young fellow who liked to talk and laugh a lot. Thinking about it made her smile and spread a mist of joy across her eyes. She craned her neck and looked down the highway for his car to appear. She knew what he'd look like. He'd have black hair—she'd always been partial to black-headed men—and it would be combed nice and have tonic on it so it would smell good; and he'd have on a nice shirt and tie, and he'd have a wrist watch, and maybe a ring on his little finger, a ruby, or say, even a diamond, to show he had a little style and was doing all right. He'd smoke cigarettes and light them with a silver lighter. Wouldn't ever even think of sticking snuff in his mouth to make his teeth ugly. And maybe, hanging off the rear-view mirror, there would be a pair of those pink fuzzy dice, just for fun, to show he wasn't too serious or anything. They would be swinging and spinning when he stopped and the radio would be playing, "I'm Walking The Floor Over You," or something nice like that. He'd reach across the front seat and open her door for her and say, "Hi there, Darlin! Now just where would you like to go on a dandy night like this?"

"I don't care, just anywheres," she said and plucked at the hair over her ear. She took a step to the left as though to climb into the convertible with the dice swinging from the mirror and the radio playing. She could almost touch the chrome along the top of the door, feel the heat from the underside of the car against her shins, practically see the stars shine in the hood, but all at once, there wasn't anything there but the grating of crickets in the ditch. For a moment she stood with her hand outstretched to lay upon the smooth chrome. For a moment she looked hopefully up the highway as if to make certain that he wasn't just a little way off, but coming still. And then darkness gave up all its magic, and she was on an empty dusty road. It raised a painful little knot in her throat to think how badly she had been treated by her own imagination. It was only that it had been so lovely in the beginning. Little waves of disjointed music came from the house, the crickets grated in the ditch, and somewhere off down in the cornfield, the two remaining shoats grunted as though in collusion and up to something.

"Well, I set him straight on not milkin no God Damned cow," she said, the sound of her voice shocking her with its near sobbing edge, as though it could barely get passed the painful little knot in her throat. "I ain't milkin no God Damned cow!" she said, each word as painful as if it had to tear flesh to get out. She assured herself she had milked all the cows she was going to milk. She had done it as a girl until she was sixteen and seventeen and eighteen and had to be whipped more than once for refusing. And whipped for spilling the milk, which she had done on purpose. And whipped for not getting all the milk and letting the cow begin to dry up. Her father didn't understand, or care if he did, that she couldn't get the smell of cow off her. It wouldn't come off. It didn't just get on the hands. It clung to clothes and hair. The warm, sweet, disagreeable odor of cow, and milk, and cow shit would not be washed away, and she had cried many times because of it, and had often not even seen the few boys who were interested in her because she was certain they could smell it too. But she had not told Dan that. What she had told Dan was that she wasn't a nigger, whatever he might think to the contrary, and she wasn't about to take over a nigger's job just because he couldn't afford to pay a nigger to do it.

She thought about what she had told him again, and went over the words in her mind, rephrasing them and making them stronger, but the little vengeful pleasure they gave her was soon gone. It was a pitifully small victory, after all. It gave her little pleasure when she measured it against the winter coming up, which would be as cold and rainy and lonesome as the summer was hot and stifling. Or when she set it over against her birthday, the rest of her life, the possibility that sooner or later, she probably would, in fact, be found milking a cow, because things got worse and not better, and a person's will did not last forever.

She reached into the pocket of her house dress and got out her cigarettes and a kitchen match and squatted down in the road to strike the match on the metal eyelet of her shoe. In the flare of light she saw what she could feel, and it infuriated her: along the top of the right hand side, her shoe had begun to wear out, and part of the knuckle of her little toe was beginning to peep through. It felt bad. It felt awful, like her life. They were the flat-bottomed, crepe-soled shoes, she had bought herself when she worked in the dime store.

She stood up, lit her cigarette, took a long shaky drag, and started back toward the house, but when she entered the yard, she couldn't bear to go inside, and walked around by the mimosa tree where she could see against the sky four or five of the dumber, or anyway, wilder, chickens gone to roost in the branches. They would be safe from the occasional weasel up there, and from the rat or snake that might steal their eggs; but likely as not, sometime in the early morning, at least one of them would lay an egg right into space. "Stupid things," she said.

When she was small, she had thought it was fun to take a sharp stick and draw a line in the dirt and watch the chickens cock their heads and stare at it with their idiot eyes. You could go off and come back in half an hour, and unless something had disturbed them, there would still be a chicken or two staring at the line, waiting for it to wiggle so they could peck it. When she was a little girl, she had played with chickens, for there wasn't anything else around. She'd catch them and fold their heads back under their wings, and then hold the wings down so they couldn't get their heads out again, and then swing them around and around and around, and then lay them down on the side where their heads were, and they'd stay that way for maybe ten or fifteen minutes sometimes. Asleep. Sometimes she would try to see how many of them she could put to sleep at once. And sometimes she played with them as though they were dolls. Dressing them in rags, feeding them, putting them to sleep. Chickens running around in diapers and bonnets, with her running after them crying: "Oh my baby, my baby!"

She laughed bitterly, threw down her cigarette, stamped it out, and immediately lit another one. Well, she had run off from all of that, got herself a good job in the five and ten; and then what had she done? What indeed, but marry the first drag-assed man who had asked her. And now here she was again. She looked at the black open mouth of the barn and her head nodded continuously and of its own volition, as if she were a palsied old woman, and the knot in her throat would hardly even let the smoke around it. She went on towards the barn as if to test herself against it, entered it, and stood in the gloom. Around her, the stringent odor of hay and chaff and fertilizer, the musty odor of earth, and worst of all, the warm, sweet cow-shitty odor that clung and stayed with a person better than any perfume ever put in a bottle and set out for sale.

She could not see the cow at first, but she could hear the small, gourdy sounds she made chewing her cud, and she marked a large, solid section of gloom in the stall. But she could have walked straight to her through her nasty stench alone. In another part of the barn she heard the intermittent scurry of mice, taking their portions of chicken feed. From the stall came the soft, steady, gourdy sounds of the cow chewing, the silky swish of her tail against her flanks. A moment more, and she could see the easy, loose motion of the cow's tail, and see the cow lift her soft muzzle to let out a low, nasal, groaning *moo*—content, self-satisfied; even, Charlene thought, a touch uppity, as though standing in her stall with all she could use of water and food and care, she had a right, after all, to inquire into Charlene's presence. "Ahhhh, damn you," Charlene said, "It's me," and her hatred was so strong it made her shiver. All at once the three bony prominences of bovine hips, the ridiculous swell of belly, the warm odor of her—all that was far too much, and exactly as a man would have done it, Charlene snapped her cigarette viciously off the end of her thumb. The spark of light arched, winked against the cow's flank and bounced away. It got no more response than a fly would have gotten. The cow shuddered her hide and gave her flanks again a loose contented switch with her tail. But even if the cigarette had hit on the hot end and caused the cow to kick, or hunch her body, or bang around in her stall, it might have made no difference. The moment Charlene snapped the cigarette away, something had already gone wrong with her beyond the cow's smug, bovine ability to aggravate. But she could never tell herself, afterwards, she hadn't known what she was doing. She knew quite clearly, although in a strange way, as though the part of her that knew and the part that acted, had somehow severed relations, as though half of her could only watch while she dug into the pocket of her housedress in a frenzy.

The first match she tried to strike, broke without igniting as she scraped it along the top board of the stall. And her hands were shaking so badly, she fumbled the next one in the dark. But then she had two together, and the instant they popped and flared, she flung them into the bales of hay stacked by the wall. The cow stepped to the side with her hindquarters, the high, clumsy steps of a startled, awkward creature; but that was only a decoration on the most remote fringe of her consciousness, for she was shaking head to foot, watching one match perversely go out, even nestled as it was between a broken bale on the floor and the corner of another above it. And the flame of the other merely crawled along its stem as if it too would extinguish. But it did not. With excrutiating slowness, it ate into the broken bale, seeming to make a little gold and rosy nest before the weak, yellowy flames began to brighten and spread haphazardly, like flowers blooming. The cow groaned, rubbed against the far side of her stall, stumbled, and for a moment, went down on one foreleg. But Charlene was watching the fire. She could feel it as though it were inside her, burning all her grief and filling her with a sense of release that was exquisite. She stood rooted where she was, long after the flesh of her face had merely begun to warp and stiffen from the heat. She was suffering pain from the fire without even knowing it when the cow bawled and seemed to shock her awake enough to stumble back. "Now, now, we'll see, by God!" she told it, but before she rushed out, she caught a glimpse of the huge, liquid eyes of the cow, reflecting the flames like a mirror, and saw her stretching her neck and lifting her muzzle to let out a long, resonant bawl that was to follow her across the barnyard and into the house. While she was calling Dan, the bawling turned to screams.

Chapter
Twenty-Two

From the moment Charlene called,
every muscle in his body drew tight. Even the brain in his head
seemed to draw in upon itself and would admit neither thought
nor speculation. It was like the moment of shock, after some
terrible wound has been sustained and before the pain starts,
except that moment was fantastically and unnaturally prolonged.

Tom Kamm, the county road superintendent, happened to be
at the station when the call came, and Dan abandoned the station
to him without a word of explanation. Left him standing by the
pumps. Left the orange county truck with the hood raised, the
cap off the radiator, and the nozzle of the gas pump rammed into
the tank with the feed locked on.

Even before he turned off the road to the Experiment Station
he could see the light in the sky, and he knew what it was without
thinking about it, as though the knowledge entered his body
through his eyes and spread to all its parts. He was stiff with
knowing, even though he would not think it into words, and the
simple matter of steering the pickup seemed as ponderous as if
he were made of steel and squeaked in every joint.

When he came down the highway toward where his own road
turned off, he saw that his house, barnyard, hog pen, and even

the upper edge of the cornfield were lit by the fire. In the pasture behind the hog pen, the cow's salt lick glowed like a yellow square of moon. Coming down the rutted dirt road, he could see people standing about toward the rear of his house. He stepped on the brakes, forgetting the clutch altogether, and stalled the pickup at the edge of the yard. Charlene and Sheila were standing by the corner of the house under the mimosa tree, and three of Sammy's children were clumped together away from the others. When he came up to the mimosa tree, he could see Sammy, himself, on the roof of the hog house, banging at sparks with a wet croker sack.

"Come on here with that pail!" Sammy shouted, and his son struggled toward him in a running walk, one arm waving wildly for balance and the other angled stiffly out from his side with the weight of a peck bucket. Water licked over the rim like silver in the light. The boy passed it to his father on the low roof, arching his back and lifting with both hands, and Sammy took it and went to the far end of the tarpaper roof and dashed it across. It dripped, sparkling from the eaves.

Dan didn't move from beneath the mimosa tree.

Sammy came up to the far corner of the house where the spigot was, filled two more buckets, carried them down to the hog house and dashed them on, and then took a third bucket from his son, went down to the far end of the hog pen where the sows roiled and squealed and dashed the sows, which made them scream as though he had drenched them in fire. And even when Sammy came up to him after that, shiny with sweat and reflecting the flames like dark polished wood, Dan didn't move or speak.

"Ain't nuthin else goan go, Mr. Dan, I don't guess," Sammy told him. "But I couldn't get nuthin out the barn." He wiped the sweat off his face. "That cow screamin when I come up. Lord." Sammy shook his head in sad wonderment. "But it couldn't nobody have got inside," he said.

Dan looked straight toward the barn. The door was swirling yellows, and smoky reds. Something inside made a punky exploding sound, not loud, but it caused Dan to flinch and blink his eyes.

"I sholy am sorry," Sammy said, "I'll hep you any way I can, you tell me what to do."

Dan looked at him, not quite knowing who he was, and at Sammy's son, as shiny with sweat as his father, the whites of his eyes glistening. He turned his head and looked at Sammy's other children standing in a clump apart from the rest of them, three girls, two in washed-out dresses, and the middle one in a slip, their limbs thin and long and their elbows and knees somehow unnaturally large in the firelight. The lighter color of their palms and the soles of their feet unusually noticeable where it could be seen, like with the girl in the slip, who stood with one leg bent at the knee and the toes of that foot knuckled under and the heel up, and the foot resting lightly on the tops of the knuckled under toes. She rotated the foot very slowly back and forth, had her arm around the shoulders of her younger sisters, and kept her face turned to the fire. Dan did not know exactly what he thought about them being there with their long, frail limbs, and placid faces. He turned his head the other way and even Charlene and Sheila put him in a strange quandary, at least until Sheila spoke and said, "Papa, is the cow dead?"

But he had not admitted anything to himself yet, and while he struggled with it, Sammy answered for him. "It sho is honey," Sammy said. "It couldn't nobody get inside to get her out."

"Is the cat dead too, Papa?" Sheila asked.

"I don't know," Dan said at last.

There was another punky explosion from inside the barn, a wet sound just audible above the sound of flames, but again Dan flinched.

"Hit's a shame . . . God, the way that cow scream . . . but you got surrance on it, ain't you, Mr. Dan?" Sammy said.

"I don't know," Dan said.

Sammy seemed, all at once, to notice his daughters and called to them: "You youngins git on home. Ain't nuthin here for you to watch. You take em on home Samuel," Sammy said.

The three girls shied off to the left, but didn't leave. The boy said, "Git on!" But they looked at the fire and didn't start until the boy picked up a stick not quite as big around as a broom handle and half as long and threw it at them. "Ain'tchew heard him?" the boy asked with vehemence, "git on to yore Momma!"

"Here!" Sammy said, "I ast you to take em home, not take a stick to them. They ain't stock you drivin."

"They sho ack like it," the boy said.

"They people," Sammy said, "little gals. You doan know that, you doan know nuthin," Sammy told him in a voice full of soft impatience and disappointment.

"Yes sir," the boy said and followed his sisters out of the yard. "Shoo on, now," he said plaintively from the dirt road, "you goan git me in trouble."

For a while then, none of the four of them who remained in the yard, spoke. Sheila left her mother's side and came and stood by Dan. She sucked her thumb and looked at the fire. After a while she tugged at her father's britches leg and said, "Papa, if the cat ain't burned, will it come back?"

Dan bent very slowly against the enormous resistance of tense muscles and picked her up.

"I'll leave you lone," Sammy said. "Yawl get holt of me when you want me to help. I'm countin on it." He stood where he was a moment longer. Although he had wiped it only a moment before, his face was again beaded and shiny with sweat but it wore no expression whatever. "I'm sholy sorry," he said.

Dan gave his head the merest hint of a shake, and Sammy started off for home.

"If the cat ain't burned, will it come back?" Sheila asked. "We can git us another cow if the cat ain't burned," she said thoughtfully.

"A dollar, it was that nigger boy that started it!" Charlene said. "I've seen him a smokin in the barn before. I've seen him smokin four or five times. I've thought time and again to say somethin about it, but I'd forget before I'd think to tell you. If there's two things you can count on to bring you trouble, it'd be a nigger and a farm. I wish I'd a thought to tell you about that nigger boy smokin in there," she said. "Probably why his Daddy is so anxious to help, cause he knows what done it. I'll just bet he's guessed how probably that barn got on fire. Course maybe it coulda been somethin else. Moldered hay kin do it."

It ain't no moldered hay in this country, not this year noway; Lord to God in heaven, the cow. And that tractor near about overhauled. Wasn't nuthin left but to see to them two galded joints and put in new wirin, and hit woulda been as good a tractor as ever I'd want. And that sorry little sight of tools I had scraped me together, and even the hay run me thirty-five cents a bale. Lord to God. Lord to God in heaven, and the cow.

"Poppa, don't hold me so hard," it said.

Lord to God.

"Papa. Papa, you hurtin my laigs!" it said.

Nary cow, ner tractor.

"Set her down! You hurtin her!" it said.

Ner barn, ner nothin.

It made a grinning noise, or was it weeping? But then it would be Beau Jim more than Sheila, for Sheila did not weep. Stiffly, he bent down, and the grinning noise went away from him, so he could stand up again.

It had begun to hurt, to run all through him like an electric current, nor did it ever cease. Not even by daylight. He had not even gone inside. Twice, without even knowing he was doing it, he wet down the hog house and the sows, for before it began to die down, the heat was fierce even in the furthest corner of the hog pen. But by daylight nothing was burning.

Chapter
Twenty-Three

He wasn't paid teamsters' wages,
but he didn't have to join the teamsters' union either, nor even
get a chauffeur's license. Strauman Brothers Construction Co.
was a nonunion contractor, and Beau Jim never drove the dump
trucks off Bond Chemical Company property. He worked from
eleven-thirty at night until eight in the morning, driving dump
trucks full of burning debris. Time after time he raced his headlights two miles across the strip-mined countryside to a lake of
burning slag and rubble where he'd slue the truck around, pop
it out of gear, engage the dumping mechanism, race the engine
until the truck bed was halfway up, and then ram it in gear again
and string out his load. By the time he got back to the furnace
building, the payloader would have loaded the second truck with
flaming rubble, and he would back around, jump out of the first
truck and into the second and tear out again.

The operator of the payloader wore goggles and a gas mask.
The Negro laborer, who hosed the trucks down with water as
they were being loaded, wore goggles and a rag over his face like
a bandit. Beau Jim counted on perpetual forward motion to drag
the fumes and smoke behind him and wore no protection at all.

What Bond Chemical Company made in the furnaces was

phosphorus, and when they wrecked the burned-out furnaces in order to build new ones, phosphorus seemed to get around. Burns from it were a constant danger, and everywhere stood red barrels of water for men to jump into if the need arose. But even the air seemed full of phosphorus and not fit to breathe, and the ground was not fit to walk on. In the mornings after work he wet down his army combat boots, only to find their soles smoking when time came to put them on again.

Still, it wasn't a bad job. He was either moving as fast as he could move, driving like a maniac, jumping from one truck to another, sweating, swearing, struggling with the wrecks of trucks he was given to drive—no one would put a decent truck on such a run—or he wasn't working at all. When they had just uncapped a furnace, things were too hot to handle, and he'd likely spend the night hunkered down talking, or sleeping in the cab of one of the trucks.

After he had survived the initial lie he'd had to tell to get hired, *that he could drive a dump truck*, it wasn't such a bad job. And what he'd told them wasn't altogether a lie: he *could* drive a dump truck; he just didn't know how to make it dump. Lucky for him, on his first trip, they sent a black laborer with him to show him where the dumping ground was.

When they got there, Beau Jim had backed around, stopped, and began to push and pull every lever, knob, and button he could find. He pulled up the emergency brake, turned on the heater, the windshield wipers, the directional lights. Finally, but not before the paint on the cab had begun to puff and crinkle, the Negro yelled: "Kick her out of gear and push that doohickey yonder forward!"

"What doohickey?" Beau Jim shouted, kicking the clutch in and slamming the gearshift in neutral. But the Negro's hand was already on the proper lever. "Race de shit outta de motor, man!" the Negro shouted, and Beau Jim did what he was told, and the truck bed began to lift. When it got up a ways, Beau Jim popped the truck into low and strung out his load.

The Negro shook his head and whistled. "Mmmmmmh, mmmhh," he said, "mother fuckin truck driver, shit! They goan pack yo ass with cotton. This here's bad enough eben if you knows what you doin! Shit, they won't eben find yo ass to pack it!"

Beau Jim stopped the truck and asked the laborer to show him

one more time how to make the bed of the truck lift. They went
through it again, and Beau Jim winked and thanked him. "You
got to start somewhere," Beau Jim said.

"Mmh, mmh," the Negro said. "Not me. I ain't. One o these
evenins when that gas tank goes and yo ass hits the back of yo
fuzzy head, you'll read me, man!"

But if you didn't count that, it didn't seem a bad job. There was
something pleasing about going to work when everyone else was
going to bed, and getting off when they were going to work. He
liked getting to Yancey's house where his bath would be drawn
and waiting for him. He liked Yancey popping in to dump a
handful of Tide in the bath water with him. "Daddy use to do
that," she'd told him the first time, "it gets you cleaner and don't
leave a ring."

Sweet Yancey, good Yancey—she acted as though not going to
his classes was only a temporary thing. But Hilda seemed to take
a different view of him. It was nothing he could put his finger on,
but something seemed different now that he was only just another rough, dirty, working man. If Hilda had been another kind
of woman, not so quiet and shy and good, she might have begun
to tease and joke with him, might have been suddenly capable of
telling him to clean his boots before he came into her house, or
asked him, point blank, what his intentions toward Yancey were.
But since Hilda was only the sort of woman she was, she did none
of those things. Yet he got the feeling she had subtly readjusted
the standards by which she expected him to live.

He wished he could do the same, but dropping out of Senneca
was not a matter he could face easily. Still, moments did come
when he seemed to see into the future. It looked hideously like
the present except for one tiny, telling detail, and that was the
sure and certain knowledge that some day he would be unable to
make any new promises to take the place of those he had broken.
There would come a time when what he was, was what he would
be to the end of his days. Such moments of insight descended
upon him like a sickness of his heart's blood, and strangely, made
him deny that he had ever really wanted anything out of college
to begin with. So you couldn't hack it, right? he'd ask himself. So
what's lost? What did you want to become? You were only win-
dow-shopping! There was never anything real you wanted out of
it!

He supposed it was true: he had not wanted to become a doctor or a lawyer, or any such person. But there was something he wanted. He struggled to think it into words without telling himself again that he merely wanted to make something of himself, be somebody. What had he wanted then? Although it seemed a weak, pathetic sort of thing to admit, he had wanted to know that ontogeny recapitulated phylogeny, by God, not to do anything with it, but just to know it, to turn it over in his mind and mull its facets. Oh, but it was foolish to try to sort out what he had wanted or lost, as foolish as, say, trying to remember his parents. He didn't see why he couldn't give himself a break. Ease up on himself a little.

He needed to learn tolerance. He needed to be more tolerant of Beau Jim Early. Of everyone. Of Yancey. Even of Claire, although with Claire, he didn't think it would help. He didn't like it, and he didn't know what to do about it, but they couldn't seem to find the right things to say to each other. He could feel the friendship dying of awkwardness. It made him mad, but there seemed no help for it. They tried to talk as before, they had beers at Tuckers, Claire even played head, but it wasn't the same.

After his fourth night's work, when they had uncapped a furnace and he'd spent most of the night asleep in his truck, Beau Jim made up his mind to explain to Dan that he had dropped out of Senneca. Dan had seemed to take such a pride in it, Beau Jim had been dreading it and putting it off. He hated to give such disappointment. At Yancey's he had his bath and breakfast and took a nap until such time as Dan would be at the service station, and he could go down and get it over with.

At twelve o'clock on the dot Yancey tugged on the lobe of his ear and said, "Come on now you lazy lout, get outta there if you goan go see your brother."

Perhaps he had been dreaming of her, but for whatever reason he opened his eyes, found Yancey with them, smacked his lips sleepily and said, "You know, you're gettin skinnier," which seemed perfectly to the point; and having said that, he closed his eyes again. Once when they had been studying together, although he hadn't asked her, she told him she wanted him to know that she wasn't having anything more to do with Mr. Wynette; and somehow that seemed to the point too, and snuggling that thought to him, he drifted again toward sleep. But she poked him in the ribs with a broom handle. "You told me to get you up, and if you ain't outta that bed in two seconds, I'm goan sit on your face!" she said.

He opened his eyes again, coming more awake. He blinked and squinted at her. "You," he said, "why you red-headed, country . . . I'll have a little respect around here!"

He caught her wrist and sprawled her across his knees. "I'm a workin man, and I needs me sleep!" And with great, good cheer he goosed her, and she bucked like a heifer.

"Stop it whoop dadgum you let me get off of if I get aholt whoop stop it!" she yelled.

They fought all over the bed and off on the floor where she found her broom again and began to poke him in the ribs with the handle of it. He turned her loose and rolled under the bed.

She banged around after him with the broom handle as if he were a shoe to be scraped out, or a mouse to frighten away. She bent down to look at him, her face flushed and pretty, and her foxy red-brown eyes glowing. "Get out from under there," she said.

"No," he said.

Her face disappeared upward, and he was left with only the freckled calves of her legs to admire. She was getting thinner. No doubt about it. He had seen her, now and again, at her mother's sewing machine taking things up a pinch at a time. "You ain't as juicy as you used to be," he said. He did not want to see Dan. She pounded the top of the bed with the flat of her broom and caused it to shake.

"Come out from under there," she said.

"No," he said. It was cool and safe under the bed. He liked it where he was. He didn't know why Dan had to take such a pride in having him in college.

"Come on," Yancey said, "maybe your brother can talk some sense in yore head. Anybody can drive a silly dump truck."

Reluctantly he rolled out, and she hit him twice with the broom, and then ran giggling through the house.

Somehow, out in the sunlight, Dan's disappointment seemed manageable. And although he didn't know exactly how he was going to put it, by the time he stopped at the pumps of the service station, it didn't seem such a hard thing for a man to explain. Only it was not Dan who came out of the station toward him, but Willard.

"Where's my brother?" Beau Jim asked.

"Well, that's a question that don't mean a damn thing to me, I'll tell you!" Willard said, and with an angry slap of his hand, he cleared the pump, and flipped open the panel over Beau Jim's gas tank. He paused with his hand on the cap. "You want gas?"

"Sure, I guess," Beau Jim said, wondering if he'd heard right.

Willard took off the gas cap and slammed the nozzle of the pump home. "I come up here last night with the station wide open and your brother gone! I mean, he stuck his ass up between his shoulder blades and walked out and left it!" Willard said and bugged his eyes for emphasis. "Any swinging dick that come along could have helped himself to the cash register! Gas! Tires! Don't ast me where the son of a bitch is," Willard said, the veins ropy in his neck and his face purple.

"What happened?" Beau Jim said, too confused for proper fury, but beginning to feel anger tighten a screw somewhere in his head anyway.

"Sammy yonder says he had a fire out to his house, and I'm sorry for that, but that don't excuse him not to call me, ner lock up, ner nothin! I mean he don't work here no more, and you can carry that message to him!" The feed on the gas pump kicked off at three dollars and eighty-eight cents, and Willard withdrew the nozzle, gave the gas cap a twist and flipped the panel shut.

The information had come too fast, but still, anger was twisting the screw tighter behind Beau Jim's eyes. He got out his billfold and withdrew a five dollar bill.

"Don't nobody just run off and leave a man wide open like that!" Willard said.

Beau Jim barely noticed himself crumpling the bill or turning his hand over to let it fall. He was trying somehow to see across the distance between Sharaw and his brother's farm, trying to apprehend what sort of thing might have happened there, and that effort and his anger almost cancelled each other, although if Cass Willard had touched him, his response would have been furious and violent. But Willard only cursed, and Beau Jim got back in his car, hearing none of it.

When he topped the hill beyond the Experiment Station, he could see, at least, it wasn't the house, for that still stood. It took another fraction of a second for his memory to reconstruct the barn that should have risen behind it, and another for him to see the black, scorched remains. He felt a huge relief that it hadn't been worse. Surely, there would be insurance, and he could borrow some money himself, from the bank, and even perhaps from Claire, to help Dan get back on his feet if he needed it. Now that he was working regularly, it wouldn't be hard. There would even be days when he could do without sleep and drive for Claire's uncle if much extra money was needed.

He parked behind Dan's pickup, which was crossways at the edge of the yard, and went on around the house. He could see Dan scratching about in the ashes where the barn had stood, and he went on, Dan looking at him now, watching him come. Dan's eyes were on him, two cold and nearly colorless orbs beneath his wiry brows, so intense, they stopped him when he was still two or three feet away. He even almost took an involuntary step backwards before recognition suddenly lit his brother's fierce pale eyes and Dan said, "Well, hit's Goosh!"

The name came from so far back in his childhood, it took him by surprise. It came from a time he had long forgotten when he was four or five and would eat almost nothing but cornbread and applesauce, crumbled and stirred into a glass of milk. It had to be eaten with a spoon, and his father had called it *goo*, and him *Goosh*, for eating it.

"I just heard about it," Beau Jim said. "How'd it happen?"

But Dan was not looking at him now. He had his head cocked at a peculiar angle and appeared to be looking over Beau Jim's shoulder—his eyes bleak and depthless again beneath the wiry colorless brows, his jaw rigid. It made Beau Jim uneasy and he moved his feet and looked about the ruins of the barn. "Got the tractor and all . . . Christ," he said. "Well, you're bound to have some insurance on it." Dan was filthy with soot and ashes, and still staring just past him rather than looking directly at him, but he appeared to be listening. "And look, well . . ." Beau Jim said and wiped his forehead, "I sorta gave up on being a college student for a while, and I don't want you to take this wrong, but I've got all kinds of money I don't know what to do with, and if you could use any of it, I sure wish you would, cause I won't do nuthin with it but throw it away."

Beau Jim realized suddenly that Dan was grinding his teeth, and it made his heart pain with equal parts anger and sorrow that his brother should be so proud, but before he could say anything further, Dan held up his two enormous hands, the fingers slightly curled as though in wrath and said, "See, don't these dogs ketch hit!"

"What?" Beau Jim said.

"Hit don't matter," Dan said in a cold, softer voice. "Hit don't matter, boy."

He's just had no sleep, Beau Jim thought, *he's just tired and mad and hasn't been to bed probably.* "I know," Beau Jim said, "except I've got all this money now that I'm not going to college, and I'd just appreciate it, if you'd let me loan you some of it, so I don't just throw it away on nuthin."

"You quit where they got that nigger a'goin?" Dan asked, and his eyes blazed.

Burned up all his labor. Might even have been better if it was the house. "Just for a little while," Beau Jim said. *Worked his ass off, and lost it. He's just tired and fucked up.* "Just till things get straightened out; then I'll go on back probably."

"That's right," Dan said. "You just rest easy. You'll be back directly. You kin read and figure with the best of em. Still yet," he said, "you might make a proper man with it. Hit ain't saying you got no chanst."

Dan was grinning, and Beau Jim decided that maybe he was teasing. Dan had never understood how to tease or joke, and likely, having been stunned by the fire and dead on his feet, he was only just trying to joke. What else could he do? *Christ Jesus!* Beau Jim thought, *he doesn't even know yet he's been Goddamned fired! I ought to kill that fuckin Willard!* He tried to think what to do, how to help. "Why don't we take a ride into town," Beau Jim said, "and just see about that insurance?"

"Insurance?" Dan said.

"It can't hurt, can it?"

"Hit's no time fer that!" Dan said, and again his eyes turned fierce. "Hit ain't even sech a thing as insurance, boy!"

Was he joking? What in hell could he mean? For a long moment the two of them stared into each other's eyes while Beau Jim struggled to understand. Why was it he felt the army years that had separated them, and even the ocean, were somehow palpably between them now? *Come on now,* he insisted to the fierce, pale eyes beneath the wiry, grizzled brows, *you're my brother, you raised me, I could always count on you, come on now, just let me get hold of this thing and find some way to help.*

"You kin hep me drag the cow on off down to the river," Dan told him, softly, at last, as if he understood.

All right then, all right, Beau Jim thought. For a while he helped Dan clear a path through the rubble but there was no rope to use, and while Beau Jim continued to clear rubble out of the way, Dan went down to the corn field to cut some barbed wire from the fence.

Beau Jim decided he could not deliver Willard's message, not at least, until he had found some way to make it easier. He would look into the matter of insurance himself. He could borrow money, as much as he could lay his hands on, and make Dan take it. He could tell whatever lies were necessary. By the time Dan got back with the wire and truck, things didn't seem quite so bad to him. Probably the insurance would cover a good bit of the loss, and he himself could make up a fair amount of money, enough to cover the miserable wages that sonofabitch Willard paid for even as much as a month, maybe more.

He tried to deal with the cow, but he couldn't. After his first awed and sickening sight of her, he tried to keep his eyes turned away, but the odor of her assaulted him. It was not the smell of old death, not rotten, but powerful just the same—the strong almost medicinal smell of new death; and although he tried to tie onto her with the barbed wire, he could not; and once Dan had got the far end of the wire twisted around the bumper of the truck, he had to take over Beau Jim's job, while Beau Jim buckled and groaned and walked away to keep from being sick. Beau Jim was afraid she would come apart when they began to drag her, but she didn't, although she left flesh behind.

They left her down by the river, bloated, her fist-sized eyes staring, and her legs propped as stiffly out as a sawhorse lying on its side. When Dan had got the barbed wire off her and off the bumper and had straightened it as well as he could, he seemed to fumble with it a moment more, his filthy hands taking small bends out, seeming to test the barbs before his eyes rested on Beau Jim once again, light hazel, almost colorless, and somehow it seemed, this time with warmth and kindness. "You go on, boy," he said, "go on and look after that insurance."

Beau Jim stood where he was a minute. There were things he wanted to say, but they did not come to his lips, and ultimately he could only bob his head.

At the Farmer's And Merchant Bank in Sharaw, he found that

Dan did have insurance on the barn, and within a week or so could expect a check for six dollars and some cents. The gentleman who sat behind the desk explained it very clearly and seemed not to notice Beau Jim grinding his teeth. As a condition of granting the mortgage, the bank had a policy which covered the buildings on Dan's property, or at least, his house and barn. The house was valued at six thousand dollars, and the barn at fifteen percent of that, or nine hundred dollars. Since the barn no longer existed, the bank would collect the nine hundred dollars and apply it against Dan's mortgage; therefore Mr. Dan Early would not be paying for a barn that did not exist. In addition, Mr. Early was entitled to get back such equity as he had in the barn. A little better than six dollars. On his livestock, the tractor, and the rest, he had no coverage, at least none handled through The Farmer's And Merchant's Bank. As for loaning Mr. Beau Jim Early money: after Beau Jim had explained his situation, the gentleman said they would be glad to do so, although Beau Jim would need a co-signer since he had no collateral and had had his job for only four days.

Beau Jim was polite. Carefully, meticulously polite. He could not help the noises that escaped his throat and entered upon the cool and ordered atmosphere surrounding the desk where he sat; they were like steam escaping a teakettle and nothing could be done about them. Apparently the gentleman across from him understood, for he took no notice of them and remained polite himself, even solicitous.

Still, it was moments after he left the building before Beau Jim could stop making the noises in his throat and cool down enough to think. He thought how Friday was payday at Strauman Brothers, although his first check would be one day short. He thought about selling the Studebaker, rejecting that notion out of hand for the little money it would bring and the trouble it would cause him trying to get to work without it. Finally, he drove to Senneca, but Claire was not in the apartment. He was not in Tucker's. He was not in the poolroom in Senneca, or the poolroom in Bolivar, or the poolroom in Sharaw. Beau Jim did not expect to find him in Sharaw, and he didn't. What he expected was trouble with Big Poke, and he was in no mood to be tolerant of it. But he didn't get that either. He'd gone in the poolroom, stiff with anger over what he thought Big Poke might say, but Big Poke didn't appear to notice him. He went back to the apartment, back to Tuckers, and back to the poolroom in Senneca. He could not face Dan again, somehow, without good news to give him. What money he could find, he was going to lie about. He was going to call it insurance money, for he knew, somehow, Dan would not know otherwise. Ultimately he drove out to the honky-tonk by the Bear Creek Pike and bought himself a pint of Fairfax County and took it back to the apartment with him to wait. Miserable and sober, he had almost finished it, when, somewhere between six and seven in the early evening, Claire came in. He had gone to Greenville, not to drive for his uncle, but to hustle pool.

Beau Jim told him about the fire and what he wanted. "I'd like a couple of hundred, say, if you can spare it," he said. Somehow, things being what they were, it made him shy to ask, but ask he did, calmly and without any embellishments and looking straight into Claire's doleful bloodshot blue eyes. Claire looked back only a moment before his eyes seemed to slide obliquely from Beau Jim's face to the windowsill by the kitchen table where Beau Jim sat. He patted his paunch. "Sure," he said.

In the small freezer of the refrigerator there was an ice cream carton jammed behind cans of frozen, concentrated orange juice, and two or three flat packages of frozen vegetables. Claire dug it out, opened it and dumped the money gently on the table by the almost empty pint bottle of bourbon. "Take what you need. Take it all if you need it."

Claire didn't say how much there was, but Beau Jim could see three one hundred dollar bills, a fifty, and many twenties.

"Lord, but I cleaned me some plows in Greenville, today," Claire said. He opened the bottom part of the refrigerator and got himself a beer. "Them fellers up there are so free with their money, I think I could take a liking to that town."

Out on the street, before the house, a siren went by, but neither of them thought anything of it.

Chapter
Twenty-Four

And no matter. For already that
same morning, long before Beau Jim had ever even gotten off
work to go home to Yancey to bathe and eat and sleep and rise
to see his brother, it was already too late.

Dan Early had sat on the warped back steps of his house watching the morning pale tediously behind what remained of his
barn: one low section of the left-hand corner still standing, the
burned hulk of the tractor, one upright of the cow's stanchion,
black as pitch. And he could not name what filled all the cham-
bers of his heart, but it was more than grief, for although he could
not yet think it into words, he knew, at last, he could carry the
farm no longer. His mouth tasted of brass, and there was no room
in him even for incredulousness. How was it that in Deep Gap
he'd had to do no more than turn his back on the rubble for his
mind to fetch it up again, every board and nail of it, every worn
sill and faded curtain, every table and chair, every sight and
sound of his mother snapping beans, or trading a cold flatiron for
a hot one on the stove, or humming some tuneless ditty to herself
at the churn? But no more. He had not once imagined the barn
intact: the tractor all but finished in its repairs, the oil and gaso-
line promise of power hovering over it; the cow shuddering her

hide and blowing softly into her feeding trough. He had worked sixteen hours a day and what had it gained him? He had added a second mortgage to the first, sacrificed all his shoats into the bargain, lost his feed crop, and now this last had come down to finish him. In a little while he would have to think it into words and admit that the best he could do was not good enough; he would have to forswear all he had labored for as far back as he could remember, everything he had laid any store by; but he could not do it quite yet.

For a moment the senselessness of it, the absence of any way to take hold of it and turn it around, boiled in his throat. The machinery of his body went stiff with rebellion: his whitleather hands, rough and chapped and dirty beyond cleansing; his back, humped with stubborn strength; every muscle and joint; all of him went taut. Oh, but there was no longer any useful purpose in pretending not to see what was plainly there. What tolerance was there in flood, in drought, or fire? In a fourteen year old boy tucking up his legs and cannonballing into the cottonmouths? He did not have to think it into words to understand that there was no tolerance. No mercy. No forbearance. There was none anywhere. He understood, at last, that a man might work all his life and gain nothing. Why pretend it was not so? But he did not ask for tolerance or mercy. He never had, and it made him tremble with anger to think that he had been brought to such considerations even for a moment. He only needed to know where to take hold. He only wanted some understanding of where to grab on, and then let anything or anyone try to shake his grip. It was his ignorance of any way to go that boiled in his throat.

the screen door slapped to behind him and the load brushed brightly down his forearms and rumbled in the woodbox. oh lord and yes *vernon said* i'm goan take in the country from mountain city on the tennessee side clean down to lenoir on this side and buy me up ever country ham that's right. now you can fool me about a whole passel of things but can't nobody fool me about a country ham. you take and run an auger in him and smell the hole and if it makes yore eyes water and yore pecker twitch then that there's a country ham. we'll start her out sellin em to the daniel boone hotel and over to blowin rock and once them rich folks aquire the taste we'll have us a mail order business can't nobody touch. early hams got the proper ring now ain't it. hellkatoot. we'll have

money like pourin piss outta a boot. *he could smell it in his nostrils.*
feel the hot flood begin to chafe his thighs. the reins in a big mule-eared
knot between his shoulderblades to take up the slack. stumble down to his
knees. sam plodding on a few steps and draggin him and the plow and
all. got his mouth mashed somehow. cut his lip. scooped his mouth full of
dirt. so. the old a model got hot coming up the black mountains towards
ashville from old fort. had to leave beau jim wheezing with asthma
hunkered on the seat. found a milk can in the weeds. someone had run over
likely. hole rusted in it. down the steep bank thick with dewberry and
blackberry briars. scoop it in the creek. crawdads dart backwards dart
backwards dart backwards. get it nearly full. get the palm over the
flaking rusty hole. pin holes on the other side. kneewalk back up the steep
bank and over the lip of the road. forgot to take the cap off the radiator.
too hot for beau jim. twist it loose in one motion but all the water gone.
back down the steep bank. briars dug in the sweat and dirt. so. look
mister you ain't got the work these dogs can't catch. *something*
rising in the throat. well all right. all right. all right then hoss *cass*
willard's father said i'll give you thirty-five cents an hour and allow
you a week to show me. *so. it was not ever again the mist rising off*
winkler's creek but the steamy smell of concrete and him hosing it down
of a mild may morning when it was not yet good light but spreading up
the pale vault and dome of sky like the wick being turned up on the world.
it was ever the worst time. always the ache to get him back the land he
had lost sings in his heart. grieves his soul. and times descend when he feels
it must break him. so. for all the sights and sounds in this place are the
wrong ones. people are always about with their talk talk talk. and where
is peace. bell. bell. rrregister. the compressor saying down the years stanta
tanta tanta. sammy's squeegee down the glass. could they be the cause of
it them niggers? sammy deep in the blue-black shadow of himself. hidden
away. out of reach under a rock down a hole. cass said the niggers were
to blame. his tongue ever ready to say any sort of thing. and charlene. and
charlene's too. but there were all manner of others. it tainted the very air
a man breathed. it turned him nearly crazy not to understand. oh but this
was the oldest of his griefs. there was ever something he could not get his
mind around. them others always caught on so easy. but which of them
could stay up with him on a job of work. and he was almost just as proud.
so. so. but it was the oldest of his griefs. and what if them niggers had
yet been before him like a book and him staring and puzzling and never
sorting them out. hidden back behind the words where he could not take
hold of them. dogging him like his shadow. his negative. dragging and

pulling him down. what was it did charlene say. what was it. nary man
could hear such talk when his barn was burning up like that. him smoking.
him smoking in it. it began to stretch his eyes and pull his mouth ajar.
wait now. hold up just one minute. sure there was nothing of tolerance
in god but there were ever signs if they could be read. it did not snow on
a man or come winter all of a sudden without tokens of warning. the
leaves turned colors and fell from the trees which was not snow. frost came
which was not snow. though it might yet kill a man's crops it was neither
snow nor winter not december and january and february. and sure it did
not come down rain from a clear sky and sure the clouds came up first
and the breeze freshened and the leaves turned belly up. and what man
was there who had been more tempered and tested. so. so at last then. he
ground his teeth and spoke from the middle of a thought:

"They's just trees makin noise in the wind, and they don't for
a fact understand it. And me thinkin all the time they wuz smart.
That's all right. It fallen to me to get things done as ever. That's
all right," he said and stood up, "and you had to take it all away
from me twicst." He began to tremble thinking of all the years
of labor he had lost and of the nigger boy who had done a good
job, and him not half grown, and done it for months, and how
the fire, even then, was an accident. Well. Well. It was clear
enough, at last, that if the taint was upon even such a one as that
small black child, then it was upon them all. "That's all right,
sure," he said, "but you'll be obliged to wait. You'll be obliged
to wait, for I've got me some chores."

Where there had been hay, the ashes were as light as down; and
even as slowly as his feet descended the ashes billowed up, feath-
ery, fragile, adhering to his shoes, his cuffs, his sockless ankles,
coating him like the body of a moth. Here and there beneath the
ashes were hot spots, beds of live coals, which he made no effort
to avoid. He looked at his cow, and he looked at his tractor. And
then he began.

Those things he found, he collected with such grim avidity he
might have been stealing. He took what had survived the fire. He
picked up the head of an axe with no conscious notion of fitting
it out with a new handle, nor did he give any thought to whether
or not its temper was destroyed. He gathered things without
even quite knowing what they were. Someone would have had
to tell him that what he held in his hands was the head of an axe,
or a smoked, cracked fruit jar half full of nails. He was just

enough inside the perimeter of reason to stop short of collecting stones and laying them grimly aside with his cache of axe and hammer heads, the jar of nails, a coffee can of staples, the pronged head of a potato digger, the blade of a sickle.

He looked at it only a moment before he knew what it was. Somehow he knew even before he could read its charred deformity: there, a paw with fur and flesh burned away and only three of the claws remaining, distended and unsheathed; and there, the head, hardly recognizable save for the glint of teeth and smear of gum; and there, the hips and thighs, rotated impossibly on the spine, as though fire had caught the cat by head and tail and wrung it as a woman might wring out clothes. Just to one side of the needle teeth and small, pink ellipse of gum, like the grin of an opossum sulling, there was a roll of chicken wire, and stiffly, he bent and picked it up.

When Charlene came to the screen door and began to call, "Come on and git you some breakfast. Come on. Come on. Come on now, fore it gets cold," her voice was a thin ringing in the chamber of his ear, like the chimes of a clock striking the hour, and he had missed too many to count them and had to guess at what she might have meant. He began to thread his way through the rubble and ashes toward his house, but he forgot almost immediately where he was going and why. He bent and put the things he had gathered beside the steps and was looking back toward the barn when she came to the screen door and said, "Come on. Clean up and eat you some breakfast and git on to bed." And again the words got away too quickly, and he responded only to a vague memory of what they might have been. He went inside, although he did not wash, and he did not eat, and when he was spoken to, he did not answer. There was only one thing in his head to say, and it roiled in him to come out. But the fabric was of one piece and vexed his tongue, and oddly, before he found any words to render it, he grew afraid. As though it were a promissory note that might be taken away, he grew queerly afraid to trifle with it. And in a moment the fear became so strong, it was no longer fear, but conviction. Still, he wanted to tell Charlene he understood, at last, why they had been cursed with bad luck, why everything went stubbornly wrong. And he wanted to tell Sheila. He wanted to tell Sheila especially, but he had bought his understanding at too dear a price, and somehow, speaking of it, seemed a serious breach of faith. *The earth knows what it knows and don't need to speak it,* he thought, *the tree knows what it knows. Hit's only a man that's got to talk, and when does he ever do more than confuse his mind and weaken his will with it?* It was a secret within a secret, and a truth within a truth. Still, when Sheila was leaving for her school bus, and her lips, cool and sweet as dew, touched his cheek, he wished to tell her, although he did not raise his arms to embrace her until she was gone. Only after he had put out his arms to hold her, did he remember he'd heard the front door close.

"Look at you!" Charlene said. "If you ain't goan eat, git on to bed. You can't do no good pokin around out there. Git on now."

It seemed to take minutes for her face to come into focus, but when he saw her, his secret knowledge generated something like pleasure. It was not quite pleasure, nor even quite pity for someone who did not understand. But there was yet something of smugness in it. "Hit's a whole lot I can do," he said in a low even voice.

"What?" Charlene said, "work on that burned-up tractor? Milk yer dead cow?"

He would not say more. Charlene looked into his face, and her own expression changed from defiance, to incredulousness, to horror. She put her hand to her mouth and wiped it so slowly and so hard, she twisted her lower lip askew. "You're a fool!" she blurted suddenly, and her eyes welled up. "You got no sense at all!" She looked all about the room as though she were addressing a host of listeners. She scooted her chair back as though she were going to appeal to each of them, although she got no more than halfway up before she sat abruptly down again. "You know what you are?" she demanded, "you're a God Damned snappin turtle that's grabbed onto a stick!" She wiped her nose and laughed suddenly, although her eyes were still swimming in tears. "You're just like the snappin turtles I used to watch my Daddy kill! Hold right onto the blessed stick even after they heads wuz cut off!" she said and laughed. "You ever seen that? Huh? Didja?" she asked him. "You can cut the heart out of one of them ole cooters and lay it all by its self and . . ." she stuck her hand in front of his face and made a fist which she gripped and relaxed and gripped like a pulsing heart, ". . . and it'll go just like that!"

If what he had felt was pleasure or smugness at having, once in his life, answers no one else had, it was also like the pleasure of suffering and surviving some terrible wound that would have killed another man; and with much more determination than satisfaction, he put it away. "I got to git the cow drug on off," he said flatly, not to throw her off, nor even to offer himself a small consideration to forestall, for a time, the much larger one, but because all the things he had to do, seemed at last, to have the same magnitude. And he had determined that first, first of all, he would see to those few things that remained his. Almost as an act of rebellion he would do it. "She's goan commence to stink," he said, unaware that he had spoken aloud or that he was grinding his teeth.

Even though Charlene reared back in her chair, her full eyes did not spill over. "Christ, I'd call the vet!" she said, "or maybe if you've actually give up on saving her, you could butcher her. She's even already cooked up for you!"

But he was no longer listening to her. He scooted back from the table and went out. He found the harrow, which was not hurt and dragged it clear, and the disks, which seemed to have lost their temper, but he could find nothing that would help him with the cow, for all the rope had burned. He found two bags of hog chow that were no good, and four that were scorched, but usable. Still, he puzzled over the cow, and had only just figured out how he could cut some barbed wire loose from the fence around the corn field and use that, when the man appeared. He recognized him immediately without knowing exactly who he was, and had, at once, the feeling that the man had come, at such an hour, as a messenger, the bearer of yet another token; but in the next instant he was overcome with gratitude and joy. "Well, hit's Goosh!" he said.

Who, if not blood of his blood and flesh of his flesh, could hear it? The urgency of it demanded telling, and it was upon his lips; but again, before he could frame the first word, he knew it was no good. He, himself, from among all men, had been chosen; and what he knew was not his to tell. There seemed in him a weakness, a demon, who wished him to fail, wished him to break faith and babble away his understanding, as perhaps other men had done. It made him suddenly so angry he ground his teeth. Even a child knew the old verity that what God gave, He gave in His own time, and at His whim, and He could not be courted, nor tempted, nor taken for granted. Even a child knew, if a man did not, that there were contracts with Him one did not trifle with, or speak of, or even think into words, for He would not have it so. And if he could stand being taken for a fool all his life, when he figured it was true, he could stand it a little longer, when he knew it was not. "See, don't these dogs ketch hit!" he said and held up his two hands.

"What?" Beau Jim asked him, and he realized that Beau Jim had been talking, although he had not heard what he'd said.

"Hit don't matter," he said in a cold, low voice. "Hit don't matter, boy."

"I know," Beau Jim said, "except I've got all this money now that I'm not going to college, and I'd just appreciate it, if you'd let me loan you some of it, so I don't just throw it away on nuthin."

"You quit where they got that nigger a'goin?" Dan asked, but then he understood that God had granted him another sign and token after all.

"Just for a little while," Beau Jim said. "Just till things get straightened out; then I'll go on back probably."

"That's right," Dan said. "You just rest easy. You'll be back directly. You kin read and figure with the best of em," he said, and he could not keep the bitter grin from twisting his mouth. "Still yet," he said, "you might make a proper man with it. Hit ain't sayin you got no chancet."

"Why don't we take a ride into town," Beau Jim said, "and just see about that insurance?"

"Insurance?" Dan said.

"It can't hurt, can it?"

It was painful for his own brother to be so wide of the mark as to think that insurance could be the cure of anything. "Hit ain't no time fer that!" he said. "Hit ain't even sech a thing as insurance, boy!" he said. He looked Beau Jim in the eye and tried by sheer will power to tune his thoughts. Beau Jim's lips moved and his forehead wrinkled, but he didn't say anything. It was no use, he could not teach him. The Lord did not wish that he should. "You kin hep me drag the cow on off down to the river," Dan told him.

They cleared a path, and down at the corn field with a worn out pair of side cutters he kept under the seat of the pickup, and with much more grip than cutting edge, Dan worried the barbed wire in two.

When Beau Jim was trying to tie onto the cow, he groaned and buckled and had to walk away in order to keep from being sick. Dan said nothing. Beau Jim was doing the best he could; he just didn't have the grit.

They left her down by the river, her legs propped as stiffly out as a sawhorse lying on its side. It came to him, at last, that he must send his brother away, that he had no allies in this, and it could serve no useful purpose to have Beau Jim stay. "You go on, boy," he said, "go on and look after that insurance."

Before Sheila got home, he cut a young cedar tree, whittled a handle for the potato digger, and buried her cat. He couldn't name what it made him feel when—after changing her school dress, which itself, was somewhat faded and outgrown, and after taking off her school shoes—she came out to watch him search the ashes. She stood quietly in the barnyard, one bare foot on top of the other, her thumb in her mouth, and watched him with her round eyes. It made him impatient although he had not quite finished his work, and it was not yet time. But he had suffered the curse all his life, without even knowing what it was, and he could suffer it a little longer, particularly now that he was the instrument, and it was God who would have to wait. It was God who would have to be patient, whether He wanted to or not, and perhaps learn what a man's labor was worth. He winnowed the ashes with the potato digger, and because she haunted him, he spoke to her often about the small things he found. "Well look here Punkin," he'd say, "here's a file ain't one thing wrong with!"

But she would neither move nor speak.

And again: "Well, what's this? Won't need nuthin but a handle to be as good a grain scoop as it ever was!"

He began to carry the things he found out of the ashes and lay them down beside her, but she wouldn't even look at them. Round-eyed and gravely noncommittal, she looked at him, unless he came near; then she looked off into space. After a while, she grew tired and squatted and wrapped her arms about her knees, but she did not go inside. He found two good bags of fertilizer and a sack of chicken feed, and although the top two thirds of the chicken feed was parched almost black, the bottom third seemed all right. He carried the sack out to her and reached down for her arm. "Bet'em ole hens is starved," he told her. "Why doncha scatter em somethin to peck at?" He carried the sack and steered her up toward the house where a few of the chickens, suspicious of the odor of fire, scratched and pecked disconsolately.

He waited for her to call, "Chick, chick, chick, chick, chickee," as she always did and laugh her little crystal laugh at the awkward rolling trot of the chickens, but she neither called nor laughed. Dreamily, never ceasing to suck her thumb, she dipped a hand into the sack and turned slowly round and round, letting the feed sift through her fingers. The top button on her dress was missing, and she had buttoned it unevenly so that the neck and hem were crooked. *The first button goes in the first button hole, don't it Punkin?* he thought; *you know that much, doncha Darlin?* It seemed, somehow, a sad piece of knowledge to have, since the first button was not there. Again she dipped her hand into the sack and turned, drawing a circle of grain around her, and he could not name exactly what it made him feel. But nothing would be wasted that could be saved, and he had, still, a little more to do, and with the same cold, patient, even vengeful avidity, he winnowed the last remaining space of ashes.

When he was done, he propped the potato digger against the house and set the three bags of hog chow and what remained of the chicken feed inside the screen door on the porch. He took the bags of fertilizer by the ears and dragged them to the house and stowed them beneath the back porch so that if the rain should come, they would not be harmed. He looked at the sun and gauged it to be five-thirty, and for the moment it took him to remember the barbed wire he had taken from the cow and put in the bed of the pickup, he was terrifically uneasy. But then he remembered it and that he had yet to replace it, and a modicum of peace settled over him again. He got the barbed wire, his sidecutters, and the chicken wire too, for he knew the barbed wire could not be made to stretch again between the last two posts. Charlene called Sheila into the house to help her, and he went off to patch the fence.

He was piecing out the last span with strips of chicken wire when Sheila came down to tell him supper was ready. But he did not go with her until he was finished. Carefully he took the final brittle ends of wire and twisted them together. Slowly, savoring it as though he were making love, he gave each pair of wires two careful turns of the wrist, and then he was done. And miraculously when he was done he was no longer of that moment. Even as he turned to follow her, Sheila had slipped as far away from him as his own childhood. He watched her climb the hill as though from a distance of many years and could not even grieve, for across such a gulf, emotion seemed to have no proper claim. It was no longer pertinent to something sealed in history, something as unalterable as his own childhood.

On his way up to the house he recalled, queerly, that for the first time since they had been married, Charlene had prepared him no lunch, although he couldn't think how that mattered either. He was not hungry. Still, he went up the hill behind Sheila and sat down with them. It seemed important to finish the day, to do what he always had done. Although again, he neither washed nor ate, he sat with them. And despite there being no help for it across such a gulf, he could see that Charlene looked pale; that her lips were thin and blue; that the motions she made, setting the table, or passing food to Sheila were of such economy they were constituted entirely of habit; and that what she said to either of them held so little, she might as well have been reciting the alphabet. He could not even regret that there was nothing in her eyes he knew, no shared knowledge, no common history. All of that seemed, somehow like the rest, foregone, sealed, and unalterable. And although Sheila, even across such a gulf, was a creature of strange and wonderful proportion—her head tilted like a flower on her slender neck, the collar of her dress askew to show the frail bones of her breast and shoulder and the delicate tracery of blue veins beneath the skin—he could not say what she meant. He could not drag such a fragile meaning across so much time. Still, he sat where he was until they had eaten and he could rise from his chair and go get his one good suit coat and put it on.

He retrieved his shotgun from the corner by the chifforobe. Slipped five shells in the magazine. Racked one in the barrel. Set the hammer down to half cock and slid another, the last it would hold, in the magazine. He filled the pocket of his coat with what shells remained, and it was perfectly predictable that Charlene's face would be before him then with her startled eyes and blue-lipped mouth from which even the questions were predictable and useless; and without heat, he swept her aside as he might have shooed a fly or a mosquito.

And once again, on his way to the door he saw Sheila, caught in time, the collar of her dress forever askew, and she, forever unmindful of it. As though she knew. And once again without heat or haste, he brushed Charlene aside.

And Sammy's wife knew. With his first step inside their door, she knew. "My God," she said, and her hand went out for the butcher knife, but he cut her down before her fingers much more than took hold of it, and it gave a little flip and skittered across the sideboard of the sink where she had been standing.

One of the girls was sitting on the ragged blond couch in the living room, and the way she shivered and stretched against the couch would have been too quick for the eye to see if there had not been the settling afterward.

Her two sisters were playing jackrocks on the floor and both were knocked winding as they scrambled up to run.

The boy flushed from the nearer of the two bedrooms, like a bird or a rabbit, and got past his mother and almost to the kitchen door twenty feet away before the shot lifted him, loose, as though all his bones had come unstrung, into the corner where the sideboard met the wall.

"Sammy," Dan called. "Sammy." And though he did not speak loud, the name cast upon the silence of the four small rooms, seemed almost the equal of the shotgun blasts. Although it was time for Sammy to be home, Dan did not search for him. The quiet he heard did not dwell where there was life. He let the hammer down to half cock, slipped five more shells in the magazine, and left, closing the door carefully behind him. He knew immediately, and as though he had known it always, that Sammy was in Sharaw, and it cost him nothing to accommodate that either, for driving to Sharaw was no less distant than driving from Deep Gap to Cocke County with Beau Jim breathing asthmatically beside him.

Cass—inside the yellow nimbus of his office, one foot on top of his desk, leaning forward, calf to thigh on that leg; twisting his head around to look so that his adam's apple stuck out like a broken joint—seemed more surprised to see him than Sammy did, who only stopped dead halfway between the near bay and the pumps while he got out and pulled the shotgun out behind him and leveled it across the windshield of the pickup. And Cass, who was not shot, went down at the same moment as Sammy. Sammy knew, he did. Knew it all, and so was trying to get up again before he even quite fell, and Dan gave him two more to put him away even though his head was still being whipped around by the second when the third pitched him backwards. He put the hammer down to half cock and slid the last shell in his pocket into the magazine.

In Senneca he asked the first man he met, "Where does the nigger live?"

The man was standing on the curb waiting to cross the street. He was dressed in overalls, a baseball cap on his head, a kitchen match in his mouth. "Huh, what is it?" he asked, touching the bill of his cap.

"The nigger," Dan said, "where does he live?"

The man made a face as if he were tasting something sour, and tugging on the lobe of his ear, stepped off the curb and came towards the pickup. "What nigger?" he said, "You just come through a whole passel of em on the edge of town."

For the first time Dan felt an edge of irritation and impatience, but he was careful to rein it in and ask once more. "The one that goes to school here, where does he live at?"

"Beats me," the man said, pulling his ear. "I don't even . . ."

But Dan had let out the clutch, and the pickup had already lurched away. He asked another man halfway down the block, and a little further along, a lady who was getting into her car. And all the time he got more impatient and angry. How was it that they did not *know?* Now that it had begun, they would have to enter in and help sweep it all away. He could not kill every last nigger by himself.

There were two well dressed men crossing the street from right to left in front of the campus, but they were already across the center line and he had to swerve to the wrong side of the road in order to cut them off and had to lean across the barrel of his shotgun in order to talk. "Where do they keep him at?" he asked them.

They looked at each other. One was young. The other was old, with white hair. They looked at him and the barrel of his gun, and then with a simultaneous awkward and jerky motion, started to walk around the truck, and he had to pull up again and cut them off. "Where do they keep the nigger at!" he demanded.

"Look here!" the older one said.

"Where does he live at!" Dan said.

"We don't know," the young one said. "Down at married student housing. We don't know."

The pickup was in motion again, but something was happening. He could feel it happening, as though time were telescoping, as though he were sliding back toward the present moment. The old affliction was beginning in his stomach. He fought it down and drove the streets, seeing no one for long minutes close enough to put his question to. He did not know where married student housing was. It had grown almost full dark, although the campus and the town were well lit, and he searched for someone to ask with a fatal and desperate urgency. In some far off, abstract way he heard a siren go by.

He swung all the way over to the left hand side of the street when he saw the three of them. Women. Girls. He couldn't tell which. His left front tire bumped up on the curb before he could stop. "Where does the nigger live at?" he asked them, and in his impatience, got out of the cab and dragged the shotgun after him.

"Oh Ardell," one of the women said and clutched at her neighbor. The woman, the girl, nearest him stumbled back and squeezed her bag of groceries so tightly it split.

"The one that goes to school here, where does he live?" He demanded.

"Just down the street! Just right down the street there!" she said, stumbling back against the other two. "Oh Ardell," the other said.

But he had already turned and started off, feeling it all begin to slip. Still he kept on down the sidewalk. Even talking to himself as he drew in sight of the patrol car, parked at the curb, the light blinking and the deputy standing in the doorway of the new brick building with the black man, and the woman and the child. "I can tote it up what it cost me," he said, "Ain't leavin nuthin off." And for the first time, the present moment was upon him. He could feel the sidewalk under his feet, the sweat at his temples, his thumb drawing back the hammer; and he knew it was no good. Still, he kept on, and those in the doorway had seen him now. All their faces were turned to him, and as if snatched away, the woman and the child disappeared back inside; and the black man was struggling to get inside too, but he could not break the deputy's grip.

"Whoa, now," the deputy said, although Dan did not know whether he was speaking to the nigger or himself.

"Stand away!" Dan told him.

"Whoa now," the deputy said.

But he was halfway across the small yard and close enough.

Book
Three

Chapter
Twenty-Five

The huge building where he
worked was divided into two parts with two hundred and fifty
brick masons and helpers at work in each half, and so it was a
place of loud and constant noise. The ceaseless scraping and
tapping of trowels on bricks; the agonized metal-on-stone sound
of the two brick saws making cuts and wedges and soaps; the
rumble of the overhead crane, rolling on railroad rails from one
end of the building to the other, grinding its winch and wailing
its siren when pallets of bricks or tubs of mortar seemed badly
balanced, or for some other reason likely to fall on the men below
—all those sounds assaulted his ears and filled his head and
helped distract him, although even in the confusion and noise,
Dan stalked him.

Nine months before, when he'd first come to Huntsville and
taken the job, the work had been very hard on him. But that too
had been a welcome distraction. Halfway through the first day,
he'd worn out his hands, and during the first week, he'd worn out
one set after another of bloody blisters. But no more. These days
his hands were so stiff with calluses he could hardly make a fist,
and nothing hurt them now. Even the heaviest work no longer
sapped his strength. He could chop mortar and carry bricks for

hours on end. He even carried tubs of mortar by himself, and a
tub a bit more than half full of mortar weighed two hundred
pounds and was not a one man job. He had done it in the beginning for the pain and struggle there was in it, but he did it now
because he could. He had learned how to pick the tubs up and
set them down again with his back straight, and it did him no
harm.

These days, there was the heat to deal with, for it was July,
summer again, and very hot. August could only be worse. But
already it was so hot that even someone who did not actively
work—a foreman or an engineer, say—was no less slick with
sweat. And there was the brick dust floating in chalky clouds
from the brick saws so that a man had to breathe it, and was
wiping it constantly from the corners of his eyes and mouth, and
eating it at lunch time, and feeling it forever on his sweaty skin,
as thick and gritty as if he'd rolled on a sandy beach. But he paid
it little mind.

In another week he would be on the other side of the tubs of
mortar and stacks of bricks, laying bricks himself, and the extra
money would be very useful. He would be far from a journeyman
bricklayer, but he'd gotten in the union and the apprentice pro-
gram and had passed the first phase of his apprenticeship, which
meant he'd get seventy-five cents more an hour, and a dollar and
thirty-five cents an hour would become two dollars and ten cents,
and double time on Saturdays. It was hard to get into the union
without pull, with no relatives in it to help, and he couldn't have
done it without the mason on the saw, who had become his friend
and had spoken for him. Still, perhaps as some sort of final initia-
tion, a month ago they had put him on the line behind Doc and
Satchelass. But if that was one last attempt to wash him out, it
had failed, and he had survived that too.

Doc and Satchelass had run many a helper off, many a water
boy too, but something about Beau Jim stopped them short of
their usual torture. He knew it, and they knew it. They read it
in each other's eyes. They called him Speed—a name they called
all their helpers, meaning just the opposite by it—and they
harassed him, but there was a point beyond which they did not
go. No doubt because what his brother had done had gotten
around the job.

He had lost his anonymity the very first day, and that, more than anything else, had almost made him drag up and move on. One of the construction men had asked him as a joke if he was any relation to the Early who had killed seven niggers and wounded a deputy before a 357 magnum had put him away. Early was a common enough name in those parts, and the man was only teasing, and Beau Jim might have lied. It would have been much easier to believe a lie than the truth, but as badly as he wanted it all to be forgotten, he could not deny Dan. It had been in all the papers, and the man had asked him in order to tease, but no matter who had asked, or for what purpose, he would have had to claim his brother. He was unable to do otherwise, although he no longer knew what the word *brother* was supposed to mean. Sometimes he wondered what a brother could be if not a form of one's self. It made no difference that, after six years in the army, he had not even been able to shake Dan's hand or speak to him without self-consciousness. Perhaps, after all, that was the one time when *selfconsciousness* was exactly the right and proper word. Sometimes he had such thoughts.

But there were very few things he trusted any longer, and least of all, the machinery of his own thinking. But that too, had a virtue: nothing could ever take him so completely by surprise again.

Still, things were not so bad as they had been, nothing like the first month in Huntsville, before Yancey had come down. In those first days he never had a moment that couldn't be ambushed by a vision of Dan executing one of the seven as easily and skillfully as he might have caught a pig or killed a chicken. "Well, he didn't act right all day," Charlene had said to one of the investigating officers, "but it couldn't nobody have told what he was up to. When he taken his gun down, I tried to stop him, but it wasn't no stoppin him. That little nigger a'settin his barn on fire and all, he'd went crazy was what he'd done!" Deputy Earl Wagner, a puffy gauze bandage taped to the side of his neck and his shirt made lumpy by another, absolutely agreed. And Cass Willard agreed. And Beau Jim, himself, had agreed, although he scarcely knew what he was saying or doing through any of the legal matters and investigations that had taken place. He had only wanted to get away from Cocke County, and as soon as they'd let him, he'd done it.

But Dan had come with him all the way to Huntsville. Rode

to work with him in the mornings, came home with him in the evenings. His good brother matched him step for step everywhere he went, and never once during all that time did it seem possible that his craziness could have produced such murders. Why hadn't it taken another form? He couldn't believe Dan owned any such craziness as that. The children, for the love of God! Dan had breathed it in, somehow, like the smoke of another man's fire. Sometimes he thought that craziness might be only some sort of vessel, filled and stirred by the quality of the times, but he didn't trust himself, for why couldn't the same thing be said of sanity, and how was a man to guard himself against it? He didn't know. He couldn't sort it out, and even almost a year later, he could feel Dan quietly, deferentially, stalking some corner of his mind.

But Yancey had made his brother withdraw a merciful step or two, and things were better, much better. And maybe soon, Hilda would get ready to come. "She's just not ready yet," Yancey kept saying, "sellin the house and all, you know; she's just got to think it over and get ready." But he wanted Hilda to come and live with them.

Sheila was coming for certain. He had written and asked for her; and Charlene—who had sold the farm after the insurance paid it off, and gone back to work—left no doubt that she was happy to let them have Sheila to bring up. They felt sure Charlene would even let them adopt her, although they hadn't asked that question yet. Still, they were going to have her very soon, before school started in the Fall. Yancey was already making clothes for her and had finished three dresses, although she constantly worried that Charlene hadn't bothered to give her careful enough measurements, or that Sheila would up and have a spurt of growth.

Beau Jim was thinking about Sheila when Doc said, "Lemme see a two inch soap there, Speed," and automatically he took the soap from a stack behind the tub of mortar and gave it a sharp little smack into Doc's palm. He anticipated all the cuts of bricks they might need and had them ready, so they would not have to wait while he went to the saw for a soap or a wedge, and they didn't like it. They were accustomed to little breaks from their labor while their helper went on such errands, but these days, they were only able to dog off when a water boy came by.

At that moment Beau Jim saw a brand new one coming down
the line of masons, and he shook his head sadly in anticipation
of what would happen to him. He looked about seventeen, just
old enough to lie about his age and get away with it. He was
shirtless, brown from the sun, and smoothly muscled. Satchelass
had already spotted him and had poked Doc in the ribs and given
him the fish-eye.

Beau Jim got his brick tongs and set up a row of bricks for both
Doc and Satchelass, knowing that once again, he would take no
side. One day perhaps he could, but not yet, and maybe not ever.
Satchelass spat some tobacco juice on the scaffolding and began
to mortar a brick with his strange little flair. Eight hours a day
he'd scoop his trowel in the mortar and lay it with expert swipes
on one edge and two ends of the brick, and then give the brick
a little pitch-turn and catch it before he mortared the remaining
edge—into the tub again for a little mortar to lay down the
center, and then he'd set the brick in place and give it three taps
with the butt of his trowel, never fewer, never more; and he
never got mortar on his fingers. Doc, however, put mortar on all
four edges of the brick without turning it, and with every brick,
he got mortar on his thumb, which, after he had set the brick in
place, he habitually wiped on his left thigh. Doc might tap a brick
once, or he might tap it ten times, and he did a lot of scraping
of seams; whereas Satchelass allowed every seam one quick swipe
of his trowel. Beau Jim watched quietly while each busied himself until the water carrier had come up behind them and set his
buckets down.

"Water," the boy said with careful, studied disinterest, but it
did him no good for Doc turned around, made a face of great
surprise and happiness, and said, "Hey, Satchelass, look what
come to see us! Lordy, ain't this boy got the purtiest little titties
you ever saw?"

Satchelass looked at the boy, his snaky eyes and grim face
showing no sign of humor. He turned his head and spat. "Watch
out for him," he said to the water boy, tipping his head toward
Doc.

"Jesus, in all my days I ain't seen no titties purtier than them,"
Doc said, and at the same time reached out his hand as though
to take a dipper from one of the peck buckets. But he was looking
at his partner and he stuck his hand into the tub of mortar

instead. "Shit," Doc said, and the boy laughed. Doc flicked his fingers as though to clear them of mortar and reached again toward the dipper; but before the boy could move, Doc had caught a nipple between his thumb and forefinger. He pinched and twisted while the boy danced in pain. "Feel em Satch," Doc said, grinning around the stump of his cigar, "they feel so goooood."

The boy made a strangling sound through his clenched teeth, managed to wrench away, and looked at his bruised, smeared nipple where the mortar had taken the skin as effectively as any sandpaper. He tried to laugh, but what came out of his mouth was not laughter, and his eyes were full.

"Kiss me, Honey," Doc said, holding out his enormous hairy arms in invitation.

"I told you to watch him," Satchelass said, leveling his red, snaky eyes at the boy and tipping his head again toward Doc. "Don't you see them pistol grips he's got for ears. He's a cock-sucker."

"Awwwh shut up," Doc said, "ever damned time I fall in love, you try to mess me up."

But through an effort of will, Beau Jim turned his thoughts to Yancey and how this was her late shift at the supermarket and how he would sit out in front in the car, have a beer, and watch her through the big plate glass window while she punched the keys on the cash register and slid groceries behind her to the bag boy. It seemed odd to him that only a year or so ago, there was a girl on every other street corner who could break his heart. He wondered if he should tell Yancey how completely they had lost their power over him. He decided that he should.

He was thinking of that and only superficially aware of Doc harassing the water boy and of Satchel rinsing out his mouth and drinking from one peck bucket while he slipped his trowel into the tub of mortar and out again and let mortar slide from the trowel into the other bucket, never ceasing to drink, or to watch the boy over the edge of his dipper. The boy hadn't seen him, although it wouldn't have mattered if he had, Satchel wouldn't even have changed expressions.

Beau Jim courted his vision of Yancey and thought of the curtain rods she had asked him to pick up for Sheila's room, of the curtains she had made: yellow daisies on a white background. She had made a bedspread of the same bright, pretty material.

"Lemme see a three inch soap there, Speed," Satchelass said to him, and he realized the water boy had moved off. Beau Jim reached behind the tub and got the soap and put it atop a stack of regular bricks rather than in Satchel's outstretched hand.

Satchel picked it up and mortared it, studying Beau Jim out of his snaky eyes and chewing his tobacco slowly and thoughtfully as if he were considering spitting in Beau Jim's face. He and Beau Jim regarded each other a long moment before a mason down the line cursed, and dashed out the limey, mortared water on the water boy's feet. Even then, although Doc laughed, Satchelass never changed expressions; he merely turned his head and spat disinterestedly on the mortar speckled scaffolding and laid his soap.

Even though he was calm, and even though he had lost, altogether, the capacity to judge other men, Beau Jim continued for a moment to gaze into the space where Satchel's eyes had been. But he was mesmerized only an instant before he blinked, wiped the brick dust from the corners of his mouth, and became aware that the mortar in their tub was getting low. Thirty feet behind him was a pallet of full tubs where the crane had set them down, and he went to get one, even though they would use no more than half of it before quitting time. He took the handles at either end of the tub, allowed the muscles of his back and arms to align themselves, and picked it up. When he got almost back to his line, Doc turned around, saw him coming and clamped his cigar in his teeth so he could talk around it. "Hey Satch," he said and gave his partner a poke with his elbow, "Ole Speed swells up like a fuckin toad when he carries that mud don't he?"

It would have been an easy thing for them to move the almost empty tub off the stack of bricks which supported it, but they did not. He set down his load and removed it himself. They watched him pick up the full tub again, Doc grinning around his cigar, and Satchel's face as empty of expression as the face of a reptile. Beau Jim set the new tub in place and Satchel said, "Wet it up some," and turned to move his plumb line and use his level.

Beau Jim took up a bucket of milky water, which had chipping hammers and extra trowels soaking in it, wet down the mortar, and mixed it thoroughly. He got his brick tongs and set all the bricks they would need within easy reach, looked over his cuts and soaps and wedges, and went to the saw for those that would be required for the rest of the day.

Around an hour later, he began to wash all their tools, and when the whistle blew, he put their trowels and chipping hammers in water and poured two inches of water over the top of the mortar.

With droves of men, he left the enormous furnace building where someday carbon electrodes would be baked. He climbed out of the red clay pit and went on towards the dusty field where cars were already beginning to pull out. Inside the Studebaker he breathed the stifling odor of upholstery while he jockied for a place in the traffic that had begun to stream through the boiling red clay dust toward the highway.

Since Redstone Arsenal, Huntsville had begun to spread in every direction. Highways, clover leafs, by-passes, housing developments, and shopping centers were being built constantly. Still, in a little more than half an hour, he could get to their apartment, which was in one of the few old houses still remaining in Huntsville. In spite of the expense, he had insisted they get a place big enough for the two of them, Sheila, and Hilda too; and since a hundred and fifty dollars a month was more than they could afford, even after eight months it was hardly furnished at all.

Without Yancey in it, it seemed extremely empty and lonely, and as quickly as he could, he drew his bath, threw in a little Tide, and cleaned himself up. When he had bathed, dressed in clean khakis, a clean work shirt, and plastered down his stubborn hair, he took a damp rag outside with him in order to wipe down the front seat of the Studebaker so Yancey wouldn't get dirty.

At five o'clock, when she came out of the supermarket for dinner, he was waiting. They went to the dingy little Cafe where they always ate when Yancey was on the late shift. He could get a meat, two vegetables, rolls, and iced tea for seventy-five cents. Yancey always had a bacon, lettuce and tomato sandwich and a glass of tea with no sugar.

"You're gettin so skinny I can hardly see you," he told her when she ordered her sandwich, "You ought to eat more." At first he had been pleased with the pounds that melted from her, but lately it had begun to make him a little uneasy. He didn't want her to vanish after all. She had gotten so frugal with everything, her eating as well as the rest, it had begun to worry him. There was no question that they had done well, saving for the time when Sheila would arrive and Yancey would quit work: They had saved every penny of her pay checks and lived entirely on his, but he had no intention of letting her spend her very flesh.

"Oh, I could still stand to lose a pound or two," she said, turning her happy, foxy eyes on him.

"No you couldn't," he said and meant it.

She threw back her head and laughed, a good laugh to the end. "I eat when I'm hungry," she said and gave him a look that warmed his heart, "I just don't eat when I ain't hungry these days."

"Why don't we see if we can get Sheila here next week," he said, surprising himself no less than Yancey. "We don't need to wait until right before school starts."

"But I haven't got her little room fixed up yet," Yancey said. "I want to get her a little dresser and paint it, and we haven't . . ." she stopped talking after a moment and gave him a funny pursed-lipped smile. "Shoot yes, let's see can we do it. I've been wantin to anyway." She laughed again. "It's been like having the itch, knowing she's goan get to come and not having her here."

"And let's ask your Momma too," Beau Jim said.

"We just ask her," Yancey said.

"Let's ask her again," Beau Jim said. "She doesn't want to be up there all by herself. You know she don't."

"Well, you ask her," Yancey said, "I can't do anything with her."

"I will. The two of them could come down together on the bus. I will ask her."

"You sholy do like to be surrounded, don'tcha?" Yancey said quizically and rubbed his leg with hers under the table. She cocked her head. "I'm just not altogether sure I like it," she said. "Don't know but what I'm a little jealous." She smiled at him and rubbed his leg again with hers, but he worried that there might, after all, be some unhappiness in her, and the worry must have shown in his face, for she reached across the table and patted his cheek. "Why I was only just teasing you," she said with a rising and slightly amazed inflection. "Don't you know that?" she asked him and laughed again. It was such a good happy laugh that it turned heads in the cheap little cafe. "You silly thing," she said.

By the time he dropped her again at the supermarket, she was excited and flustered and had thought of a dozen things that needed to be done. But most of all she wanted him to pick up, not only curtain rods, but a little bedside lamp for Sheila's room, and

had scribbled down a list of material she wanted him to be sure
and get at a Remnant Shop. "I want to make that child a doll, and
if she's honest to God goan get here next week, I got to get started
this evenin, if I'm goan get done," she told him.

Buying the bedside lamp and the curtain rods caused him no
more embarrassment than buying anything at all caused him. He
didn't like to buy things. Something about it made him feel
foolish. But at the Remnant Shop, it was impossible. While the
saleslady smiled patiently, he struggled to read the names and
amounts of fabrics from Yancey's list. But it might as well have
been written in another language, which in fact, it seemed to be.
The only things he could make out were cotton batting and
yellow yarn. After some abortive movement of his hands and
feet, he told the saleslady that his wife wanted to make a doll and
gave her the scrap of paper with the list on it and let her deal with
it while he probed one of his ears and then the other with his
index finger, discovering in each, despite his bath, a great deal of
brick dust. The sales lady picked out the odds and ends of
material and yarn with great care and enthusiasm, holding up
scraps for him to admire, laughing and talking and sighing to
herself. It was all the more amazing to him when it turned out
that everything put together, cotton batting included, came to
under three dollars. He thanked her, and she thanked him, and
he thanked her again.

He carried all that back to the Studebaker and put it with the
curtain rods and the bed side lamp he'd gotten at the dimestore,
and then he started out again to get himself a beer to take back
with him to the parking lot, so he could sit and drink it while he
watched Yancey through the big plate glass window. But half a
block down the sidewalk, he decided he didn't want a beer bad
enough to take the time to get it. The possibility of Sheila coming, in so short a time, had excited him, and he wanted to be near
Yancey. He carefully did not think of Dan, but when he passed
the Remnant Shop again, he almost glanced at the window to
catch a reflection of this new man he was. He'd see no one in
buckskins, he knew that much. But he wished to try to discover,
somehow, the specific gravity of the man who went there; but
ultimately he didn't do that either for he understood, all at once,
it wouldn't work; no man ever was able to catch himself
unawares.